THE SOLDIER

M. K. Jones

Maze Investigations –
The Genealogy Detectives
Book 6

This story is a work of fiction. Names and characters are the product of the author's imagination and any resemblance to actual persons, living or dead, is entirely co-incidental. Where real historical persons, places or events are featured, they appear only as the author imagined them to be.

Cover design: Alison Morgan at AliCat-Design

Cover Image: ALBA Photo 11-0944, With kind permission of Tamiment Library/Robert F. Wagner Labor Archives.

ISBN 9 781739 228422

Chapter 1
Barcelona, Spain 1938

Helen, I am not coming home.

We marched yesterday, strong and proud on the outside, cheered on by crowds, given a wonderful speech by a woman they call 'La Pasionaria'. I wanted to cry, but I held my tears. The lads are looking forward to going home, despite worries about what authority will do when they arrive.

Tonight there is relief, anxiety, defeat. It's clear now the war will be lost. Hitler and Mussolini armed the Fascists too well. We had what the Russians sent and even that is running out. We hear Europe is trying to appease Hitler. If he turns on them what he has bombarded Spain with, God help you all.

My mates say I am lucky, a lucky mascot, they jibe. I have survived Teruel, the horror of Belchite, the failures of Gandesa and the Ebro. I have seen friends, comrades, buddies as the Americans call us, injured and killed. I didn't know what Fascist meant when I came here. Now I know that I must fight against them and everything they stand for, to my dying breath. I have made trusty friends and learned what it means to be a family.

Harry is still here. He's made it. He knows I am not leaving with him tomorrow. I have given him the postcard for you and I will give him this journal once I have finished my thoughts.

They are saying war will come in Europe, that Hitler is already stretching out from Germany. God help you all, if that is so. His troops and his Luftwaffe have had valuable practice here in Spain. They are ruthless, as are the Italians. I have heard that groups of our boys who surrendered were just shot. Executed. No prisoners of war here. I am eaten up with anger and sorrow when I remember those good buddies.

I am done now. Dawn will break soon, and I must be on my way. It will take me a couple of days to reach what remains of the XVth International Brigade.

What will be, will be. If my luck runs out, know I love you all and I never meant to hurt anyone. 'Lo siento mucho'.

Chapter 2

Maggie Gilbert sat with her feet on her picnic table, gazing out over the canal at the end of her garden, beer bottle in hand, suspended half way to her mouth.

Despite a few remaining restrictions lockdown had been lifted and she had caught up with one of her long-time school friends, at a reunion coffee morning earlier in the day.

Jude Crawley Winters threw her head back and laughed.

"That was interesting, Maggot." She paused to take a swig of beer. "Didn't you think?"

Maggie grimaced. "Should we have gone, Worm? Nostalgia's all well and good, but it's false memory." She took her feet down, sat up and put the bottle back on the table. "Interesting, though."

Footsteps heading down the garden distracted their thoughts. Zelah Trevear, glass in hand, sat on a spare seat and turned her face up to the early autumn sun. "Enjoy your reunion? Coffee, memories, unforgiven grudges?"

"Interesting," Maggie said. "Quite well attended. But some people missing I had expected to see."

"Poor organisation, maybe?" Jude added.

"By your 'old girls 'group?"

"No, by the still dreadful Cath Harris," Maggie replied. "Surprising not one of her groupies turned up."

"Maybe they grew up and felt shame."

They looked at each other, and in unison shook their heads and said '*no*'. "I'm amazed she turned up at all," Jude went on. "People who get expelled don't usually want to return to the site of their humiliation."

Maggie looked away, shaking her head.

"Didn't stop her getting in a couple of digs, did it?" Jude took another mouthful of beer and banged the bottle back down on the table.

"Every girls' school has one," Zelah muttered. "Thank God I never had to go through that."

"I had a chat with Belle Harrington," Maggie said to Jude. "You remember Belle, tall girl with curly brown hair, or it was then. She told me that of the original gang of seven, apart from Cath three are dead and three are untraceable."

Jude shrugged. "What's curious? We were in our teens, and it's almost forty years ago. Accidents and illnesses happen, people move on."

"Well, Belle thinks it's curious. She brought a photo of them."

"I saw it. Didn't they look so smug? And what about little Jane Perry? Still following Cath around like a dog begging for scraps. You know, I never understood her, after what they did to her best friend. What was her name?"

Maggie took a deep breath. "Josephine McKenna."

Jude sighed. "Thank God they threw Cath out." She glanced at Maggie. "Everyone believed she did it, didn't they, held little Josie's head in the toilet 'til she passed out." She turned to Zelah. "Given what she'd been getting away with for so long, under their noses, they had to act after that."

"Sounds nasty," Zelah said.

"She was an evil cow," Jude replied. "Still is, from what we saw today."

"What happened to the toilet girl?"

"She came back. She had told the school it was Cath, but she stayed away until she knew Cath had been expelled," Maggie said.

"Too scared to face the rest of the gang," Jude added. "They all swore Cath was with them. But their story fell apart when someone else came forward to confirm she'd seen them and Cath wasn't with them." She turned back to Maggie. "Your evidence nailed her."

"What did you see?" Zelah asked.

Maggie shook her head and didn't reply.

"Maggot saw Cath leaving the cloakroom and when she went in she found Josie on the floor, unconscious," Jude said. "Pretty traumatic."

What's with the 'Maggot'?" Zelah asked.

Jude laughed. "Just a nickname. I am cursed with two surnames, one being 'Crawley', so Maggot decided to call me 'Worm'. I retaliated, in a friendly way."

"You must have been close friends," Zelah remarked.

"We were," Maggie replied. "Cath organised a 'send to Coventry' on me, and persuaded almost the whole year not to speak to me for two weeks, which may not seem like a long time now, but when you're thirteen, it's like dog years. When Worm found out, she deliberately befriended me and made sure I always had a companion. You were a great friend," she said, leaning forward to hug Jude. "You ended Cath's spite towards me."

"Anyway, about the rest of Cath's groupies, Belle thinks there's something not right. What did Cath say to you, Worm?"

"She told me I'd put on weight and looked frumpy now. And she presumed my life had turned out the mess it had always promised to be. You?"

Maggie grinned. "She told me I hadn't amounted to anything.

"And your reply?"

"Oh, I told her she was right. Then I asked if she'd listened to my radio spot lately, or seen our internationally acclaimed Maze website? She tried to change the subject by telling me she'd heard my husband died, and was he not connected to some kind of fraud? I told her it had been tragic, but I've moved on since and my partner is an Acting Detective Chief Inspector of police. Then I asked about her before she could try to stick another knife in."

"And?"

"She just walked away and avoided me until she left. I think she left when she couldn't find any of her former friends and no-one else wanted to speak to her, apart from Jane Perry. Who has only grown a few inches taller, I was surprised to see. She still has that hunched shouldered, beaten look."

"Miaow," murmured Zelah, who had closed her eyes again and faced back towards the sun, now setting over the mountain in a magnificent display of red and orange.

"Well, it's over and I loved seeing Knyghton House again. I miss the old place; I'm glad it's been restored and opened up to the public."

"Me too. Zelah, you OK? You're quiet."

"Enjoying the sun, and your school horror stories."

"It wasn't so bad," Jude said.

"Oh yes it was," Maggie replied. "I had four years of being taunted, until Cath finally got thrown out."

"You've never mentioned it before," Zelah said. "Explains why you were so upset about the treatment Alice suffered when she went up to the High School."

"Yes, it does," Maggie replied. "Anyway, Alice is happy now."

"I'm looking forward to meeting her at the weekend," Jude said.

"And she wants to meet you. She's always fascinated by my past. I've no idea why. Jack, thank God, isn't interested. Anyway, what about you? We've got a lot of catching up to do. How long are you back here for?"

"Whereabouts in the States were you living?" Zelah asked.

"New York," Jude replied. "I won't be going back."

"No? What happened? What about your husband?" Maggie asked.

"Ex-husband, or he will be when the divorce comes through," Jude said. "I left."

"Sorry," Maggie said. "I didn't know. Can you talk about it, what happened?"

"We had a final, big disagreement, the final one of so many I've lost count, and he reacted in the way he usually reacted to people who disagree with him."

"Which was?" Maggie asked, taking another mouthful of beer and not certain she wanted to hear the answer.

"He shot me."

The beer came flying back out onto the table and Maggie scrambled to grab a pile of napkins to wipe it up. "Are you serious?"

Zelah stared at both. Jude rolled up her sleeve, revealing an ugly raw scar on her forearm with a speculative look at Maggie and Zelah.

"I don't know what to say," Maggie said.

"Puts your arguments with Bob into perspective, though, doesn't it," Zelah remarked.

For a second, the three exchanged glances, then they burst into laughter.

Jude wiped tears away with a trembling hand. "I haven't had a laugh for weeks."

"Good joke?" They hadn't heard Nick and Stella walking down the garden to join them.

"Sorry," Maggie managed to get out. "No, not that. Nick, Stella, this is my school friend, Jude Winters. Worm, Nick is the third partner in Maze Investigations and Stella is his fiancée."

Jude stood up, pulled back the mass of black corkscrew curls that had fallen over her face, and shook hands with each of them. "We were talking about our partners, my contribution being my psychopathic ex."

"I'll explain later," Maggie said, indicating to them to take a seat.

Zelah hadn't stopped sniggering. "What's brought you two here? I thought you were going to take advantage of our being out on national parole and go away somewhere?"

"We're on our way," Nick replied. "But an email came in an hour ago I thought you'd want to know about." He turned to Maggie. "This one's for you."

"OK. Give me a precis."

He took a bottle of beer each for him and Stella from the cool box at the side of the table and carefully took off the tops. Maggie smiled, waiting. She saw Jude's puzzled expression and made a mental note to explain later that their colleague Nick was the most unhurriable person they knew, who required patience and understanding of the way in which he thought and considered before speaking.

He took a sip of beer, then said, "It's from a prospective client in Scotland. Her mother died recently. Last week she steeled herself to begin sorting out her possessions. Her mother had died in a care home. Dementia. Nothing had been done with her stuff, as she'd not been there long. Covid." He sipped again. "The client found a load of papers, going back to the 1930s, belonging to her grandmother, a woman called Helen McAlister Stewart. They have revealed a secret no-one in the family had known about. I only know a summary so far. Helen and her three siblings had been abandoned young. Three of them had gone into care, in one of those notorious Catholic orphanages." He paused to drink his beer.

"Are you getting to the point soon, or can I go and get a refill?" Zelah asked.

Nick ignored her. "The client had known about four children, not five, and she's found out not only was there a fifth, but he disappeared when he left the orphanage. The single trace of him is a postcard, postmarked London. But, the message written on it was in Spanish. It said—"

"*Lo siento mucho*," Maggie interrupted, sitting forward.

Nick nodded. "We knew it would find us."

"And off we go, again," Maggie replied, raising an eyebrow at Zelah.

Chapter 3

Maggie had invited her friend to stay through the weekend and the offer had been gratefully and rapidly accepted. Maggie thought Jude seemed relieved but didn't push it. Jude wanted to hear the story of Maze, how it began and the cases they had worked on and the more she heard, the more interested she became.

By the time they sat down to dinner on Friday evening, she bristled with excitement about the new case.

"If there's anything I can do to help, just let me know," Jude said. "What about talking to the medium again? Might there be further information?"

Maggie shook her head. "We know Claire Lewis well enough now to know that if there were, she would have called."

"I can check," Zelah said. "Just to be sure, although I agree with Maggie."

"Let's do it Monday first thing," Maggie replied. "Nick will be back and he can give us some detail."

"If there is any more," Zelah said. "He's told us what he knows."

"Can someone tell me, please?" Alice asked. "It sounds interesting."

"And me," Bob added.

"Ok," Maggie said. "To summarise, the client is called Delilah Sadler. Her mother died a couple of months ago and she's just gotten around to sorting out her mother's effects she'd boxed up and put in the loft after her Mum went into a dementia care home. She found some papers that had been there longer than the recent effects, amongst which she found a postcard from London, postmarked 1939, with the words '*lo siento mucho Helen*'. No signature, addressed to Delilah's – or I should say Lolly's, because that's what she likes to be called – grandmother, Helen McAlister Stewart. She also found family birth, marriage and death certificates of her grandmother's siblings, including a birth certificate for a brother called Brodie. Neither she nor her sister had ever heard about a great uncle Brodie. She'd always thought her grandmother had three siblings, not four so she did some research and what she found has horrified and traumatised her and her family. Grandmother Helen was one of five children, a boy called Brodie being the youngest. The others, in order of age were two older brothers, Malcolm and Lewis and one younger sister, Julie. Now, here comes the traumatic horrifying part. Their father was a drunk, sadistic wife beater, called John McAlister. In 1927, he attacked his wife Grace, beat her to death and did a runner. The police caught him and he was hanged, but that's not a relevant part of the story for us. The two older boys were aged 17 and 16. They were left to fend for themselves. The other three, Helen herself, Julie and Brodie, were taken into care. Brodie was five or six at the time. Grace McAlister had no siblings or family on her side and the McAlister family refused to take the younger children in. So, they went into a Catholic care home. It turned out to be one with a history of both physical and sexual abuse."

She paused and took a slug from her beer, as they sat, silent, anticipating.

"Helen left the home in 1931 and Julie the following year. She managed to set up house on her own and get a job, so she could take in Julie when she left the orphanage. They petitioned for Brodie to be allowed to join them. But the court continually refused. Two years later Helen married. Her husband was a man of good character and standing and prepared to take in Brodie. But again, the court refused. It turned out the home insisted the boy needed special care he could only get with them, as his family could not provide it and they dug their heels in, when Helen and Julie appealed."

"That's odd," Bob interjected.

"Fishy," Zelah added.

"Agreed. Now, fast forward to December 1937. Brodie, who's been in the orphanage for ten years, is about to turn seventeen in a week's time and can leave the home on his birthday. But an incident occurs and instead he runs away. As far as Lolly can tell, Brodie's brothers and sisters never heard from him again, nor did they speak about him. Apparently there's a criminal case, but Lolly hasn't given us any details. That's something we can pick up on Monday. Anyway, to finish what I know, the postcard is stamped 1939, and the location is London. But the message is in Spanish. That's it."

"So this Lolly is just putting two and two together and assuming the card came from Brodie?" Bob asked. "But her family doesn't know if he went to Spain. Or why?"

"That's right," Maggie replied. "They know nothing about the International Brigade volunteers. We're guessing it might be from him because of Claire's message. Lolly thinks he might have run away to London, but she's at a loss to understand why the message was written in Spanish."

"What does it mean?" Alice asked.

Jude replied. "It means '*I am very sorry Helen*'. Does it mean he went to Spain but managed to find his way back to London? I know hardly anything about the war in Spain."

"There was a criminal investigation and Brodie went on the run, so I suppose it's possible he went there to feel safer in another country, but he was so young. Could it have been a possibility, Bob? Didn't the international volunteers leave around that time?"

"Not quite. The International Brigade, what remained of them, left Spain in November 1938," Bob replied. "The Spanish Government decided they shouldn't rely on international help, and expected Hitler and Mussolini to reciprocate by withdrawing their help to Franco's rebels. Big mistake. There were over thirty-five thousand from around the world over the five years of the war, but just a few thousand were still there at the end."

Alice stood up. "I think I'll go read about the Spanish Civil War. It sounds interesting."

"Check the books in the office," Maggie called out to Alice.

"Will she do it?" Jude asked.

"Oh, yes. When my daughter decides on something, she's one hundred percent in. Before she goes back to school Monday morning she'll be able to tell us the entire history."

"Should you be careful with some of those books?" Bob asked.

"I don't think so. She's fifteen, but I'll warn her about the horror stories."

"I agree," Zelah added. "She can take it. But, perhaps let the school know?"

Maggie nodded. "Yes, I should do that. Now, if we're done, another drink beckons and Jude and I are going to relive the good old days."

"That's the signal for me to go," Zelah said. "I'm meeting up with Michelle and the brat tomorrow. Help sort out the latest crisis." She rolled her eyes.

Maggie pulled a face. "Yuk." She turned to Jude. "Michelle Quinn and her son Gerard are the sole heirs to Kennet Quinn's estate. It's the story I told you briefly yesterday, that started with the investigation we did last year into the proposed statue for the Quinn ancestor, Adolphus Quinn, the politician."

Maggie turned back to Zelah. "I presume they're encountering yet more bumps since they came home?"

"""They sound like a slimy bunch and I sense an ongoing story," Jude said, eyes lighting up.

"Let's get those drinks and go talk. The saga of the Quinn family is one of those where you say, '*you couldn't make this up, could you*? 'Come on, I'll tell you the whole sordid tale."

They left the room as Maggie began to explain the details of the Quinn story over her shoulder to Jude. She didn't notice Zelah and Bob exchanging a quick glance, and Zelah's rapid escape from the house.

Chapter 4

Detective Constable Ben Scott smothered a yawn and smiled at his sister as she pointed to a café on the harbour wall.

"You look tired, bro," she said. "I see that yawn. Come on, let's sit and revive you with coffee." Sarah found a free table and ordered coffees and pastries in rapid French.

"You've gone native," Ben said.

"Marriage to a Frenchman. The kids are bilingual now." She sat back and admired the view. "I love it here."

"Business going well?"

"Before Covid, yes. Now, I'll admit we're struggling. We've had a better number of visitors lately and the gites have been taken for the next six weeks. We'll get through, somehow. So, how were Mum and dad?"

Waiting for their drinks to arrive they talked about their parents in happy retirement in the Dordogne, where Ben had spent a pleasant two weeks before driving overnight up to Normandy to take the ferry from Cherbourg. He put his sunglasses on and sat back in his chair, looking at Barfleur harbour. He had been here before and knew how crowded it should be. Today, at the start of a warm September day, there were just a few visitors, of varying nationalities. He caught a morsel of English on the breeze and glanced in the direction of a group of women on the roadside who were hugging and saying goodbye. He couldn't catch the conversation, but took a second glance. One of them looked vaguely familiar, but he felt too tired to take any further notice.

An hour later he said goodbye to Sarah, promised to visit again when the pandemic allowed and headed off on the short journey to Cherbourg harbour. Sitting in the queue to board, he spotted one of the three women again, getting out of her car and crossing the road to the café and toilets, then hurrying back to join the queue as it started to move towards the ferry. He again thought he recognised something familiar about her, but he couldn't put his finger on it. Perhaps he had met her somewhere in his hometown of Bristol, where he was a regular on the social scene. That must be it and he forgot about her as car engines started and the queue began snaking towards the bowels of the huge ship.

Ben had decided to sleep through the journey. There weren't hordes of passengers, it being a Monday afternoon, so he searched for a comfortable bench to accommodate his six-foot-three-inch height, where he could stretch out for the three-hour crossing to Portsmouth, to sleep before the final leg of the journey back to Bristol. He found the ideal spot in the bar area, which also meant no bored kids running around. He had just settled down when he saw her again, on the opposite side of the bar, queueing for a drink. Now it bugged him. He had a tight feeling in his stomach, a gut instinct prompting him that he shouldn't just leave this.

As carefully and surreptitiously as possible, he took out his phone, held it up and raised his free hand as if to ward off the sun from the screen and took a couple of pictures, just as she turned around and looked directly at him, a sharp penetrating gaze. He took a deep breath to stem a sudden feeling of panic and turned to one side, keeping the relaxed posture, and peered closely at the screen, as if trying to make out its contents. The woman paused for a moment then took her drink to the far side of the bar and settling in an armchair, took a book out of her bag. Ben turned his back on her, made a display of stretching out on the seats and, when he thought she couldn't possibly see, texted the pictures to his colleague and partner in Bristol, with a question mark and a plea for a check.

Ten minutes later he received a response. '*Stay alert. Do not approach. We're on it' and* then gave a name, one Ben knew well. He didn't sleep for the remainder of the journey.

Chapter 5

On Monday morning, once Alice had been delivered back to school and Jack had driven into Newport to meet up with Max Howell and a group of their friends, Maggie, Zelah and Jude sat around the office table and began a plan of action for the McAlister case.

"And, it's a paying client this time," Zelah said.

"We took on both the Blackstock and the William McRoberts cases pro bono, sort of," Maggie explained to Jude. "But our waived fees came back ten times over from the amount of publicity the latter case generated and the additional clients we signed on."

"That's aimed at me," Zelah said.

"Is it true?" Jude asked.

"Reluctantly, yes," Zelah replied. "But as I'm the one who does the publicity and marketing, I still had to put in a lot of work to make it happen."

"And we are so very grateful to you." Maggie gave her a wide, falsely sycophantic smile.

"Bollocks," Zelah muttered. "Right, let's get on. Nick's bowing out of this one in any active sense, for now. Strikes me he's spending more time contemplating what to do about his relationship with Max and less time actually working on it." She turned to Maggie. "What do you think?"

"He's not a natural man of action. His brain is what I guess a game of chess is like, not that I've ever played. He wants to work out several potential moves in advance and the consequence of each one before he decides how to act. But I'm sensing growing frustration in Max, who is an action man.

"Perhaps they need their heads knocking together."

"Perhaps they need someone to act as mediator?" Jude said.

Zelah shrugged. "Give it a shot, why don't you? In the meantime, we have work to do. Between Claire and this woman Lolly Sadler, what can we put together as a starter for ten, before we speak to her?"

Maggie was about to reply when Bob joined them.

"Oh hi, we're going to discuss Brodie McAlister. Do you want to sit in?"

"Um, yes OK, for this part, then I'm off to the office, after I've had some breakfast," he pulled out a chair, ignoring the loud scraping noise and scowled as he sat down.

"Too much paperwork in his promotion," Maggie explained to Jude, who gave Bob a sympathetic grimace. "Right, let's start with Claire. She told us the third message, '*lo siento mucho*', had a Scottish connection involving someone called Charlie. Bob, you knew something about him, didn't you, and the International Brigaders who stayed on in Spain?"

"Yes, but I got some of it wrong, I've found out. Turns out, just a handful of Internationals stayed on. Some of them who did withdraw with the majority when they were ordered to go home, sneaked back. The wanted to join the final line of defence to allow the main army time to get away across the river at Flix, up to the north. I think I said Charlie was a young man?"

Maggie nodded.

"Well, more recent archaeology puts him in his forties, and most likely Spanish, a local Catalan. Towards the end there were a lot of older men and boys. So if this Brodie was seventeen, he would have fitted in." He glanced at his watch. "I have to go. Good luck."

"Thanks for the info," Maggie said as he made his way to the kitchen. "What else do we need to know before we call Lolly Sadler?"

"I've sketched out a brief timeline," Zelah said, handing Maggie and Jude a sheet of paper. "I did some research into the McAlister family and I found some of the details about the death of the mother. As you can see, John McAlister married Grace Adair in 1910. They had five children over ten years, with Brodie the youngest, in 1920. John McAlister was a petty criminal with convictions for theft and assault, in and out of prison from the time he married Grace. But if he was so violent as to kill her outright in 1927, he wouldn't have started there. She must have been an abused woman before that."

"I know about that," Jude muttered.

"Anyway," Zelah went on, "As we know, the two eldest boys Malcolm and Lewis were left to make their own way and Helen, Julie and Brodie were taken into a children's home. The first place they were in wasn't too bad. But in 1930 they were transferred to the hell that was the orphanage. There's an ongoing enquiry in Scotland about the whole disgusting affair, and it's already found the children there, including those in the nineteen thirties, were

… hang on, let me find the quotes." She hammered her keyboard.

"Here it is, they were subjected to '*threat and abuse*', were sexually assaulted and were beaten with leather straps, crucifixes and hair brushes and it confirms the children received, and again I quote, '*no love, no compassion, no dignity and no comfort*'." She sat back.

Maggie and Jude sat in silence for several seconds.

"And that's where the McAlister children were sent?" Maggie asked.

Zelah nodded.

"Well, we had some verbally offensive nuns teaching us, but that's a whole new level," Jude said. "Ours leaned towards mental cruelty, with the occasional slap. Those poor, poor kids. Helen was lucky to get out when she did. I'm guessing she didn't pass on anything about what happened to her, to her own children?"

"Seems not," Zelah replied. "She married James Stewart and they had three children, James, Janet, and Ewan. Janet Stewart is, or was, Lolly's mother. We can ask when we speak to Lolly if there's ever been anything that gave her a hint about her grandmother's experiences, from anything her mother or her grandmother Helen said. Janet died earlier this year but the enquiry has been in the news for a couple of years, so she would have read about it, or heard it on the news."

"But as we well know, Zelah," Maggie said," some people's interest in their family history begins with the discovery of an unexpected event. It's possible they knew nothing about their connection to the enquiry."

"True; we'll find out when we speak to her. There's more. Shall I go on?"

Chapter 6

Maggie and Jude nodded.

"The case, in which Brodie McAlister's name comes up, was an inquiry, not a trial. It took place in Glasgow in December 1937 and into 1938, around a month after Brodie's seventeenth birthday and after he disappeared. It was an official enquiry into a suspicious death at the orphanage. A boy aged fifteen had been beaten to death. A doctor gave evidence of long-term abuse, probably within the family home although that was hinted at rather than said explicitly, and the ultimate cause of death was a blow from a blunt instrument. A nun who gave evidencc at the inquest stated the boy came to the orphanage at the request of his mother, due to beatings from his father, and had shown behaviour of mental instability. She also said there had been an ongoing feud between Brodie McAlister and the boy and they had fought often, and viciously from her account."

"Was there any questioning of why the boys were allowed to fight '*viciously*'?" Jude asked. "And did anyone question the evidence about the '*mental instability*'?

"I haven't found more information yet," Zelah replied. "It's a good question but would it have been a matter for the inquiry?"

"It should have been, but it's a good possibility no-one questioned the word of the Church, given in a court of law. Can we get the transcript?" Maggie asked.

"Again, don't know," Zelah replied. She checked her watch. "Time to call Lolly Sadler. You ready?"

"As I'll ever be," Maggie replied.

Zelah punched the number into the conference phone in the centre of the table.

"Delilah Sadler."

"Good morning, this is Zelah Trevear, of Maze Investigations. Before we begin, can I ask if you prefer Delilah or Lolly?"

"Lolly, please. Don't know what my mother was thinking." The voice was soft, with a strong Scottish lilt, and confident. "Sorry. I'm so pleased you've called. Nick told me you have some information that might help to clear up this mystery we've found."

"We'll do our best. We can tell you what we know and how we received our information, which may be a shock to you," Zelah said.

"Ah, Nick told me about the medium, if that's what you mean." Lolly replied. "I don't mind. If it's real, it makes life more interesting, don't you think? So, shall I begin?"

"Please do," Zelah said. "Just so you know, there are three of us at this end. My Maze colleague, Maggie Gilbert, and a friend who's working with us at present, Jude Winters."

"Right. Well, you know my mother died earlier this year and my sister and I have been trying to sort out probate and during the search we didn't find any documents regarding ownership of her house. I knew she and my dad took it over in the nineteen sixties, when Grandma Helen passed on, but I'd never thought about who owned it. I'd never been up in the attic, but when I couldn't find anything in Mum's bureau, I decided to go up there to check if there might be anything stored away. You wouldn't believe how much stuff I found. I won't go into that, but in one old, taped up box I found family papers going back to my grandmother's time and, I believe, my great grandmother." She paused and shuddered. "I cannot tell you the extent of my horror when I found the newspaper clippings, about my great grandmother's murder by her husband. I felt sick." She paused again. "But that was nothing compared to the paperwork about the children, including grandma, being taken into care and moved around, and when I saw the name of the place, I knew the outcome wouldnae be good."

Jude raised her hand to ask a question and Zelah nodded.

"Hi, Lolly, my name is Jude and I'm working with these guys at the moment. I have a question, if that's OK?"

"Of course."

"Do you think your mother knew about the box of papers?"

"I've thought about that, and no, I don't think she did. I found the box stacked up against the back wall of the attic and at the bottom of a heap more boxes. I should explain the house is an old one, built back around nineteen hundred and the attic is large, with its own staircase. There were pieces of broken furniture up there hiding the boxes, and it looked like no-one had rummaged amongst any of it for decades, judging by the cobwebs and the undisturbed dust. So, no, I don't think my mother knew about it, but if she did, she never said so."

"Thank you, Lolly."

"Are you an American?" A note of caution sounded in the voice.

Jude smiled. "No, I'm Welsh, but I've just returned home after fifteen years in New York. I guess some of the accent has rubbed off."

"Oh well." Another slight pause, then "Let me pick up the story again."

Jude gave Maggie a quizzical look and a shoulder shrug, which Maggie returned, as Lolly went back to her story.

"I found some other bits and pieces in the box, including this postcard, sent from London in 1939. Nick said you understood the words written on it, and it means '*I am very sorry, Helen*'. Pity we can't read the other bit."

"There's more?" Maggie interrupted, leaning forward. "Sorry to interrupt, Lolly, but we didn't know there was more."

"Och, yes. Another sentence or two, but it's so faded it's nae more than an impression on the card. You canna make out the words at all."

Zelah spoke this time. "Lolly, we're going to need to see the original copy. We can ask a forensic expert to tell us what the sentence says. How about one of us comes up to meet you? This might all be easier face-to-face, instead of over the phone."

"That would be fine with me. When would you like to come?"

Zelah glanced at Maggie and Jude, pointed at herself and mouthed 'tomorrow'? They both nodded back.

"I can fly up tomorrow," Zelah said into the phone console. "If that's convenient for you."

"Aye, tomorrow is fine. It'll be nice to meet you. I'd prefer a face to talk to, too."

"Good. I'll check out flights and let you know the time. What's your address?" Lolly told her.

"I think we should end this call now," Zelah went on. "Then tomorrow you and I, Lolly, will pick up again and we can go into detail."

"Agreed."

"Good. I'll call you back in about half an hour. Goodbye."

They all sat back in their seats. Maggie spoke first. "W

hat an unexpected turn-up."

"But hopefully one that'll give us a big jump forward. I'll start on sorting out the flight. What will you two do?"

"Take an hour to think about the best options," Maggie replied.

"I have an idea," Jude said. Maggie and Zelah turned to her. She smiled. "Maggie, let's go to Spain. This week."

Chapter 7

As the ferry entered Portsmouth Harbour and passengers were advised to return to their cars, Ben Scott followed the woman he had seen in Barfleur down the narrow staircases, half a flight behind her and, he hoped, hidden by the people descending ahead of him. He breathed a sigh of relief when she exited onto his car deck. Her car sat two rows across and ahead of him, but he thought that, with luck, as the cars moved off she wouldn't get too far ahead. As he stood next to his car, apparently fumbling with the key in the lock, he noted the make, model and colour of her car, but couldn't make out the licence plate without being too obvious. Once in his driving seat he had time to send a quick text with the information to his colleague, who would relay it to the local non-uniformed police who were waiting on the dockside in unmarked cars. Drivers started their engines and the first line of cars moved towards the now open end of the ferry. Again he was relieved she hadn't once looked back in his direction.

The queue inched forward. He calculated there would be about forty cars between them, which would even out when they reached passport control and the single queue divided into half a dozen, but he still twitched with anxiety. His partner had texted that local police would tail the woman's car once she cleared customs and passport control, both of which had been told to wave her through. Still, Ben wanted to be part of this. He would follow for as much of the journey as he could.

His calculations were correct. His car had also been given a wave through and, although he could see hers waiting, they cleared passport control in tandem and he followed her out and onto the motorway, with just two cars between them. He planned to tail her as far as Bristol, where he would drop out unless told to stay on the case, which he hoped would happen.

But, to his regret, no-one contacted him again, so he exited the motorway at Bristol and made his way home, hoping for sleep, but knowing he wouldn't relax until he knew the outcome of the incident. This was too important to sleep through and, after all, he had been the one to set the chase in motion.

With a start he realised he had forgotten, in his tiredness and excitement, to let his partner know there had been three women at Barfleur harbour. He had just closed his eyes when its significance hit him. He leapt out of bed, grabbed his phone and rang his colleague, who passed him to a senior office, who swore and took the information and descriptions then told him to get some sleep then get into the office. He would be needed.

He had been asleep for just forty minutes when his phone rang again. His senior officer didn't greet him, but said three words before ending the call. "Get here now."

**

After the discussion about Charlie and Spain, Bob Pugh sat in the kitchen, contemplating life over a strong coffee and two steaming croissants. As he waited for both to cool sufficiently he thought through his day ahead, and grimaced. He had more forms to complete than he had known existed in the modern police force. Completing them would be followed by two appraisals, both with old-timers who would be resentful and non-compliant when faced with questions about their goals and aspirations. Their desire to retire in one piece without nightmares would be what they aspired to. Fortunately, neither had had any issues or complaints in the past twelve months. Both were good, solid constables. He would have to find a way to have them comply without realising they were doing so. 'Not much chance,' he mused. They had been around long enough to know when the wool was being pulled. He hoped they had sufficient respect for him to … his musings were interrupted by his phone ringing. He pulled it out of his pocket.

"Pugh."

As he listened to the message he jumped up from the chair, grabbed a croissant and stuffed it into his mouth as he ran through the hall, snatched his coat and slammed the door on the way out. Reaching his car he saw Maggie standing at the office window. She waved to him. He returned a perfunctory wave, adequate, he hoped, to forestall any concern she might have at his sudden, noisy departure. She moved away. Just as well. He couldn't tell her what he had just heard, she would have been hysterical. And angry. The reckoning would come later. In the meantime, he had to get to the station, then up to Hereford, as fast as his vehicle would take him, knowing the alert was out and no eagle-eyed traffic boyo would try to stop him.

Despite the fear, he felt excitement streaming through him. A break, at last. The hunt was on.

The first one.

Chapter 8

Maggie sat up and folded her arms, staring open-mouthed at her friend. "What?"

"Why the hell would you decamp to Spain? Apart from one message relayed by a medium and a postcard we haven't seen, what possible reason could you have?" Zelah asked.

"Much too soon," Maggie agreed. "We need to see the postcard and research the unlawful killing of the boy from the orphanage before we decide to go anywhere." She sat back. "Which brings me to my next thought. What is our purpose here? We haven't fully established what Lolly wants from us, have we?"

Jude held up her hands. "OK, sorry, impulsive. Just seems to me that whatever Lolly wants, there's a connection with Spain that needs exploring."

"Yes, there is," Maggie replied. "But not yet. That's not how we do it." Turning to Zelah, she said, "Can you get a flight tomorrow to Glasgow, do you think?"

"Might be Edinburgh then train or hire a car, but yes, I can get there." She paused. "I might even go up tonight."

Maggie nodded. "We can go on with the background research." She didn't look at Jude. Zelah picked up the hint.

"Right, I'll leave you to it." She leaned down to pick up her briefcase then paused, turning to Jude. "It's not a bad idea, and someone might need to go, but not yet, not until we have a better understanding of what happened in Brodie McAlister's life, if he went to Spain, and if he did, why and when. Once we have that information we can re-visit the idea of a continental jolly."

Jude nodded, not looking at Maggie.

The slamming of the front door caused a momentary distraction and Maggie got up and walked to the window, where she could see Bob jumping into his car. She waved.

"Unusual for him not to say where he's going in such a hurry." She turned back. "See you later, Zelah."

"Message received and understood," Zelah muttered and departed.

"Kitchen," Maggie said to Jude.

"Garden," Jude replied. "I need some air and we need to talk some more, huh?"

The weather had held, with the sun shining and although the slightest of chills suggested autumn-to-come in the air, it was still sufficiently warmish to not require anything more protective against the gentle breeze than a thin sweater. As they sat, drawing in the warmth, Maggie waited for Jude to begin to talk, which she did.

"OK. You've guessed there's more to my story than I've admitted so far."

"Of course, but I've been leaving it to you to decide on the right time and situation to tell me. I think we just arrived, Worm."

Jude smiled. "Yep. So, the old man. A total bastard, which I didn't find out until we got back to New York and he went back to work."

"Back to New York? From where?"

"Las Vegas."

Maggie stared goggle-eyed at her friend. "You aren't seriously going to tell me …"

"You got it. Three days. Love at first sight. Married in an Elvis chapel. We just hit it off from the get-go. We seemed to share a sense of humour, he loved English girls, etc etc. At the time it seemed like a dream come true. He's exceptionally handsome." She stopped and took a drawn-out sip of coffee as Maggie sat back and folded her arms.

"When we got back, the apartment was great, he was great. You know, loving, caring, introduced me to his friends. I felt wonderful."

"How long did it last?"

"Difficult to say. The changes happened so gradually I hardly noticed."

Jude looked down at her hands and picked at her nails, which were rough and jagged, at odds with her otherwise smooth appearance. "After a couple of weeks I decided to go back to work and found a job. He didn't like that, said how I disappointed him, thought I should stay at home, his job being so stressful, dangerous, and so on. I felt guilty. I kept going for a couple of weeks then I quit and started my own business so I could work from home. That didn't work out so well either. He didn't like me talking to clients. Next, he complained about my looks. I didn't dress to impress him. He wanted me to do my hair and make-up every day. I didn't want to. Then he didn't like my domestic skills, wanted me to cook what his mother had cooked." She tried a grin which was more of a grimace. "He soon found out I'm not a skilled cook. But, all the time he was kind, charming, loving, particularly when colleagues and friends were watching. Bought me flowers and chocolate, but warned me against getting fat."

She paused and looked up. "The first time he hit me I packed a bag and walked out. He found me after three days and persuaded me to come back." She laughed. "He showed such abject sorrow, crying, hugging me. Told me how deeply he loved me, he got angry because his job ensured danger and I needed to behave in a way not to stress him further."

"You've never told me about his job," Maggie interrupted.

"No, I didn't. He's a policeman," Jude said. "One of New York's finest. He even has a medal for bravery; he confronted a gunman and saved a woman's life, de-escalated a dangerous situation in a drug store."

"Wow. And, let me guess, you thought no-one would believe you if you accused him of abuse?"

"Exactly. I had no friends; he didn't like me to have a life in any way separate from his."

"How long did this go on?" Maggie asked. She could see Jude's increasing distress, but an instinct told her Jude was speaking openly for the first time and needed to get it out.

"Six months, getting worse all the time." She looked up, her expression contorting between rage and desperation to explain. "I've read about these situations. We all have, but I never, ever, once thought this – let's call it what it is – this abuse applied to me, until the day his violence put me in hospital." She laughed, sharply and bitterly. "I thought I could manage the situation, but those few days convinced me if I stayed any longer the consequences could be fatal and I should get out, before it was too late." She took a deep breath. “A nurse in the hospital kept giving me odd looks when I said I had fallen, I was clumsy and careless, I had been drinking, which I hadn’t. The night before the hospital discharged me she came to talk to me. She didn’t ask any questions; she told me about how something had happened to her and gave me the address of a refuge. Then she walked away.”

“What did you do? Did you go to the refuge?”

“No. He picked me up the following day. He cross-examined me when we returned to the apartment. He was paranoid someone might not have believed my excuses. That was when he told me he would kill me if I ever told anyone what he had done. Something in my face must have told him someone did suspect. He grabbed me by the hair, demanded to know. I told him about the nurse but insisted I hadn’t told her anything. He started to shout, got wilder and wilder. Then he pulled out his gun. He wasn’t even supposed to have it with him. He put it to my head. I don’t remember what happened after that. I screamed and yelled and fought and tried to pull away. Somehow, in the struggle, the gun went off, and back I went to hospital.”

“Did you tell them this time?”

“Yes. They held an inquiry. I told them everything.”

“So they charged him?”

“No. He insisted I was hysterical when I got back. I had been planning to leave him and had staged the ‘accident’ and I had taken the gun and pointed it at him and he had disarmed me, but couldn’t prevent the gun going off. He got off and they wanted to charge me.”

"What? Are you kidding me?" Maggie shouted, despite Jude's sagging shoulders.

"They let me go home, but kept him to complete some details. I grabbed my passport and as many clothes as I could stuff in a backpack. Then, my lucky break. I didn't know a neighbour had overheard one of James's threatening rants at me, and she offered to help. Boy, was she a life saver. I told her I planned to head to the refuge and begged her not to tell him anything. I stayed at the refuge for a month. I told them the full story and they arranged for the neighbour to give a statement, anonymously. That kept him away and the charge against me got quietly dropped. Once my arm healed I got on the first flight back, to Paris. From there I hired a car to Brussels, then the Eurostar to London. And here I am." She stared fiercely at her friend. "Maggie, I arrived here the morning of the reunion. I have nowhere else to go."

Maggie stood up and bent over Jude, enveloping her in a breath crushing hug.

"You have been through hell," she whispered. "You can stay as long as you like and need."

Jude began to sob. "I hoped I could rely on you, Maggot. Thank you for trusting me," she whispered back.

"Always, Worm. Another thought. Does he know where you are?"

"Honestly, not sure. He'll have found out I got on a plane to Paris, which I did because I knew he could check and didn't want him following me to the UK. I don't think he can find out about the car and the Eurostar, but I wouldn't put it past him to try."

"Did you ever talk about Cwmbran and Newport and any friends you have here?"

Jude turned her head away, nodding. "I'm so sorry, Maggot. I did."

Maggie squeezed her arm. "No worries. No reason why you shouldn't have done, but it's best for us to know and be prepared, just in case. Are you OK with me telling Bob and the others about your story, Bob particularly?"

"Of course. Now you know, I feel I can trust the people you trust."

"Good. OK, let's go and start some work. We have a shedload of background researching to do." She paused as they turned to go back into the house and office. "You want to go to Spain in case he turns up here, don't you."

Jude nodded. "Running scared."

Chapter 9

Maggie put an arm around Jude's shoulder. "You are not a scared woman and you never have been. You have always been strong and brave. This was an aberration and they happen to the best of us. Just remember that. Come on, things to do."

"Good, I need to be busy. Your colleague, though? Is she always so … what's the word, brusque? Abrupt?"

"More so than usual. We're all tense right now, constantly looking over our collective shoulders." She sighed. "I'm twitchy, too. The three witches would harm us without a second thought, and not just us. If they find you're here, this could put you in their spotlight too. How do you feel about that?"

"From what I've seen, you're a great team. You have each other's backs. I'm OK being part of that, I think."

"We're going to have to keep close for the coming weeks. They'll start to appear. Then, watch out."

**

Zelah called mid-afternoon to report she had booked a flight to Edinburgh, a car to Glasgow and back and a hotel in Edinburgh overnight. She would be back late-ish evening so they shouldn't expect to see her until Wednesday. If something happened for Maggie's attention, she'd call after her meeting with Lolly Sadler.

Maggie had set Jude to learn as much as she could about the end days of the Spanish Civil War, when the last of the

International Brigaders escaped Spain and returned to the UK and elsewhere. With Maggie's collection of books piled up on the arm of the settee in the office, Jude settled down and was soon immersed.

Maggie had decided to look up news reporting about the institution to which the McAlister children had been sent. It didn't take long for her to snort in disgust and call Jude's attention to what she had discovered.

"Listen to this. At another of the institutions run by this order, searchers found a mass burial of over four hundred children and babies. Babies! What were they doing? What were they thinking?"

"How many babies?" Jude asked.

"It says here around a third of the bodies found were children under five years old. And what's more, the nuns can't provide the records."

"Sounds suspicious."

"Seems a lot of them were natural deaths. They do seem to have registered most of them, but there's no record of a burial."

"They were orphans, weren't they?"

"Mostly, yes. And if they had families it appears they made no effort to trace them." Maggie shook her head. "They just threw them in to the ground with no record to mark their memory."

"How does it connect to the McAlister children?"

"Same order of nuns, different location."

Jude wheeled her chair across the room to sit beside Maggie and look at her screen. "Is there evidence of abuse in this place?"

"No, but they only have the nuns' word for that. Look here," Maggie pointed to a paragraph where a man had related a story to the newspaper. "This poor chap lost his brother, literally, never knew what happened to him. Disappeared when he was thirteen. He found the death certificate," she moved the story further down the page. "Here, it says cause of death was a brain haemorrhage, but he had heard stories of his brother being struck with a golf club."

"Which would have caused a brain haemorrhage, wouldn't it?"

"Possibly," Maggie replied. "But too many years later and there's no proof."

"But it does suggest a pattern of abuse."

"I agree, but to make a case we need proof. And I suspect we aren't going to get any, just hearsay."

Jude returned to the settee. "I'll carry on with the Spanish Civil War, although I think I have the sequence of events and the politics. I think I'll go onto one of the books Alice was reading over the weekend. What do you recommend I start with?"

"Umm, there's an excellent history there, but it's a longish read. Perhaps keep that one for bedtime. How about reading the personal experiences? The Welsh miners' books of their memories and experiences are good. Then there's one called *Testimony of Women.* That's the book Zelah cautioned about Alice reading. And there's also the archaeology book Bob bought recently. I think that's where you'll find the story of Charlie he mentioned earlier." She glanced at her watch. "I should start on dinner. Jack'll be home soon. Bob though … There was something about the way he left …" She shrugged. "Whatever. He'll call or just turn up when he's ready."

Jude already had her head down in a book.

An hour later, when Maggie had joined Jude back in the office, she had just decided they would go ahead and eat when the front door opened with the sound of voices and something being dragged in. The 'something' turned out to be a seriously drunk Max Howell, muttering and pulling at his hair and being held up by one arm and shoulder by Jack. Maggie jumped up to take the trailing side.

"Let's get him into the lounge," she said. "He can sleep it off on the settee and you can tell me what's happened."

They took off Max's jacket and Maggie put a bowl on the floor close to his head, just in case. "He'd better not miss it," she muttered to Jack and an amused Jude, as they headed to the kitchen and sat down to eat.

"He's going through a bad patch," Jack said. "You know why."

"I've already told Jude the story," Maggie replied, "with Nick's permission."

"Poor boy," Jude said. "Is he getting counselling?"

"No," Jack replied. "He talks to us for now. But, I think he's starting to open up to Nick and to Stella. She's been great, apparently."

"Good," Maggie replied. She threw Jack a quizzical look. "Is that all or is there something else?"

Jack nodded and rubbed the back of his neck. "When he gets properly drunk he's said a couple of things that bother me." He took in a deep breath. "I think he had an affair with Helen Redland."

Maggie dropped her fork onto her plate. "What makes you think that?"

"I can't tell you some of what he's said. Too embarrassing, for him and me. But, I'm certain every time he mumbles it out, she got him into some heavy stuff. Weird sex, vicious sadism, with drugs." He shook his head. "Bad stuff."

"She's a malevolent woman," Maggie said, sitting back. "She must have known he was abused in India after he lost his mother and how he hated his father for abandoning them. He is so fragile." She put a hand on Jack's arm. "Thanks for telling me. Do you think Nick knows?"

Jack shrugged. "It comes out when he's so bladdered he doesn't know what he's saying and can't remember afterwards. Do you think we should tell Nick?"

"No," Maggie said decisively. "It's a tough one, but Max trusts you and that would be a betrayal of his trust."

"Does he have any idea you know, Jack?" Jude asked.

"I don't think so, it's mostly mumbling. Should I let him know I know?"

Maggie put her elbows on the table. "Not sure. You could suggest he's been muttering some odd things, see how he reacts. If he shuts you out then no, don't even hint you understood. Let me think about it, OK?"

"Ok. Right, I'm going to see how he's doing; if he's puked on the carpet." He grinned at Maggie, who returned an exaggerated grimace of horror.

"Call me if he has. No, on second thoughts, don't."

"That's a hell of a burden for a boy of his age," Jude said when Jack was out of earshot.

"Agreed, and that worries me no end," Maggie replied. "From what I know of most teenagers of his age, when a friend is in this much trouble, they can't handle it and walk away."

"Well, I'm no expert on teenagers, but what little I know tells me you're right. Are they that different to how we were?"

"It's a more superficial society now. Anyhow, let's not go there or we'll still be here at breakfast." She yawned and set Jude off yawning.

"You know, I think I'll go to bed with a couple of those Spanish Civil War books."

"Carry on," Maggie replied. "I'll wait a while for Bob, and for the potential puker to wake up, or not. I'll see if we can get him up to a bed."

When Jude had gone, Maggie's phone pinged with a text from Zelah, telling her she had arrived in Edinburgh, would be meeting Lolly Sadler in the morning at eleven and would call afterwards with an update on what she had learned. The text also said she had decided on an extra night in Edinburgh in order to visit some archives for information on the enquiry into the death of the boy in the orphanage.

Maggie returned a '*thumbs up*' emoji and began to clear away the dinner detritus.

From the hallway the sound of low voices and some stumbling on the stairs told her Max had recovered somewhat and was being helped up the stairs by Jack. She left him to it and shortly after he reappeared in the kitchen.

“He didn’t throw up and he came round, sort of, so I’ve put him in my room, on a mattress on the floor. I’ll keep an eye on him tonight. Is that OK?”

“Of course. It’s what I was about to suggest. I’ve just made myself a fruit tea. You want anything?”

No thanks. I’ve been thinking about what to do. We have to tell Bob. There’s a national hunt for Helen Redland and the others. He needs to know.”

Maggie’s cheeks reddened. “OK, agreed. He was furious when we left him out last time and rightly so.” She paused, hearing the front door opening and closing. “Here he is now. Let’s tell him once he’s settled down.”

As he had closed the door Bob shouted her name and the urgency in his voice told her her earlier instinct had been right. Something had happened. She went out into the hall and found him standing ashen faced outside the office. The muscles in Maggie’s stomach clenched so tightly she thought they would solidify.

“What?” She had expected an outburst, but instead, he grinned.

“We’ve got one of them. You’re not going to like the story, but it’s turned out well. Come on, let’s go and sit down and I’ll tell you both what’s happened.”

“Kitchen,” she said. “I’m guessing you haven’t eaten all day?”

He nodded.

As she warmed up a plate of food and put it on the table with some force, none of them spoke. After swallowing a mouthful with a sigh of appreciation he looked up at Maggie on his right, then Jack on his left.

“Sherry Martin. She was on her way to Hereford.”

Chapter 10

Maggie leapt up from the table. "Hereford? The school?"

Bob nodded. "They stopped her trying to get into the grounds." He held out his hand to her. "There was never any danger. Please, sit down Maggie."

She put her head down, remained with her arms wrapped around herself, clutching at her sides. Bob stood up, gently unfolded her arms and lowered her back into her seat, then put his hands on her shoulders.

Maggie turned to look up at him, frowning and questioning, before the reality struck her.

"Of course; Matthew."

"Who is Matthew?" a voice from the doorway asked.

Jude stood in the doorway, face pale with concern.

"Come and sit down," Maggie indicated. "Matthew is Alice's best friend at school. His father is a big cheese in national security services, head of something or other." She held up a hand as Jude went to speak. "Don't ask me which service. I've never wanted to know and I don't think anyone would tell me if I did ask."

Bob had returned to his seat.

"Finish the story," Maggie said to him. "When did you find out?"

"When I left this morning," he replied. "A text alerted me to a major operation underway with Sherry Martin and told me to head up to Hereford. I had started to put two and two together already in the car when the detailed intel came through. She'd been detained trying to get into the grounds. The school had been warned. They have protocols, with Matthew living and studying there, so they stopped her before her feet touched the ground on the school side of the fence."

"Did they think she targeted Alice?"

"Not just Alice. They found pictures on her phone of Matthew with Alice, so the assumption was Matthew could have been the target too. I'd told them about her dinner here and how she showed what I thought was an unnatural dislike of Alice. And Alice being Matthew's friend, they took notice." He stood up again, walked back to Maggie and knelt down, taking her hands in his. "She wasn't ever in danger. Being Matthew's friend ensured that."

Maggie nodded. "Well thank God for Matthew and his spooky father."

Jack, who had slouched in his chair throughout the exchange, sat up and said, "It must have made the bitch shit herself, being pounced on by … what, men with fucking big guns?"

Bob nodded. "You bet. They were screaming at her, pinning her to the ground with weapons pointed at her, treating her like a terrorist. Serves her right. Despite everything I tried to teach her, Sherry never properly did her homework."

"Language, Jack. What happens now? Does Alice know; or Matthew?"

"No, Maggie, the kids don't know," Bob replied. "And I need to make this crystal clear to all of you. Nothing must ever – ever – go outside this room. Please don't even tell

Zelah or Nick, yet. I'll get clearance for you to tell them. For now, Sherry's been carted off to London to be interviewed by security services."

"Can you be there?" Maggie asked.

"No, no chance," Bob replied. "Can I get up now? My knees are killing me."

"I suppose."

"I should get information, though, on where she's been and what she's been up to. And who she was with. They'll get it out of her, guaranteed."

"Well, I'm not sure what that means, but I don't care. You believe she'd partnered up with Helen Redland and possibly Emer McCarthy Miller."

"And we think they're all back in the country now. Look, I have to go back to work. Are you OK?"

"Yes. We should all go to bed," Maggie said, looking at Jack, then Jude. "We'll talk about this in the morning. Oh, Bob. Jack will need to talk to you tomorrow. It's relevant and urgent."

"Ok. I'll get back tonight, but it could be late, maybe not til early morning. Is this really important?" he asked Jack.

"I think so," Jack replied. "It's about Helen Redland."

"Right, that's important." He glanced at his watch, hovered for a moment then frowned. "I must go. They want us on the end of a phone and I'm leading the briefing. I'll be back in the morning, by seven latest. Can you talk to me then?"

Jack nodded. "Max is here. Perhaps, if he's awake he'll talk to you, too. He has to, now."

"See you later." Bob gave Maggie a brief kiss and squeezed her arm, then left them.

"Go up and check on Max," Maggie said to Jack, then to Jude "I need a drink. A strong one."

"I'll join you," Jude replied.

"Never a quiet moment here," Maggie replied. "I have no idea what comes next but, like I said, it's going to be pretty scary."

Chapter 11

Zelah had spent an uneventful evening at the hotel in Edinburgh. She picked up her hire car at nine the following morning and set off, having already booked herself in for an extra night and changed her plane ticket.

Having spent the evening alone with a room service dinner, she had read through her notes again and reviewed the online information about the children's homes and the active enquiry. By eleven she had formed a plan. She was expecting additional information in the archives, in both Edinburgh and Glasgow. It would be crazy to lose the opportunity to visit, as they were both currently open to the public. The others could manage without her so when she had finished talking to Lolly Sadler she would go to the archive to put in as many hours as she would be allowed to stay before heading back to the hotel.

She already had an idea that public procedures in Scotland differed significantly from those in England, Wales and Northern Ireland and her research had confirmed this.

For starters, the system of public inquests differed in Scotland. Here, once a death was registered, which had to be done within eight days, the Procurator Fiscal would determine if a Fatal Accident Enquiry were appropriate. This would happen if the cause of death had not been established in the 8-day period, or if there were circumstances requiring further investigation. Zelah presumed a child beaten to death in an orphanage might prompt such an enquiry, but you never knew, given the age period in which it had occurred. Responsibility for the enquiry would then be handed to a local Sheriff's court, and in 1938 a jury would have been involved.

She had made two phone calls, one to the National Records of Scotland Office in Edinburgh and one to the Glasgow Family History at the Mitchell Centre in North Street, close to the city centre. She would go there after her meeting with Lolly Sadler, and spend the remainder of the day there. She had then arranged a visit to the National Records of Scotland Office in Edinburgh the following day, booking a desk in the Historical Search room in General Register House. Before her visit she would also go to New Register House to find out if she could get her hands on a copy of the death certificate of the boy who had died as a result of the beating, if she hadn't sourced it in Glasgow.

After hours searching on the internet she had found the name. He was David Laird, aged fifteen when he died. She also found the approximate date of the incident in which he died, hopefully adequate to obtain the certificate.

She had booked herself on the final flight back to Cardiff and later on, after meeting with Lolly Sadler, would let Maggie know what she planned.

It came to Zelah, as she drove and thought over her plans, that she felt excited about this case, and with it shock that she felt this excited. The past year had taken its toll and now the worst seemed to be over, she knew she had lost some of her previous enjoyment in her work, any pleasure in discovery being hampered by a constant sense of disquiet and occasionally, although she would never admit it to anyone, fear. She knew, of course, it wasn't over and wouldn't be until the three witches, as she thought of Sherry Martin, Helen Redland and Emer McCarthy Miller, had been caught and dealt with. She wouldn't care if any or all of them died as the outcome of their efforts to inflict damage on herself and her friends and their families. They were her family now, these newly acquired relations and relationships and she would fight for them as fiercely as Maggie fought for her children and Nick for Stella and his newly found Max. She and her husband Martin had lived in a bubble, needing no-one else, and when he died she had been so devastated she put up a barrier against all humans, gaining the reputation of a grumpy harridan, a person to be avoided at all costs. Meeting and teaming up with Maggie and Nick had changed her life, had given her the courage to re-visit her youth and as a result, she had discovered a family. She now had Mischa Quinn as a surrogate daughter, two nephews in Stephen and Niall McCarthy Miller and Rick Mathis in Canada as an increasingly close friend. She loved them all. A year ago she had been tempted to ditch them, worried the increasing love she felt for these people was an emotional vulnerability she would be better off without. But no longer. Zelah Trevear, she admitted to herself with a smile as she drove along the M8 motorway to Glasgow, had become a nicer human and happier for it. But the barrier wouldn't come down yet. She could still enjoy her ability to wind people up and she would never not speak her mind.

Zelah's thoughts had sped her along to the outskirts of the city and were interrupted by the satnav telling her to take the next exit. Ten minutes later she pulled up outside Lolly

Sadler's house. Stepping out of her car she looked up at an imposing end-of-terrace, double fronted sandstone building on three floors, she guessed Victorian, if not older.

Two central sets of steps led up to a wide black front door with tiers of plants on either side down to the low wall marking the front boundary of the property. Zelah had just reached the second step when the front door opened and a woman came running out towards her holding out a piece of paper.

"Mrs Trevear?"

"Yes."

"This is a visitor parking permit. You'll need it to make certain your car isn't towed away."

Zelah took the permit and put it on the windscreen of her car. When she turned around again the woman stood waiting in the doorway. As Zelah reached her she stood aside.

"Do come on in, Mrs Trevear. We're going through to the back, follow me."

"Thank you, and please, call me Zelah."

"And I'm Lolly. My sister is joining us this morning."

Lolly Sadler strode along the conventional Victorian black-and-white tiled corridor until they reached a door on the right three quarters of the way along. Ahead Zelah caught a glimpse of an ultra-modern kitchen with a substantial picture window onto what looked like a magnificent garden. When she entered the room just ahead of the kitchen, following behind Lolly, a library with an original fireplace, cases full of books and a set of French windows leading out onto the garden, Zelah had a better view which confirmed her first impression.

"Wonderful garden," she said. "Do you look after it yourself?"

"Yes," Lolly Sadler replied, with a wide smile. "It's my passion. I ..." Before she could elaborate a sharp cough came from the depths of a high-backed armchair. Her smile disappeared.

"Let me introduce you to my sister. Zelah, this is Michaela Wilson."

"Nice to meet you, Michaela."

"Mrs Wilson, to you."

Zelah's hackles rose, but she gave back a perfunctory smile and held out a hand. "My apologies, Mrs Wilson." Michaela Wilson folded her arms. Lolly Sadler bit her lips and blushed, but she said nothing, instead indicated the armchair opposite her sister, placing herself on a settee between them.

'*Ready to referee,*' Zelah thought.

Lolly leaned forward to the flask and cups on the table. "I'm forgetting my manners. Tea or coffee, Zelah?"

"Coffee please, cream and three sugars." Which produced another grimace from the po-faced sister.

The two minutes it took to pour and hand over the cups gave Zelah time to observe the sisters and make some guesses regarding the order of the family hierarchy.

'*No-one would ever connect these two women as relatives, never mind as sisters*', she thought as she glanced from one to the other. Lolly had long, honey coloured, bouncy hair and dark green eyes sparking with humour. Zelah had mentally placed her in her early fifties. Michaela had grey hair, pulled back into a tight bun, exposing over-sized ears. The eyes were a steely grey, watchful and intent, the nose long, the lips thin and prim. The woman looked positively Dickensian. She sat on the edge of her chair, her back ramrod straight. Zelah guessed her to be anything up to ten years older than her sister.

She decided to take the bull by the horns. "What is it about this discovery and research you don't care for, Mrs Wilson?"

Lolly Sadler bit back the grin creeping towards the corners of her mouth, as her sister stretched further upright, stiffened her shoulders and put her cup and saucer down on the table with a deliberate crash.

"It is not seemly. Two murderers in the family. It's shameful, not something to be exposed. Our family will be the subject of gossip."

Zelah speculated from the glint in her eyes, Michaela Wilson was not actually averse to gossip, so long as she was the one dishing it out.

"It's possible there will be interest. But, you'd be surprised how little people care about you as an individual. It's the story provides the interest every time."

Before the woman could react she returned to Lolly. "Can we talk about the information you have about your great uncle and might I see the postcard?"

"I have it all here," Lolly replied, indicating a cardboard file on the table.

"We've done some preliminary research into the death of the other boy," Zelah said. "His name was David Laird. He was a year or so younger than Brodie. This afternoon I'm visiting the records office in the city centre to look for the death certificate and anything else relevant. In England and Wales there would be an inquest, but I know you have a different system here."

Lolly nodded. "I haven't gone so far, but I'm glad you're visiting them." She flashed a defiant look at her sister.

"And tomorrow," Zelah added, now with some relish knowing Lolly was on board, "I shall be spending the day in Edinburgh at the Historic Records office. I'm hoping to find an account of the Fatal Accident Enquiry, assuming there was one."

"I would prefer you did not," Michaela Wilson interrupted.

"Now, this postcard," Zelah said, looking at Lolly.

Lolly Sadler leaned forward and fished into the file, bringing out the postcard, which she had put in a document holder Zelah recognised as an acid-free pocket.

"Well done for protecting it," she said, as she took thin white gloves from her bag.

"I bought a set of these sleeves. I'm putting all of the documents I found into them."

Zelah used her fingertips to remove the postcard from its protective cover. The sepia picture on the front showed a dated Piccadilly Circus, with cars from the pre-war era, but she would check it out, to get an accurate date. She turned it over.

The faded writing on the back was surprisingly neat. *Helen, lo siento mucho. I …* after that the words were almost gone, leaving just a faint imprint of brown ink.

"Lolly, may I take this? I promise I'll be careful with it. We have a contact in a laboratory who should be able to restore the missing words, without damaging the original. Ordinarily I would take a copy, but with something this dated and delicate it won't work from a copy. I assure you," she added "if it can't be done without degrading this original, then we won't do it. Is that acceptable to you?"

Lolly Sadler pursed her lips, weighing up her options. Zelah remained silent. This postcard had become a precious family document and she sensed that trying too hard to persuade Lolly to give it to a relative stranger, might have the opposite effect.

"You promise nothing will happen to it, to damage it in any way?"

"I give you my promise," Zelah replied. "I'll let you know what the techie says so you can decide if you want to go ahead. You can speak to her directly, if that would help."

Lolly nodded. "Ok, you can take it." Zelah put the prized postcard back in its protective case, took a hard backed envelope from her bag and inserted the casing. "Double protection. Now what else can I look at?"

"I'll have nothing further to do with this," Michaela Wilson interrupted in her gravelly voice. "We will regret this."

Chapter 12

The woman stood, picked up her bag, and marched from the room. Zelah and Lolly sat in silence until they heard the front door slam.

"Sorry," Lolly said, clasping her hands in her lap.

"She's not like you," Zelah replied. "She's dominated by fear of judgement."

"Not you, though," Lolly said.

"No, I don't care what people think about me. If they don't like me, that's fine with me. I usually find people who don't like me, well, let's say I don't like them either." She grinned at Lolly. "Now, is there anything else you think may be useful?"

"I have birth certificates for each of the children except Lewis, but including Brodie. Could you use those?"

"At this point everything is useful," Zelah replied. Lolly handed her the documents, again in a protective folder and Zelah put them into her envelope.

"There wasn't anything further relevant to Brodie." She paused, hesitating. "I found a set of photos, but none of them were annotated so he may be there, but I can't tell which one might be him, if he's there at all. There's a family group that might have been taken in the 1920s."

"Would you like me to have it dated? Again, we know an expert who can give you an opinion."

Lolly fished into her file and brought out a black-and-white print of two adults and five children, the youngest around five, and handed it across.

"If this is him, he was a cute kid," Zelah said.

"Aye, he was that. So sad."

"Lolly, what do you want to get from this research? You know, it could turn out Brodie killed then ran away. Are you prepared for that scenario?"

Lolly Sadler took in a deep breath. "You know, Zelah, I've been asking myself that question since I spoke with Nick last week. Do I want to pursue this? Michaela could be right, one executed murderer in the family is already more than we need." She had been looking through the windows at the garden as she spoke, but now turned back to face Zelah. "Thank you for asking. I want to know what happened to Brodie, here in Glasgow and afterwards. I want to know why the postcard is written in Spanish. Whatever the answers are, I can face them."

"How much does your other family know so far?" Zelah asked.

"Nothing as yet, apart from Michaela. I haven't got round to it and I wanted to meet you before I decided if I would go ahead. Now I have, I think you'll do the right thing so I'll start letting them know. That's Malcom's family, great uncle Malcolm, the eldest son. That's if they want to know. The family lives up in Dundee and we aren't close."

"There is something potentially helpful for us, Lolly. Could you draw out a family tree starting with John and

Grace, then their children and their children and so on. Please add Brodie in."

"Certainly, if it'll help. But I can't help with Great Aunt Julie."

"Why not?" Zelah asked.

"The family lost track of her after the war. She went to London, Grandma Helen said. Met a Canadian chappie, married him and went to live in Canada. No-one ever heard from her again."

Zelah sat up. "Julie lived with Helen when Brodie disappeared, didn't she?"

"Aye, she did. Oh, she might have known what happened, too. I hadn't thought of that. But no-one's heard from her in over seventy years."

"Doesn't matter," Zelah said. "She's unlikely to be alive now. She'd be over a hundred. But she may have had children. Do you have any idea of the name of the man she married?"

Lolly shook her head.

"You found nothing about her in the paperwork?"

Another shake. "Nothing, sorry Zelah."

"Don't be sorry. This is what we're here to do. It's just another strand of the investigation for us to dig into. If she remained in Canada we'll find her, somehow, or find out what happened to her. Now, if anyone else in the family has information let me know at once."

"Of course," Lolly replied. "But I don't think it's likely. Helen wasn't close to her older brothers. There's just my distant cousin, you know, the one you exchange Christmas cards with, but that's all."

"Well, anything at all, let me know, please."

"I'll call him this afternoon."

Zelah nodded. "Good. We'll find some answers for you, Lolly. I can't guarantee we'll find out what happened entirely, and I suspect Brodie's ending wasn't good, but we have an idea about the Spanish phrase."

"What idea is that?"

"We think he may have gone to Spain, to fight in the Spanish Civil War. For now, it's just an idea. He disappeared at the end of 1937 when men and women were still signing up to go to Spain. He may have met up with someone who offered him the chance to get out of the country."

"He wasn't a man, though. He was just a boy," Lolly replied.

"As I said, it's just one possibility at the moment. We'll do our best to find out what happened to him, Lolly," Zelah said. "Now, I should go. I need a couple of hours this afternoon in the library." She stood up. "Have you gone through everything else in the attic?"

"Not quite. There are still a couple of boxes. If I find anything useful I'll let you know, Zelah."

"Good. Now I'm off."

"I'll come with you to your car. I need the parking permit."

They walked down the front steps and Zelah glanced back up at the house. "This is a magnificent house," she said. "I'll be in touch in a couple of days, once I've done my research here and I'm back at home."

"Thank you for coming all this way, Zelah. Whatever this turns out to be, I do want to know. I don't care what the neighbours, or the family, think," and with an emphatic nod, a smile and a wave she walked back up the steps to her house.

Chapter 13

At seven the following morning, Maggie had just opened up her computer when she heard Jack helping Max Howell down the stairs, into the kitchen and onto a chair. Without a word Maggie handed him a mug of steaming coffee, which he raised to his lips with shaking hands. Jack sat alongside him, arms folded. After a minute of the slurping of coffee, Maggie went to sit on the chair opposite the boys.

"Jack, have you told Max what's coming?"

Jack nodded. "He's ready."

"You don't look like you'll get a word out, Max. Your face is green."

Max put a hand up to his chin and rubbed. "Face? I can't feel my face," he said in a gravelly voice.

"Your throat took a bashing, too," Jack added. "A lot of shouting."

Max put the cup down on the table, followed by his forehead.

"If you're going to throw up, get to the bathroom," Maggie said.

"Not gonna." He lifted his head and gave her a feeble smile. "It's just heavier than usual this morning. And it hurts like damn."

"Jack, go fetch him painkillers."

Jack jumped up, and arrived back in the kitchen as Bob returned.

Max put his head back on the table. "Now for it."

"You don't look too lively either," Maggie said to Bob, handing him a mug of coffee. "Breakfast?"

"Anything, please. I'm going back soon. But first, Max, are you ready to tell me about Helen Redland?"

"Yes."

"Right, let's go into the office. Maggie and Jack will not be coming. This could turn into a statement and they don't need to hear your private business."

"Jack already knows," Max said, pushing himself up from the table. "He thinks I don't remember, but I do." He lurched and held onto the door frame. "I'd like him to be with me. Makes it easier."

Bob nodded to Jack.

Left alone in the kitchen, Maggie drummed her fingers on the table, feeling edgy. Whatever it was, it wasn't pretty and if Jack had heard it before, well, so be it. Better she didn't know, so when Nick asked her she could plead ignorance. Nick! He had planned to come over this morning. She jumped up, caught them up and pushed them into the sitting room, so she could have the office.

An hour later, after writing up a set of case notes, and watching constantly at the window, she caught a glimpse of Nick. She headed to the front door, told him to '*shush*' as he opened the door and followed him into the office, to explain what was happening. Nick turned towards the living room door but Maggie held onto him by his sleeve.

"Leave them, please. I had to. They're young men, not boys, and this is what they wanted. If he needs to, Max'll tell you later; a sanitised version, probably."

Nick scowled. "That despicable woman," he muttered. "She knew his vulnerability and she used him."

"Helen Redland is a psychopathic murderer," Maggie said. "And Bob needs every piece of information he can get. If Max will help, that's a good thing, isn't it?"

"Yes, yes, I see that. But what if ..." His voice trailed off as he gazed away from her, his eyes frantically scouring the walls.

"One thing Bob will need to be confident about, is that he's no longer – what would you say – open to temptation? Just in case she might try to contact him again, which I suppose is a possibility," Maggie said, still holding onto his sleeve.

"You can let go," he replied. "I'll wait until they come out. If he wants to speak to me, that's up to him. I won't push him." He sat down at the table, took out his laptop and logged on. For the following twenty minutes neither of them spoke.

The door to the living room opened and Bob crossed over to the office, saw Nick and gave Maggie a '*don't ask*' head shake. "We're done, for now. Nick, Max is going back to bed for a couple of hours. This won't go to a formal statement, but the information he's provided is significant and will be useful. I have to go."

"You haven't slept or eaten," Maggie protested, but he had already reached the door.

Jack and Max looked in and Max gave Nick a quick nod, then they both disappeared up the stairs. Two minutes later Jack returned. "He's already asleep. Can we just leave him here until he wakes up, Mum? That was harrowing, on top of his hangover."

Maggie nodded and fought back her yearning for the information.

"Right, I have some stuff to do," Jack said. "By the way Mum, Bob got called back in because Sherry Martin has been talking. He says he'll catch you up later."

"And we're only just past breakfast," Maggie sighed.

Nick snorted. "Let's hope the day calms down a bit. If it's OK with you, I'll stay until Max wakes up."

"Of course. And Zelah should call this morning. She's going into the records office in Edinburgh today and flying home tonight."

"I've picked up two initial enquiries. I'll get on with checking them out. Where's your friend?"

As he asked Jude appeared in the door, still in dressing gown and pyjamas and yawning. "I heard voices. Did I miss the action?"

"Come on, I'll fill you in. I need a break. Then we can discuss what we're going to do today. Nick, will you call me when Zelah rings in?"

He nodded and returned to his laptop.

Maggie had just begun to give Jude a summary of the events of the morning when Nick called out "Zelah's on the phone," and they rushed to the office.

"We're here. What do you have?"

"Good morning to you, too. So, from the meeting with Lolly Sadler. I got her go ahead with whatever we need to do to find out what happened to Brodie McAlister. I told her about the potential Spanish Civil War connection. She agreed we could proceed with checking that out, although she may not sanction a trip to Spain; we'll have to decide if it becomes necessary. Right, an important piece of urgent research. Her grandmother Helen's sister, Julie, married a Canadian after the war and went to Canada. No-one in the family's heard from her since. Try to track her down; she was close to Helen and may have known something, so see what you can find. Next, the Procurator Fiscal's enquiry. A hearing took place in 1938, after Brodie disappeared. A nun gave the main evidence against him, a Sister Mary Veronica. Look for her, too. I tracked down a couple of names of two of the children there at the time, Mary Cameron and Alexander Smith. They were younger than Brodie so they'll be in their nineties, but it's worth a try as I haven't found a recorded death for either of them. I have extra information about the families of Brodie and his parents and the boy who died, David Laird, but none of it's relevant to the search. That's it; I'm off to the national records office to see what I can find from the Sheriff's court."

"Before you go," Maggie interrupted before Zelah could cut off the call, "yes, we can move on these this morning, but I also want to carry on looking for any evidence of Brodie in the archives of the Spanish Civil War. I'm going to contact a memorial organisation in London."

"Fine. Oh, and I have the postcard. We'll have to get it to Ruby's lab to ask if she can work her magic. There's more, quite a bit, I think. Maggie, give her a call, see if she's free to look at it." She ended the call.

Maggie sat back and saluted at the phone now emitting a hollow buzz. "Yes, ma'am. Well, that's ample to concentrate on and work stops me agitating. Who wants to do what?"

"You are fidgety, aren't you? Assuming you're checking out the memorial organisation, I'll take a look for the sister who went to Canada," Nick replied. "After I've evaluated these enquiries."

"And I can start on the nun," Jude said, "if that's OK with both of you?"

"Fine with me," Maggie replied, "but let me show you how we record searches. Nick, you've set up the dedicated file; can you give Jude access whilst I run her through our methods and recording?"

"Good. What about the children Zelah named?" Jude asked.

"We'll get to them, but let's get these primary issues sorted out first," Maggie said.

Chapter 14

After a couple of hours Bob returned and came straight into the office.

"Is Max still here?" he asked.

"Yes, still asleep I think. Why?" Maggie replied.

"I have news, something I can share with all of you. Get him down and come into the kitchen."

"Hmm. Today must be 'issuing instructions without waiting for a reply' day," Maggie muttered as she stood and walked out to the stairs. Nick looked at Jude and shrugged and they went into the kitchen where Bob stood with his back to the sink, swishing the coffee around in his mug, staring into it. They were followed by Jack and Max, the latter having lost the green complexion but still pale and shaking, and Maggie.

They all sat whilst Bob remained on his feet. "Right, here's what we know. We suspect Helen Redland is already back in the country. According to Sherry, who has finally understood the depth of the trouble she's in and is screeching everything she knows at megaphone level, they had planned to come back on three consecutive intervals and meet up later this week. They each had a plan, Sherry's being to kidnap Alice and get money out of Maggie. I know, I know," he said, holding up a hand in response to Maggie's open mouth and expression of fury. "Just tell yourself she didn't get anywhere close and now she'll be locked away into the distant future. She's being treated as a domestic terrorist, on the basis that if Alice had been with Matthew, she would have taken him too. I think that's a bit ropey, but I'm not going to argue. So, she's out of your hair for good. Now, Helen Redland." He paused and took a slurp of the coffee and sighed. "She wants money too. She believes she's entitled to Kennet's money, being the mother of his son, according to Sherry."

"But she abandoned the poor little sod," Maggie said.

"Still, biologically, she is the mother of his son. But, she's not his wife. Michelle Quinn is legally his next of kin so she'll get everything."

"It's all but done," Nick said. "The confirmation is expected any day now. Zelah helped with the legal side, I believe."

"Where is Zelah?" Bob asked, realising she wasn't in the room.

"Scotland," Maggie replied. "She's back tonight. I can fill her in tomorrow morning."

Bob scowled. "That's not all. There were definitely three of them, the third confirmed being …"

"Emer McCarthy Miller," Maggie interrupted. "Well, you guessed anyway, didn't you."

"I suspected she was the third person in the car the morning Kennet died, yes. Zelah needs to know. Let me know as soon as she calls you again. I'll give her an update over the phone, put her on her guard."

"I'll send her a text to call you," Maggie said. "No need for me to be in the middle."

"We'll need to have a discussion all together. Emer's the most dangerous of the three. She could go for any of you on her way to Zelah. You'd just be collateral damage."

"That trip to Spain is sounding terrific to me right now," Jude whispered to Maggie.

"Are you going back to work?" Maggie asked Bob.

"No, I need some sleep. I've taken what's left of the day. I'll grab a couple of hours, then, Max, I need to speak to you. Don't leave here." He swayed slightly, rubbed his eyes, smiled at Maggie and left them.

Maggie made up plates of sandwiches and cake for lunch, during which everyone talked about everything except Helen Redland and Emer McCarthy Miller.

"How's the case going?" Jack asked, after Max had taken a sandwich and more painkillers back to bed.

"Early days," she replied. "I'll be going to London later this week to meet up with an International Brigade expert who's going to talk to me about recruitment in the early months of 1938 and the journey to Spain. We'll check the list of volunteers for Brodie's name."

"Would he have travelled under his own name?" Jude asked.

"Maybe," Maggie replied. "He would have had to get to London, that's where the transport was organised for groups of volunteers. They had to go first to Paris on a so-called weekend trip, then a French organisation took over the arrangements for them to go down to the Spanish border on the Mediterranean side. From there, they either went by truck or they walked over into Catalonia."

"Then he must have met someone in Glasgow, because it's not a means of escape a boy of seventeen would think of alone."

"I agree, in Scotland or London. I hope I can get information about where Scotland fitted in when I meet the guy from the Trust in London."

"*We* meet the guy in London," Jude said. "I'm coming with you."

"Fine with me," Maggie replied. "Are you getting anywhere with the nun?"

"Very slow," Jude replied. "I know from a newspaper article she was in her forties, which I didn't expect, somehow; I imagined she'd be older, like the nuns who taught us. But the church records are tight. I can't find any record of her birth name. Is there some better way you know of for me to find out?"

"Electoral register?" Nick said. "Nuns did vote. And the 1939 War register. I've never had to look for a nun before on either, so you should check for registration in their birth name, and their religious name."

"I'm on it," Jude replied. "Did you get anything on the sister, Julie?"

"No," he replied. "She doesn't appear to have married before she left the UK. I've checked the 1939 national identity register for Scotland, and she was still living in Glasgow, so she must have gone down to London after war broke out. She would most likely have found work there. I'm about to move on to emigration passenger lists."

"OK, let's get back to it," Maggie said. "Perhaps we can make some progress before Zelah calls again."

"I'll stick with this for now," Nick said. "It's building up and with Zelah away, you need the help. Are you OK, Maggie? You look, I don't know, worried?"

"You think? With Helen Redland back and Emer McCarthy Miller somewhere in the background and likely to be after any one of us, of course I'm bloody worried. I'm scared. Aren't you?"

Nick turned back to his laptop. "Of course I am," he muttered.

**

Bob reappeared after a couple of hours, eyes red-rimmed, and yawning. Minutes later, Max walked unsteadily into the kitchen. Bob took him by the elbow and directed him into the lounge, accompanied by Jack. Again, Maggie and Nick were shut out.

They emerged after half an hour, each looking wary when they joined Maggie, Nick and Jude in the office.

"Mum, Max wants to stay another couple of nights," Jack began.

"Not a problem. What then?"

"I'm going back to my flat," Max said, not looking at Nick, who sat up.

"Which flat would that be?"

"The one Kennet Quinn rented out to him," Bob interjected. "Max still has the keys and he's willing to go back there."

"So you can use him as a tethered goat to catch Helen Redland?" Nick jumped up, stood eyeball to eyeball with Bob.

"Oh shut the fuck up, both of you." They all turned to look at Max. "No-one's forcing me to do anything. She needs stopping. Look, Nick, I'll have someone there with me all the time. Whoever the poor sod turns out to be, they can't leave until she turns up, so let's hope it doesn't take long. Jack and one of his mates will come by, like friends do, just in case she's watching. None of us will be in danger and I have to know she can never get at me again. Stop thinking about yourself."

Nick turned away, shaking his head.

"He's not thinking about himself, Max" Maggie said. "He'd lie down and die for you in a heartbeat, as I would for Jack." She said to Jack, "You must be exceptionally careful." Then to Bob, "She's already killed one man. She won't hesitate to do it again to preserve her own freedom."

"I know," Bob replied. "It's the best chance we have, Maggie. Sherry told her interrogators the three of them are returning in 3-day intervals, meaning Helen will be back tomorrow, or she could have come in today, then Emer McCarthy Miller in four days' time. The following day they're due to meet up. We know where and when."

"Then why not just wait for that?" Nick shot at Bob as he paced up and down the room, clasping and unclasping jerking hands.

"Best laid plans, etc," Bob replied. "There don't appear to be any pre-arranged signals, just some code words, but if one of them gets an impression all is not as it should be, they'll both bolt. We need to get Helen Redland before Emer gets back."

"Where is she coming from?" Maggie asked. "Can't you just arrest her as soon as she arrives?"

Bob shook his head, grimacing. "We don't know where she plans to enter the country. She's devious and scheming, but clever, which is how she's evaded us for so long. We can't just rely on it being directly from France or from Ireland."

"So, you're OK with this?" Nick asked Max.

"Yes, I am, Nick."

"So be it," Nick replied. "I think I'll go now. I need to talk to Stella. If you need me, you know where I am, any time."

Zelah called just as Nick reached his van but Maggie decided not to call him back. Whatever Zelah had to say, Nick could wait until tomorrow to hear it.

"I'm heading to the hotel now. I'm knackered."

"Was it a useful day?" Maggie asked.

"Definitely. Got some interesting stuff to share."

"As have we. Bob is going to call you as soon as he can," she said, nodding at him.

"Why?"

She handed the phone to Bob, who took a deep breath. "Zelah, we have news. Emer McCarthy Miller is about to return to the country."

"How? When? Where?"

That's the thing, we don't know, just it'll be in three or four days."

"Then get off the phone so I can call the boys at Rosscarbery. If she's coming for me she may well go via them. Have you told the Garda?"

"No, not yet."

"Then do it" she yelled at him and ended the call.

"She's right, Maggie," Bob said. "Stephen and Niall had no part of what happened, but Emer won't care, she'll see that Zelah has Rosscarbery House and everyone living there must be complicit. I'll make the call now. She could be in Ireland already."

Chapter 15

Zelah's additional time in Edinburgh had been productive. In Glasgow she had picked up information about David Laird and some newspaper reports. In Edinburgh she had found notes on the Fatal Accident Enquiry and its disturbing outcome. The extra time had been worthwhile, but Bob's news was uppermost in her mind throughout the day, plus the outcome of the call she had made to Ireland. When the call ended with Bob she had dialled Mischa's number.

"Hi, what's up?"

"Are the boys there?"

"They're around somewhere. Why?"

"Can you get them, please. We need an urgent call with all of you listening."

"What's happened? Something has."

Zelah took a deep breath. "Yes, something which affects all of you. Go and get them and call me back when you're together." She had disturbed Mischa, she knew, but she had to instil in the girl the fear she felt of Emer's psychopathy. The boys would understand and they would all have to be on their guard. They had top-of-the-range electronic security at Rosscarbery and when she had brought them up to date she would hire in physical security. Her phone rang.

"Right, Zelah, we're all here. What's happened?"

Zelah gave them a succinct summary of the situation, finishing with the fact Stephen and Niall's cousin Emer would soon be in the UK, but might be arriving via Ireland.

She also warned Mischa about Helen Redland and who knew what Helen might be prepared to do, to get access to Kennet's money.

"What about my mother and brother?" Mischa asked.

"They'll need security too. Helen is bound to try to use one of you to get the cash. There isn't a legal way. I'll call them Thursday when I'm back from Scotland and set up a meeting. I don't think I can tell Michelle over the phone, given her penchant for hysteria."

"What might this woman do?" Stephen McCarthy Miller asked.

"No idea," Zelah replied. "She might try to hold someone hostage, Michelle most likely; she's the weakest and would give her whatever she wanted."

"Does she have the probate yet?" Mischa asked in a dull voice.

"Yes, she does, which will make her Helen's primary target."

"And what about Mischa going to Dublin to start her medical degree?" Niall this time.

"I don't know. We'll have to think it through and discuss how to make it work. We have time. With a bit of luck the police can catch them both before the term starts. There is a plan."

"There's something I'm thinking about. We'll call you back in fifteen minutes." Mischa ended the call before Zelah could respond.

Zelah waited patiently, by her standards. When the call came in ten minutes she pounced on the phone.

"I have something to propose, and Stephen and Niall are with me on this," Mischa began. "I want my mother and …" she cleared her throat, "and my brother to come here as soon as possible. If we all need security we might as well be in one place."

"I can hear your teeth gritting. Are you sure about this?"

"Yes. It's time. We don't have any groups here at the moment and there's enough room for Gerry and me to keep away from each other, if we need to."

"OK. I'll let you know the outcome when I've met up with Michelle and Gerry."

"Thanks, Zelah," Niall said.

"I'll be in Edinburgh all day today, flying back in the evening. I'll call you again tomorrow and I'll speak to Michelle and Gerry."

Although she had wondered about broaching the subject herself, Zelah liked that the idea had come from Mischa. She had hoped for a reconciliation at some point. If this situation had given it impetus, so be it.

After a full-on day in both research buildings before she headed to the airport Zelah called Mischa again to check she hadn't changed her mind. Mischa seemed less certain – the prospect of being in the same country as Gerry and her mother being enough to dampen any enthusiasm for a family reunion - but she still thought it the best solution for all of them, to Zelah's relief.

Zelah took a taxi straight to the airport from the city centre. Provided Michelle and Gerry saw the sense in what Mischa had proposed, the three witches might have achieved something useful, albeit not something they could possibly have anticipated.

Chapter 16

From the airport Zelah had called Maggie to let her know she wouldn't be joining them until later the following morning and the reason why, and Maggie, tongue in cheek, wished her good luck.

Just before eight she took a deep breath and called Michelle. Michelle was, as usual, unnerved by a demand for an urgent meeting, but Zelah stayed firm, not explaining, just telling her to stay at home, with Gerry, until she could get to them.

Michelle and Gerry were now housed in Newport, in the former residence of Kennet and Rufus Quinn, and Gerry and Mischa's former home. Zelah had been shocked when Michelle informed her they were moving back in.

"Not much surprises me," she told Maggie, "but this is a bombshell. Her husband murdered in the lounge, her daughter beaten half to death in the library and hall and her father-in-law died there too, all within a couple of months. Still, perhaps she's developing some balls."

"It's the perfect way to say, '*up yours, bastard*' to Kennet. It had been her home, where he maimed her and threw her out, too, remember."

Zelah had laughed, but now as she parked her car and walked up the front steps she saw Michelle waiting, white face, her hands trembling. She led Zelah into the lounge. To Zelah's surprise Michelle had transformed it, with new carpets and furniture and a modern, light ambience, far removed from Kennet's adherence to Victorian tradition.

Gerry, who had been lying on a settee, tapping on his mobile phone, sat up at once. He no longer had steroidal biceps and his face had lost the arrogant look put there by years of 'training 'by his father. Zelah thought he looked quite handsome. She hoped the inner Gerry had made the same progress. Time to find out. She pointed Michelle at the settee and sat down opposite them.

As Zelah started to explain about Helen Redland, Michelle's hands flew to her mouth and she uttered a squeak. Gerry put his arm around his mother's shoulders.

"Not surprised she's back," he muttered. "I never thought she cared about Pa. I saw her face change a couple of times when she turned her back on him. She wanted the money, and the business."

"What can she do?" Michelle managed a trembling voice to ask.

Zelah gave her a selection of ideas, including threats, kidnapping and maiming, and possibly killing someone, reducing Michelle to hopeless sobs. She had over-exaggerated, but did so knowing this might encourage them to consider Mischa's proposal. Knowing both as she did, and their apprehension regarding Mischa, it would need some serious fear to get them out of Newport and over to Ireland.

"Stop blubbing, Michelle. I have a proposal for you, to keep you both safe. You haven't thought about this yet, but you're not the only ones in this family in danger from Helen Redland."

She gritted her teeth as the implication of her meaning hit both of them.

"I … I didn't think," Michelle said.

"Well, there's a surprise," Zelah retorted. "And here's another one. Mischa wants both of you to go over to Ireland now, to Rosscarbery, to stay with her and the McCarthy Miller boys. The Gardai are aware of the danger and I've hired extra private security. You'll both be safe there."

Gerry's arm dropped from his mother's shoulder. "She wants me there?" His voice wobbled as he spoke.

"Yes, and not with the intention of maiming you. I believe she's prepared to try a reconciliation. Well? Will you go?"

"I don't know. I need time to think," Michelle said.

"There isn't any. Decide now, or you're on your own."

Gerry stood up and pulled Michelle to her feet. "We accept and we'll go pack. How do we get there? And how long will we have to stay?"

"Now, today. I can have a car waiting within the hour. How long? Until Helen Redland is in police custody, either there or here. Then, we'll consider the next move, given Emer McCarthy Miller will be on the scene imminently and she makes Helen look like a minor criminal. This time she wants me first and foremost and she won't hesitate to use any of you to get to me."

Michelle nodded and walked towards the door, but turned back. "What if it all goes wrong? She can't like us, not after, you know, everything."

"Mischa's willing to try and if it goes wrong, well, it's a big house. There's room for you to stay away from each other." She paused for a moment, then walked up to Michelle and put her hands on the woman's shaking shoulders. "This is your chance, both of you. Don't blow it. I'll see myself out. Arrangements to make. I'll be here in," she glanced at her watch, "Let's say an hour. Be ready." She walked past them and out of the house.

At the foot of the stairs Michelle turned to Gerry. "Are we doing the right thing?"

He nodded emphatically. "If they're willing to do this for us, let's not screw up, Ma. We've both done too much of that. Anyway if nothing comes of it, it sounds like a nice place to spend some time."

He gave her a quick hug and ran up the stairs two at a time.

Back in her car Zelah made a couple of quick calls to arrange transport and a ferry crossing. Also realising the house would be empty for a week, maybe longer, she decided it, too needed some security, as it wouldn't do for Helen Redland to discover it empty and use it as a base.

An hour later, after a call to Maggie, she made her way back, to find the transport waiting and Michelle and Gerry with their bags packed, standing in the hallway. They ran down the steps to the transport, threw the bags in, pushed the keys into Zelah's hands and gave her a half salute as the car took off.

In the intervening hour Zelah had arranged to meet a private security firm at the house and agree arrangements to watch over it. She ensured they knew all of the entrances including Mischa's secret entrance at the rear of the property.

The meeting took her up to lunchtime and she wanted to get to Maggie's house to catch up on the Brodie McAlister case. As she drove off up the road, turning her thoughts to what she had learned and eager to share, she didn't notice the single car parked at the top of the road, in which sat a woman with short, dark hair, wearing sunglasses, head bent over her mobile phone.

When Zelah's car had passed and turned onto the main road at the top of the hill, Helen Redland pulled off her wig, lowered the car window and spat onto the road.

"Fucking witch bitch," she shouted, slamming one hand on the steering wheel. A passer-by on the opposite side of the road jumped and scowled. Helen gave her the finger and raised the window, as she watched the security consultants let themselves into the house.

"Right, Plan B it is." She smiled, started the engine and drove off down the hill.

Chapter 17

Max and Jack left after breakfast. Maggie watched them go with much apprehension. They planned to check the flat's safety and be sure no-one had tried to force an entry. The entrance had been re-inforced with a new door and locks and the windows were now alarmed. They were also meeting up with the 'tenant' who would share the two-bedroom flat for the foreseeable future.

"His name's Joe and he's amazing, Mum," Jack said when he reported back mid-morning, as promised. "You'd never guess he's police. He's a scruffy git and he's well into gaming. They've got everything here. I almost want to stay myself."

He paused in anticipation of her roar of objection and wasn't disappointed. "I'm joking, cool it. I'll be back for dinner. Max and Joe are off to the supermarket to get some food and beers. There's nothing here and the fridge stinks so I'm waiting until they get back."

"Be careful and don't answer the door," Maggie instructed. "I can see you rolling your eyes," she added, "but you know how worried I am for you."

"I'll be fine, speak to you later," and he cut her off before she could say more. He did understand but sometimes, well, she just had to acknowledge he wasn't a child. But just in case, he went over to the window and took a look up and down the street. He knew the windows had been re-fitted, were shatterproof with one-way viewing, so no-one passing by could see in, but still he took just a quick glance before stepping back. There was no-one of interest on the street, just a couple of pensioners and a woman with short dark hair and sunglasses, checking out her phone as she walked past, who didn't give the flat a second glance.

**

When Zelah arrived at Maggie's house, Nick, Maggie and Jude had just stopped for lunch but unanimously agreed to exchange news first.

Zelah brought them up to date on the Quinn/McCarthy Miller situation. "They're on the ferry now and due in Rosscarbery around five this afternoon. Mischa will let me know when they've arrived and Stephen's going to give me a sneaky call later to let me know how things are. It's unlikely to be anything other than tense this evening and tomorrow, but I'm keeping my fingers crossed for some cooling of hostilities after that."

"Sounds like the US and North Korea," Jude said.

"No," Zelah replied with a straight face. "It's far worse than that."

"She's kidding," Maggie explained to an astonished Jude. "But it won't be good. At least you're not there," she said, turning to Zelah. "Your peacekeeping and diplomacy skills are minus zero on the nought to ten scale."

Zelah shrugged. "True. Let's push on with more interesting things. Where shall we start?"

"Why don't you bring us up to date on your Scotland visit?" Nick said.

Zelah ran them through the visit with Lolly Sadler and her sister, finishing with the postcard, which she took out of her briefcase and put on the table. "I'll call Ruby Patterson this afternoon, see if she can do something with it. Those additional words could well give us the bounce we need to confirm he did go to Spain and if so, when. You can see," she added, peering closer "there's the edge of a date stamp. If Ruby can clarify it, we'll know when it was sent."

"It should read 1938 or 1939," Nick said.

"Why?" Jude asked.

"Because he ran away just before his seventeenth birthday, at the end of 1937. It would have taken a couple of weeks to get to Spain, so 1938. The men were able to send mail home. That's one possibility. The other is he asked someone returning to send it for him when they reached England, which would have been October or November 1938, or at the latest, January 1939."

"If it's the latter," Maggie mused, "That would mean he didn't return when the International Brigades were withdrawn."

"Stop!" Zelah said. "We're getting ahead of ourselves. Let's stick to the time between the fight and the death of David Laird – he's the boy Brodie McAlister fought with and who died – and what he might have done. I have the information on the boy here."

She dived into her briefcase again and brought out plastic sleeves which she spread out on the table. The first was a death certificate. "See, cause of death was a cerebral haemorrhage. And I have the post mortem result." She slapped another sleeve down. "You can all read this in your own time, but the instrument had a rounded end and the imprint on the skull left an impression of what looked like two eyes and a nose."

"That's odd," Maggie said. "Unusual for a pathologist to speculate about something like that."

"Perhaps it wasn't speculation," Nick said.

"What do you mean?" Zelah asked.

Nick turned to his laptop and loaded up a report from the children's home Maggie had researched. "Look at this. It's in the evidence from the enquiry. The children were beaten with straps, crucifixes and hair brushes."

"None of those would have a round end and a face, would they," Zelah said.

"No," Nick replied. "But a statue would."

"The ones we had in school were hollow plaster casts," Jude said. "They might have knocked you out, but they would have shattered on impact. I know from experience. I could knock off a hand or an arm with a hockey ball. They made spanking target practice, didn't they?" she said to Maggie, who nodded and grinned.

"How about if it was solid wood, or metal?"

"Miles Cooper," Maggie said. "You remember, the retired Coroner, friend of Bob's. He could give us an opinion, and he's bound to know a pathologist who could look at this for us."

Zelah nodded. "Yes, excellent idea. Get hold of him. Now, the Fatal Accident Enquiry. The 'star 'witness was the nun, Sister Mary Veronica. She said she found the boys fighting. They hated each other and fought whenever they could. She ran to intervene, but before she reached them Brodie McAlister had knocked David Laird onto his knees, then delivered a massive punch to the side of David's head, which knocked him backwards and the back of his head hit the edge of the concrete pavement."

"That wasn't consistent with the post mortem, was it?" Maggie asked.

"Indeed. The prosecutor questioned her on that aspect, but couldn't account for the injury in another way. According to her testimony Brodie took one look at the prostrate David and ran. She then called for another nun, a nurse, who tried to revive David, but found him to be dead. Eventually, they called an ambulance."

"What do you mean by 'eventually'?" Jude asked.

Zelah smiled. "They didn't call the ambulance for two hours."

Chapter 18

"Well, that doesn't sound right," Jude said.

"No, it doesn't, does it? OK, the boy was dead, but Brodie had scarpered and if the nuns truly believed him guilty as charged, they should have called the police immediately."

"What about the children? Were there any witnesses?" Nick asked.

"None, according to Sister Mary Veronica."

"Were any of the children questioned?" Jude asked.

"Not according to the existing information. They took the nun at her word."

"Then we should try to find any children still alive," Maggie said. "We have a couple of potential names."

"Agreed," Zelah replied. "I'll take it on. I'll leave these papers here so you can all read through them. So, what else is there?"

"I'm trying to track down the nun," Jude said. "No luck so far with electoral registers or the 1939 war register."

"She should be on the 1939 National Register of Scotland," Zelah said. "Mind if I take a look?"

"Be my guest," Jude replied.

"I'm looking for the sister, Julie, who supposedly went to Canada after the war to marry a military man," Nick said. "I'm checking what there is on emigration and shipping. Again, nothing yet. She would have travelled under her maiden name, as there isn't any record of a marriage of a Julie McAlister up to 1946."

Maggie finished up. "Jude and I are off to London tomorrow, to meet with a guy from the memorial organisation. I'm hoping he can give some information about men who volunteered to fight in Spain in 1938."

"Sounds like we all have a tolerable amount to be getting on with," Zelah said. "So, let's do it."

Maggie had just swallowed a mouthful of coffee when both Nick and Jude shouted, 'got her'. She gulped as she and Zelah looked across to them.

"Go on, then," Zelah said.

"I've found the nun," Jude said. "They were registered on the 1939 Register, but under a variety of names. Some were just their religious name; those tended to be the older ones. Some gave their religious name and surname and others a combination of both. Our nun is in the latter category, which is why I missed her first time around. Sorry."

"So who was she?" Zelah asked.

"Sister Mary V. Shepherd, born in 1897, so forty-two years old, like the newspaper article said. No more description. And I've confirmed her on an electoral register from 1936, when her name appeared as Sister Mary Veronica Shepherd, so it's definitely her. Same address, too, the children's home."

"Good work," Zelah said. "Nick, you've found something?"

"Yes. Julie McAlister left the UK in 1946, in November. She arrived in Canada just before Christmas. She headed for Toronto, where she married Jason Montgomery in January

1947. They were both living at his parents' home at the time of the marriage. And, I've found the birth of one child, a girl named Maria, born in December 1947. I'll see what information I can find about Maria Montgomery. There's every chance she's still alive, as she'd be in her early seventies. Fingers crossed. You, Zelah?"

"Yes, I've got something. I can confirm that the two names we had from the children at the home are still alive, Mary Cameron, now McShane and Alexander Smith. At the time of David Laird's death Mary was nine and she's now ninety-one. Alexander was a year or so younger. He'll be around ninety, and both are in nursing homes."

"They'll both be frail, Zelah, physically and mentally," Maggie said.

"Then let's hope one of them can talk to us, and we'll be allowed to talk to them," Zelah replied. She glanced at her watch. "It's almost four. I'm going home to work from there whilst I wait for the phone calls from Ireland. If you don't hear from me, assume all's well and good luck with your trip to London tomorrow."

"Thanks," Maggie replied. "We'll carry on here for a while longer. We're on a roll and I want to keep going."

"Me too," Jude added. "What about you, Nick".

"I'm meeting Stella at five. I'll give it a bit longer."

"This has been a profitable day," Maggie said. "Let's hope tomorrow we get useful info about Spain. The pieces are coming together."

Chapter 19

Maggie and Jude reached Paddington station the following morning just before eleven, in sufficient time to get to the pub where they were meeting Martin Smith from the Trust.

"I haven't travelled on the London underground for almost twenty years," Jude said as they made their way down the steep staircase leading from the main concourse. "Tell me again how we get there."

"We're going to Chancery Lane, near the Royal Courts of Justice," Maggie replied. "On the Bakerloo Line to Oxford Circus then onto the Central Line. The pub's called The Seven Stars. It's at the back of the courts. Martin says it's touristy, but it's supposed to be one of the oldest pubs in London. He thought it might be fun for us."

"He thinks we're provincials, then."

"No, I gather he lives nearby and the food is good. I'm buying lunch."

Twenty minutes later, after the usual waiting for trains and walking between the two underground lines they emerged into bright sunlight. A short walk brought them to the front of the pub in Carey Street where Martin stood waiting, carrying a tatty briefcase and wearing a traditional striped college blazer.

At well over six feet both Maggie and Jude had to look up at him. Maggie put his age at somewhere under thirty. He greeted them enthusiastically and paused for a moment as they all looked at the frontage of the pub, with its original black beams and its covering of flowering hanging baskets.

"This is old," Jude remarked as Martin led them inside.

"Very," he replied. "It's the oldest one to have survived the Great Fire of London, I believe the date is around 1602. The inside is interesting, too. I've booked us a table."

Once their eyes had adjusted to the inevitable darkness caused by the small windows and low ceilings of ancient buildings, Maggie found herself somewhat puzzled, which Martin noticed.

"It's traditional, yes, but the landlady has been here years and it's her style you're seeing. And as you can see from the legal regalia, it's popular with the barristers and lawyers from over the road. It's not pretentious, is it."

"No, definitely not. Is the food good?"

"It's beyond good. Basic, simple, cooked on the premises and wonderfully delicious. Let's find our table and order. Then we can spend our time on your project. I've brought paperwork with me."

Once they had settled and ordered, the special of the day being a fish pie, and drinks were delivered, Martin produced his paperwork and a notebook and pen.

"Before we get into specifics, why don't you give us a run-down of the Trust," Jude suggested. "Maggie's been getting me up to date, but I'd like to hear more, if that's OK with you, Maggot."

Maggie nodded, grinning at Martin's puzzlement. "Nickname," she explained. "We go back to Grammar School. She's 'Worm'."

"Oh, Ok. Fair enough," he smiled. For the following twenty minutes, until their food arrived, he gave them an account of the history and work of the Trust, and their efforts to keep alive the memory of the men and women from Britain who had gone to Spain to join the fight against Fascism. He was a gifted storyteller, holding their interest and fascination until their food arrived.

"That was excellent, thank you, Martin," Jude said, eyeing up the substantial plate of steaming fish pie. "If this tastes as yummy as it smells, I need to dive in now."

After another twenty minutes of eating accompanied by chat and questions about the work of the Trust, dishes were removed and Martin took a sheaf of papers out of his satchel.

"I've checked the name you gave me," he said. "But I'm sorry to say I found no-one of that name, either at the end of 1937 or in the initial months of 1938. It could be he gave a false name, which happened for varying reasons."

"It is possible he gave a false name to make sure no-one who might have read the newspaper reports of David Laird's death would recognise him," Maggie replied. "How about his age? He had just turned seventeen, but you said the minimum age was eighteen. Were there any very young volunteers around that time?"

Martin checked down his list, then looked up. "There's one," he said. "A twenty-year-old, name of Lewis Malcolm Stewart. From Edinburgh."

Maggie shot up straight in her chair. "That's him," she shouted.

Chapter 20

She had raised her voice enough to attract the attention of the tables around her. "Sorry, didn't mean to shout."

"Why would you think that's your McAlister lad?"

"Because he had two older brothers, called Lewis and Malcolm and his sister Helen's husband's name was James Stewart. Is there a description?"

"Yes, there is." He picked out another page and put it on the table so the three of them could see.

"Height six foot," Maggie read. "Reddish ginger hair, blue eyes. Round face, no distinguishing marks. He's signed it at the bottom of the page. Look, the writing is mature for a boy of seventeen."

"Well, he fooled his way past the recruiter."

"What would have come next?" Jude asked.

"Papers," Martin replied. "He would have been given an ID document. Nothing fancy. I'm saying this because if this isn't his real name, then he wouldn't have already had something with him."

"With a photograph?"

"No. Just an identity card with his name."

"First to Paris, then down to the Spanish border?" Maggie asked.

"That's right. With a group of volunteers, although there weren't anything like the numbers going over by then. The war wasn't going well, you see, and the International Brigades had suffered heavy losses. Lessened the enthusiasm."

"By this time, yes, I've read that," Jude said.

He smiled at her. "My grandfather was there. His luck held out. He went over in '37 and survived through to the withdrawal in October '38. He was twenty-one when he volunteered."

"Did he talk to you about his experiences?"

"Yes, he did. My dad didn't like it, I was just a kid, but Grandad said it was important to keep the memory alive. Times were different then. Grandad was a communist." He saw Jude trying not to look disturbed. "You have to remember the context in the 1930s. Hitler was gaining power and becoming threatening to Europe. He had armed Germany, against every treaty Germany had signed and no-one could stop him. The Fascist agenda was rampant; a superior race, to put it basically. Power to be held by select groups of approved people, the rest supressed and enslaved. Jews were already being marked out, attacked and put out of work. Men like my Grandad foresaw an ugly future as Hitler's rhetoric became increasingly threatening. There had been talk of a war for some time, now it looked inevitable. After the election of the republican government in Spain Franco and the monarchists, plus the Catholic church hierarchy, rose up in an insurrection against the government."

"I know the history," Maggie said. "About thirty-five thousand volunteers from around the world went to Spain to fight against Franco?"

"Yep. Biggest international gathering since the medieval Crusades."

"Your grandad was lucky to survive. He must have survived the World War as well," Jude said.

"He did. Amazing man. But his passion remained for Spain and the horrors perpetrated by Franco."

"Is that why you work for the Trust?"

"I'm a volunteer," Martin replied, "but yes. He inspired me to keep the story alive." He paused for a moment, and they didn't interrupt, seeing his attention had wandered far away. He snapped back. "I'll get you copies of these papers, email them to you later. I'll also check RGASPI."

"What's that?"

"It's a database of a fair percentage of the volunteers, Jude. There are lists, but the actual paperwork is in an archive in Moscow."

"Wow. Because they were mostly communists?"

"Yes, but they weren't all communists, although that covers a good number of the international volunteers. There were Socialists and Anarchists too and some weren't affiliated to any political party. What they all had in common is they were strongly anti-Fascist. You have to understand the state of world politics in the context of the times to understand the extent of the threat."

"Thank you, Martin," Maggie interrupted, seeing this could develop into a protracted discussion between the enthusiastic Martin and the equally enthused Jude. "That's what we need. We have further researching to do, but I think this makes it clear Brodie did go to Spain. All we have to do now is find out what happened when he got there and why he never went back to his family."

"I don't think that will have been for a positive reason," Martin replied. "But I hope you get an answer. Many families only heard their relative was MIA. That's Missing in Action."

Maggie glanced at her watch. "We need to be going, and I suggest," she said to Jude, "we start our return journey with a walk. I could do with it. Lovely to meet you Martin; this has been invaluable. You get off now, I'll pay the bill."

"Good to meet you, Maggie, and you, Jude. And good luck with your project. Do let us know what you find out. Our archives always welcome updates. The copies will be with you by the time you get home and I can do an initial check on the RGASPI lists."

Outside the pub Jude asked, "How far are we from the Thames?"

"Not far, I think. Why?"

"We've plenty of time before the train and I'm guessing you want to think as well as walk off that meal. How about we make our way down to the river? We can walk along the embankment to a street connecting up to Trafalgar Square."

"Sure you don't want to wander round here? It's one of the most historic parts of London."

"No," Jude replied. "I need to think too. A walk along the river will help and it's too nice a day to waste this sunshine."

They exchanged just a few words on the way back to Paddington where they caught their train back to Newport where Bob would meet them at the station to take them home. As the train pulled out Maggie realised she hadn't checked her phone all the time they were in the pub. She took it out of her bag.

There were eleven texts, various ones from clients, one from Zelah, one from Bob and six from Jack in quick succession. She opened these first. They all said the same thing, sent an hour earlier, just three repeated words:

"Help. Now. Urgent."

She dialled his number and he answered after the first ring.

"It's OK, Mum. Panic over."

"What were you panicking about? Six texts in a row, identical message. What's happened?"

"Look, it can wait until you get home. Bob's here talking to Max and Joe and he's going to bring me with him when he meets you at the station. We can give you the story with what's going on now. And look," he paused, "I'm sorry about the texts. I panicked, but it's all OK."

"OK, but just give me one sentence."

"Helen Redland came to the flat and called out to Max to let her in."

Chapter 21

Maggie explained to Jude what had happened and ended with "I knew I shouldn't have let him get involved."

"Now just hold on there. Jack's almost nineteen, he's a head taller than you and from the look of him, physically strong. You had a plan to stop him?"

She was right, of course, Maggie knew. Max's flat was safe and well protected and Jack would never have been in any danger unless he had opened the door, which he wasn't so stupid or naïve to have done. Warrior mother instinct taking over again. But how could Jack learn to protect himself if she didn't allow him to experience dangerous situations? Then again, the dangerous situations to which he was gaining exposure were not within the normal range of teenage experience. This was uber-dangerous stuff.

"This is not normal exposure to challenging situations, Jude," she snapped.

"I know that. So does he. So does Bob. Let's wait until we get back to find out the full story. No point speculating on what might have happened. In fact, nothing happened, did it, not really."

Maggie scowled. "It's fine for you, you don't have children." As the words left her mouth she knew she had overstepped. "Sorry. That was unfair of me."

"Yes, it was."

"Then accept my apology and help me to stay calm when we hear the full account."

**

Maggie was the first person off the train at Newport where Bob and Jack were waiting in the carpark.

"We've picked up a take-away," Jack said as she and Jude got into the car. Maggie didn't reply.

Back at the house Bob and Jack organised the food. Jude tried to keep up some conversation but Maggie sat with her arms folded and didn't react when Bob told everyone to help themselves. Despite piled up plates no-one started to eat. When he couldn't take it any longer Bob broke the silence.

"Jude, Jack, please leave us."

They closed the door and sat in the hall as the voices from the kitchen grew loud and aggressive. Jack paced around the living room and had opened his mouth to object when the kitchen door flew open and footsteps ran up the stairs. Bob came to join them.

"She's raging."

"I'll go talk to her," Jude said.

"No, leave it to me," Bob replied. Before he could go Jack interrupted. "Neither of you speak to her. I'm going up there. What happens now is down to her."

Bob shrugged. "I've been working for eighteen hours straight and I'm starving. I'm going to eat."

"And I'm going to join you," Jude replied as Jack took a deep breath and headed up the stairs. "It's been a long day for us, too. Come on, let's go eat and I'll tell you what we've found out."

They had been chatting for five minutes when Jack came back and began to pile food onto a plate.

"I'm taking this up to her. I've told her either she calms down and treats me with some respect or I'm packing my bags and moving into the flat with Max and Joe."

"You can't," Bob replied.

"I know that, but Mum doesn't. I made a mistake texting her, but I was scared and you weren't responding. Anyway, it's up to her now."

When he returned none of them felt like eating. They sat at the table, waiting for someone to say something.

"So you've found out Brodie McAlister went to Spain under an assumed name," Bob said.

"Right. He chose a name from each of his male siblings. The guy we met, Martin, is going to look for further information on something called RGASPI."

"Excellent. Sometimes there are comments about the individual as well as personal identification details. What about the email the memorial chap said he would send?"

"He's sending it to Maggie so until she opens her emails we aren't going to know if anything else turned up."

Before Bob could answer footsteps in the hall approaching the kitchen signalled Maggie's return. She walked past them into the conservatory and sat in an armchair looking out across the hills to the mountain.

Once again Bob signalled to Jude and Jack to leave. He walked out and took the second chair. Maggie drummed her fingers on the chair arms, biting her lips. He said nothing, waiting. After five minutes she gave in.

"I suppose you're going to shout at me again."

"Wrong,' Bob replied.

"Why not? Don't I deserve it?"

"If your plan is to play the martyr, or go for the sympathy vote, you are not even in the shooting zone, never mind on any part of the target."

Her lips began to tremble. She let out a low moan. Bob leapt up from his chair, dropped down and enveloped her in a crushing hug. She began to sob, uncontrollably, in heaving breaths. He said nothing, just held on until she could no longer sustain the energy and the sobs slowed to a stop.

"You've cracked," he whispered. "At last."

"What? What do you mean?" came out in a muffled hoarse murmur.

He held her out at arm's length. "Listen to me. You've been the rock, the base, the concrete shoulders on which everyone else has stood or sat or leaned. You've been through hell with Eira Probert, with Zelah getting her skull cracked, with the confrontation in Ireland and with Kennet Quinn. You managed five teenagers through months of lockdown with no thanks from your rotten, selfish sister. You lost your brother-in-law, but she hasn't even considered that. Now, Alice has been the intended victim of a kidnap and Jack has just had an encounter with a maniac. Maggie, you were never going to keep up this 'superwoman' act and I, for one, am not unhappy the wheels have come off."

"Well, thanks for the support. When you put it like that …"

"Look, I love you but I've stood back for too long. I've wanted to intervene, but I couldn't because you wouldn't have listened, you'd have just resented my interference. Now, perhaps you can admit you're just an ordinary woman under extraordinary pressure and the lid just blew off?"

She sniffed. "Maybe. What do I do now?"

"For now, go to bed. You're knackered and you need the rest. Your face looks terrible, but it'll be better by the morning. I have an idea, but not now."

She nodded into his chest. He helped her to stand and walked her up the stairs. She was asleep in minutes.

Then he summoned Jude and Jack.

"She's OK, but this is a watershed thing and to capitalise on it we need some drastic action. So, I have a plan. You're both involved, OK?"

They nodded, as for the next hour Bob explained and they discussed the details of his plan.

Chapter 22

Helen Redland sat on the bed in the narrow, cheap room she had hired and paid for with cash. For the second time in an hour she picked up the cleaning cloth and a bottle of antiseptic spray and furiously scrubbed at all of the surfaces. The bed linen provided by the house lay in a heap in the corner of the room with the paper-thin towels. She had bought her own bedding and personal items. After five minutes 'scrubbing she sat down again on the bed and took out her tablet.

The plan seemed to be working. The woman she had paid to visit Max Howell's flat and call out his name had not been stopped, not even followed. This did surprise her. The bastard inspector must have known she would try Max. Or would he? If Max had been arrested for Kennet's murder maybe they thought the boy would never trust her again. How little they knew of infatuated youth. She had had Max Howell entirely in her grip, possessed him body and soul. Once she was satisfied it was safe to approach him, Helen knew she could spin him a tale of confusion. Kennet had attacked her, she had wrestled the knife away from him, the stabbing had been accidental. She didn't know what she was doing when she left the house in a state of shock, didn't even remember putting the knife into his hands. And of course, she wanted her baby back; she couldn't let him be brought up by strangers. Max would understand that. She had seen him look fondly at James. She'd have to refine a few parts, but it would do. Timing was everything. Henry Camberwell would be next. Once she had the money she could reconnect with Camberwell. Max wouldn't be needed then.

She turned her attention to her true soulmates. This puzzled her. She had sent the message to Sherry on her return to the bedsit, but as yet there had been no reply. The agreement required a reply within half an hour. She had just stood up and paced around when the phone pinged and she breathed a sigh of relief.

'Sorry. Been sorting something out. You OK?'

She typed back, '*Fine. How's the weather there?*'

A few seconds and the reply came back. *'it's not raining'*

The agreed response. '*Heard from E?*'

'Not yet. Should be tom or day after. You OK?'

'All good. Plan on track. Umbrella?'

Again a few seconds pause, then: '*getting a new one. this one too old*'

'Let me know when you have it'

She signed off. All good. Helen cut up the SIM and inserted a new one. She would text the agreed message when it was up and running, which should be in … the phone pinged again. No message, just three dots. Satisfied all was well she inserted her next SIM and texted back four dots before switching off the phone.

On to the next stage of the plan. One further check that neither she nor Max Howell were on the police radar. This was just too easy. She stood, chose a wig and applied make-up, picked up the bag containing her belongings and left the bedsit, unaware her location had already been traced and an unmarked police car sent. It missed her by seconds.

**

Many hundreds of miles away, in a room without windows, sitting on a single bed, the solitary piece of furniture in the room apart from the disgusting toilet in the corner, Sherry Martin wept as the phone was taken from her. She had let her sisters down. There had to be some way of letting them know what had happened to her. She winced as a drug fed into her arm via a drip; within seconds she lost consciousness.

**

Helen drove to Newport and booked into another anonymous Bed and Breakfast, again paying cash and using the false driving licence and passport Emer had so thoughtfully provided. The woman was a marvel. Having deposited her bag she went out again, this time to the town centre, and embarked on a shopping spree, choosing a whole wardrobe. She'd have to be careful, though. The money was almost gone. Time for a final check on Max before arranging to meet him.

As she tried on the outfits she thought about how to approach him, what to say. She had already decided on shock as the reason for giving him the knife. Now she needed an embellishment, not too much, just enough to convince him she had not been the guilty party. An idea began to form. Never depart too far from the truth. Reverse the story. It had been Kennet who had attacked her, tried to kill her, she had to defend herself. But why run if that was the case? She feared no-one would believe her. Kennet had an established presence in the town. He had never been involved with anything illegal before. That might do it. She could weep copious tears on demand when she needed to. But would it fool Max? She needed time to think it through.

As she left the store she decided to contact Henry Camberwell. It wouldn't be an easy sell, but she felt confident he would still want to use her contacts to find the next batch of 'merchandise '. It had been her show, after all. Henry needed the money. Once she had activated the overseas accounts, she knew he would bite.

Back at the bedsit Helen changed into a new outfit that she thought Max might like, chose a wig and drove to his flat, preparing to spend a couple of hours waiting to see who, if anyone, went in or out. The girl she had paid to knock on the door confirmed there had been someone inside. She had settled down for a long wait but, after ten minutes the door opened and Max emerged, accompanied by a young man. They were laughing and chatting. She wondered whether or not to follow them, but decided against. She would wait until Max returned. It didn't take long. Another twenty minutes and they were back, loaded up with supermarket bags. Poking out of the top of one she could see a carton of beer cans. She bit her lip. Who was this unknown man?. She took a quick snap with her phone and drove away.

At the bedsit Helen spent some time studying the picture. She didn't know the man. He looked a little older than Max. She carefully examined his clothes. People gave themselves away in the detail, but for this guy there was nothing to suggest he was anything more than a friend or lodger. No designer trainers, no expensive jewellery, no stylish haircut. She decided to stake out the flat overnight. And if nothing untoward happened, she would contact Max in the morning.

At seven the next morning the front door opened and the unknown man opened the front door, glanced around, rubbing his face and running his hand through his unruly hair, yawned and picked up a newspaper deposited by a paperboy an hour earlier. Could this be a lodger? But why would Max have needed one? The flat belonged to Kennet and he had given Max the tenancy without rent. Normally she would have been extra cautious, but with Emer about to arrive and Sherry already waiting to join them, she needed to access the money. She would have to separate Max from his friend, and find out this person's identity.

She dialled Max's number. No answer and voicemail kicked in. She tried again. This time after three rings a sleepy voice answered.

"Hello. Who is this?"

"Good morning, Maxwell."

Chapter 23

Several seconds of silence followed, but he didn't cut her off.

"Are you still there, Maxwell? This must be quite a shock."

"What do you want, Helen?"

"I want you, of course, my darling. We have a lot to talk about, but I can't tell you how I've missed you. Will you meet me? Today?"

More silence. Then, "I don't know, Helen. You stitched me up."

"I can explain. Please give me a chance. I love you, you know that."

"Maybe. I'm not sure. I'll call you back."

"No, I'll call you. An hour."

She ended the call, took the SIM out, broke it in half and replaced it. Nothing changed over the course of an hour. No cars arrived in the street. No-one walked up or down. Helen relaxed a little. An hour later she called again. This time he answered on the first ring.

"Helen?"

"Yes."

"I don't think I want to talk to you."

"I can understand that, honey. What happened was horrible, for both of us. Look, all I'm asking is for you to listen to what I say. Nothing else. If you're still unhappy when you've heard me out, then I'll go away." She paused for a moment. "Are you alone?"

"Yes, well, my lodger is here but he can't hear us."

"What lodger?"

"I have to pay rent now, Helen. Michelle Quinn insisted."

"Right. What a bitch. OK, let's meet up somewhere."

"No, you can come here. It's OK. Joe keeps himself to himself. He'll leave us alone to talk. But that's all. Just talk."

"If that's what you want. Give me half an hour to get there."

Helen spent the half hour again watching the street, putting on make-up and a clean jacket. She unbuttoned her blouse, leaving plenty of cleavage on show. If he looked, she'd let him touch, with luck, guide his hands. Time to go.

Max stood at the door, opening it to let her in as she walked up the short pathway. Inside the flat there was no sign of the lodger, but she could hear the sound of a TV in another room.

Helen went to kiss his cheek but he pulled back. "You have ten minutes, Helen. Then you have to go."

He hadn't looked and now she had to think fast, change the plan. "Agreed."

"Tell the truth. For a start, you never loved me and I don't know why you used me the way you did. Was it just to get back at Kennet?"

She laughed. "No, I didn't love you, but Kennet had no imagination. He wanted an heir, a proper one. He'd grown tired of Gerard and he thought I might produce a more intelligent offspring. You were – what shall we say – good-looking but lacking experience, which I gave you, whilst getting what I wanted. Ah, you're blushing."

Max's face had gone a deep red and he looked away, blinking. When he looked back his expression made Helen take a step back.

"What do you want now, Helen?"

"I need your help, to get into Kennet's house."

"It's Michelle and Gerry's house now. Why should I help you, anyway? You killed Kennet, didn't you, deliberately?"

No point in the 'Kennet attacked me 'story now. "Yes, I did. He wanted to take over my enterprise. Our sponsor was furious, wanted Kennet permanently removed. He called me that morning and told me he suspected the police had got wind of our activities, so I had to get out." She smiled at him. "I didn't have to kill Kennet, I just wanted to, serve him right. An eye for an eye."

"What's in it for me?"

"Good boy, always look after yourself first. Money is what's in it. You're broke, I can tell. Can't even afford the rent without that knuckle dragger I saw with you. There's paperwork with details of an account, with enough in it for me to retire. I'll give you fifty thousand if you get it for me."

Max folded his arms and shook his head. "The police must have gone over the house, taken it apart. If there were any papers they'll have them already. And how am I supposed to get in and out without Michelle and Gerry noticing?"

"They aren't there, they've gone to Ireland. There's security, but they call by every couple of hours. And the police won't have found the papers. They're well hidden."

He ran a hand through his hair, giving the impression of thinking, flicking his head away so she wouldn't see his face, then back to her.

"A hundred thousand. I need to get away permanently, too. How do I do it?"

Helen Redland smiled. "Seventy-five. Get dressed and walk with me. I'll tell you what to do."

"Not until you agree to the money."

"OK, I agree. Now, get a coat and let's go. We haven't much time."

A phone rang in the flat as Max and Helen let themselves out.

"Do I follow them?"

"No, someone is already on it, Joe. Just wait for them to come back. Once we know the plan we can decide what to do next," Bob Pugh replied. "He's doing well. Let's give him space to reel her properly in."

Max returned half an hour later. The waiting Joe put a call straight through to Bob and his team.

"When are you supposed to be at the house?" Bob asked.

"Tonight, late, she's going to call and tell me what time. Do I have to actually go?"

"She's given you the keys, so you'll be going as far as the front door and you can let yourself in. She'll be there watching you. Once you've found the papers, get back to the front door. She'll be waiting to pick you up. That's when we'll pick her up and we'll take it from there."

"Good. Shame about the hundred thousand though."

"I'm going to assume you're joking, boyo," Bob replied. "Right, don't go out again until she calls you."

Chapter 24

Back at her bedsit, Helen decided to sleep for a couple of hours. She would call Max just before the time she had decided he should go to the house. In the meantime, she had two calls to make. She shouldn't, but she couldn't help herself.

The response to her first elicited the anger she had anticipated.

"You were supposed to wait until I arrive. This is dangerous."

"No it isn't, Emer. I know what I'm doing."

"We had a plan, you've broken it. Your reckless behaviour puts us all in danger. I'm coming now. Meet me tomorrow and don't do anything tonight."

Helen threw the phone at the wall. Damn Emer. Who did she think she was, issuing instructions. She adored Emer of course, but sometimes Emer pushed her too far. Someone had to come up with a pragmatic plan and God knows they needed the money. To hell with her.

The second call was received with caution.

"You have returned, Miss Redland. Why are you contacting me?"

"I have funds and contacts. They have merchandise. If you aren't interested I'll go elsewhere."

"We need to talk. Not by phone. Where are you?"

"Wales."

"A large country. I am assuming Newport. Can you come to London?"

"Not for a couple of days."

"I see. I shall think over your proposition. Can I call you back on this number?"

Helen considered. She should switch the SIM after each call, but this one was probably safe, for an hour or two. "Call me at four this afternoon. I'll turn the phone back on."

"Very well."

Without taking off her clothes, Helen sank down onto the bed, setting an alarm for three thirty. When she woke she texted Max to be outside the Quinn house at eleven. There were two incoming texts. She read both, spent a few moments deciding whether or not to comply with the instructions they contained, then dressed and went out.

**

At eleven o'clock, Max Howell hovered ready outside the Quinn house. He glanced up and down the street but couldn't see any sign of Helen. She would be waiting close by. He walked up the steps and put the key in the lock. It opened, to his relief. It took less than five minutes, following Helen's instructions, to work out where the papers were hidden. '*Genius*', he thought as the panel clicked open to reveal the envelope. If you didn't know it was there, you'd never have guessed. Rufus had been right when he'd told her about it. He had also been drunk and he hadn't remembered he'd told her. Boasting, most likely, about his revered murdering ancestor who'd had the panel installed to hide the trophies he'd taken from the women he killed.

He took a deep breath, went to the front door and stopped, giving up a silent prayer nothing would go wrong, that all hell wouldn't break loose when he opened it.

The road was empty and silent, no sign of a car, no-one walking. He tip-toed down the steps, past the open gate and onto the pavement, his heart hammering. Nothing. She must be waiting to be sure no-one approached him. Ten minutes passed. His palms were sweating. What was she up to? Had this all been a joke, a test? What was going on?

Then, a car screeched around the corner at the top of the hill and slammed on its breaks as it reached him. Running forward, he found, not Helen Redland, but Bob Pugh.

"Get in. She's not coming."

"Why not? What's happened? Is everyone OK?"

"Everyone is fine. We just got a call. A body has been pulled from the river down by the Transporter Bridge. It's a young woman, with waist-length red hair. Helen Redland is dead."

Chapter 25

Mid-morning Jude decided to wake Maggie with a steaming coffee. Starting at being shaken, Maggie jerked her head, trying to clear away the fog. "Where's Bob?"

Jude sat on the side of the bed. "He took a phone call this morning, something about Max, I think. Then he rushed off."

"Something must have happened," Maggie grunted, sitting up and taking the mug. "Thanks for this. What time is it, then?"

"Just after eleven. Nick's here, and Zelah. We're working on the next phase of the Brodie McAlister case. Join us when you're ready. There are developments." With a grin and a raised eyebrow she left the room.

Maggie sat for five minutes, sipping at the coffee, thinking over the previous evening. She still felt exhausted. Had Bob been right? Had she finally melted, or combusted? There were faint vibrations on the surface of the cup, sending tiny waves back and forth, evidence of shaking hands, a heavy head and numbing exhaustion. Maybe he was right. But what did this mean for what she had to do now, to face now. Did they all know about her meltdown? She dragged herself out of bed and into the shower. Dressed and in a presentable state she hauled herself down to the office. Everything stopped as she entered the room.

Zelah spoke first. "In case you're wondering, yes, we know what happened." She stood up and in a rare gesture of compassion, in fact, Maggie thought, for the first time as far as she could remember, Zelah walked up to her and gave her a hug, then stepped back. "We are all feeling an immense weight of guilt. We've taken you at face value for too long, assumed too much and rarely asked you how you are. You're brilliant at putting on a front, you know. So, how are you?"

"Bit much, Zelah," Nick murmured in the background.

"No, it's not," Maggie replied, a tight smile on her lips. "I can't say right now how I am, but I am glad you're all here. And you shouldn't take all of the blame. I don't ask for help, even when I know I need it and that's my bad. Anyway, I'd like to do some work. Not much, but maybe an update? Jude said there's progress." Her legs were starting to wobble and she sat down at the table, noticing rain beating against the window and wind rattling the casements. "Oh dear, the weather's broken. I had hoped to spend some time in the garden."

"It's due to clear up later. Now, here's what we've all got," Zelah said, reverting to a business-like tone. "Jude, you start."

"Yes, ma'am. Maggie, Martin said he would send us the information he showed us on the person we believe to be Brodie. Well, he's outdone himself. He's also sent us the RGASPI information, listing Lewis Malcolm Stewart."

"It's an archive of information about the volunteers," Jude replied to Nick's question about the acronym.

"Can someone go visit this archive?" Nick asked.

"You can probably get permission. It's in Moscow," Jude said.

"Oh. Right. Let's stick with these lists, then."

"What do they tell us?" Maggie asked. "That we don't already know."

"We'll get to that, but first, Martin's information. I've shown Nick and Zelah the Trust's reports. This morning I looked at a number of them and what struck me, when I saw the information in context, there's no outcome to Brodie's report."

"What do you mean?"

"I've printed off a few, to show you." Jude put five pieces of paper side by side on the table. "You can see they have details of what happened to each of these volunteers, which battles they fought in, if they were injured, if they died, the location or battle, and if they were repatriated. Also, their date of death if it occurred after their return. Brodie's record, in the name of Lewis Malcolm Stewart, has nothing. His first major engagement had been at Teruel, then he saw action at Belcite, finally the assault on Gandesa, which he survived, in April '38. Then the Ebro in July three months later. He survived that one, too. In September, when the announcement came of the withdrawal of the International Brigades, he should have returned, but he didn't. There's no further record, either in Spain or back in the UK. He just seems to have disappeared."

"Hmm. The withdrawal was well organised. The Internationals paraded through the streets of Barcelona before they headed for the French border. Do we know if he took part?" Maggie asked.

"We don't know. I've been scouring documentation, but there's nothing. And photographs of the parade. Sorry, forgot to say, we've found a photograph, just the one. Here."

Across the table she handed Maggie a black-and-white portrait. A round faced young man, strands of lightish hair poking out from under a Spanish beret, wearing a heavy military overcoat, gazed downwards in concentration, caught in the moment of lighting a cigarette hanging from the side of his mouth.

"Tough guy pose," she said. "Is this definitely him?"

"Yes, I found it in a collection and it's captioned with the name he gave. It's the only one of him. He's so young, isn't he?"

Maggie stared at the photograph. "It's heartbreaking. He was seventeen when this was taken. He shouldn't have been there."

"But what happened to him afterwards?" Jude said. "It's a mystery. Anyway, there's more. Over to you, Nick."

Nick coughed to clear his throat. "I've found Julie McAlister and her husband. He'd been an Air Force pilot, based in Lincolnshire. I'm working on their descendants; their daughter Maria married and had a son called Peter. I'm tracking him now."

"My turn now," Zelah said. "I've tracked down the two survivors from the orphanage, Mary Cameron McShane and Alexander Smith. Both are in their nineties and living in care homes. I have the names of the homes but I haven't checked yet what kind of homes they are."

"What does it mean?" Jude asked.

"Well, hopefully they'll have a couple of marbles between them, enough to give us something useful. I'll ask the homes if I can talk directly to them, with the Covid rules."

"Are you the best person, Zelah?" Nick asked. "Discretion and compassion will be necessary. And a lot of patience."

Before she could answer Maggie said," She can do it when she needs to. This is progress. What next?"

The three of them gave each other a quick up-and-down glance, but no-one spoke.

"OK. Someone spill. What have you all been talking about behind my back?"

"Bob's plan," Jude said. "It's best he explains. Do you want to work today?"

"Don't change the subject."

"We all need to be here, with Bob, so stop asking and either make some progress, or go back to bed, or whatever," Zelah intervened. "No-one's talking about you. Stop being so paranoid."

Maggie tried to argue, but found she didn't have the strength or the inclination. She shrugged, muttered '*whatever*' and went to the kitchen. The rain had stopped and the sun had come out again. A day to spend in the garden, away from everyone. She wondered where Jack had gone and panicked for a moment, until she heard his thunderous descent of the stairs. Seeing her, he stopped, looking sideways at her.

"I'm not going to re-start the shouting match, if that's what you're thinking," Maggie said. "I will try to accept what you say. I don't want you to leave."

He walked over to her and put his arms around her. "Have you talked to Bob?"

"Apparently he went out early, something about Max. He stayed here last night and left with Bob."

Jack stiffened as a ping on the phone announced a text message from Max with just two words: '*we're on*'. He typed back:' *need me*?'

'No. B says stay at home. Will contact l8r.'

"What's up?" Maggie asked.

"Don't know. Something, maybe. What are you going to do today?"

"Work. For now, some gardening. If I feel enthusiastic later I'll join the others on the project."

"I'll be in my room."

She wandered out into the garden, got out her gardening tools and began to pull weeds. Something was going on. Normally she'd be annoyed at being so obviously left out, but today she couldn't be bothered. After a while she gave up. She couldn't even find the enthusiasm to pull the weeds. Might as well head back to the office. In the end, company was better than solitude.

She found Jude in the office, chattering away in fluent Spanish. From the living room she could hear Zelah on a call, and no Nick.

Jude finished her call. "Just talking to a contact of Bob's in Spain," she explained. "Chap called Joan Torrens. He said to say hello."

"We met him a couple of years ago, when Bob and I went to Catalonia. He's a genealogist. How can he help this time?"

"He can't personally, but he has contacts in the Gandesa area, people active in memorialising the Civil War. He's going to put me in touch with them."

Maggie stared keenly at her. "You're still thinking we should go to Spain, aren't you."

Jude grinned but didn't reply. "I'll speak to the people when they call. Then we can make decisions about next steps. What do you want to do?"

Before she could answer Nick came running into the office. "I've got them," he puffed. "I've got Julie McAlister's descendants. A man called Peter Montgomery, her grandson. He says he has something in writing. Julie instructed him to keep it safe until someone came to ask for it."

"What does it say?" Maggie asked.

"That's what we're about to find out," he replied. "He's waiting for us to call."

Chapter 26

"It's early morning in Canada, isn't it?" Maggie whispered as Nick dialled the call on the conference phone.

Jude nodded. "Five hours, I think, which makes it around seven over there. He must be keen to share."

The phone rang. "At last, someone wants this damn letter! Good morning to whoever you are."

Nick spoke first. "It's Nick from Maze Investigations, Peter. Good morning and thanks for taking this call so early. I'm here with my colleagues, Maggie Gilbert, Zelah Trevear and Judith Crawley Winters. As I explained, we've taken on the case of your great grandmother Julie's missing brother, Brodie McAlister. What can you tell us about what's in Julie's letter?"

"I can tell you nothing. It's been sealed since she wrote it."

"Peter, this is Zelah Trevear. Before we get into the letter, can you give us a brief run-through of who's who in your family, just the basic line of descent?"

"Sure. Grandma Julie was born in Scotland, in Glasgow, I believe in 1917. She met my grandfather, Jason, in London during the war. I guess she worked there, or something. He was a pilot. They got engaged and after the war she came to Canada to marry him. My aunt Maria was born in 1948 and my dad, David, in 1949. He and my mom – she's local from Toronto – married in 1978 and I was born in 1979. I'm the eldest of three. I have two sisters and I can tell you, they are both dying to know what's in this damn letter."

"As are we," Zelah replied. "But again and sorry, what's the story of the letter, or what you know?"

"I know a scant amount. We don't know when Grandma wrote it. I guess it will be dated. I hope so. She said it contains important family history, but it shouldn't be opened until someone asked specifically for it. She knew someone would contact us. She gave it to my dad and when he died last year he handed it on to me. That's all I know."

"And you are happy to open it now?"

"You bet, Nick. Right. I'm gonna unstick it. Wow, my hands are shaking. This is … I don't know what to say. OK. It's open. I'm taking out the contents. There are six flimsy small pages. The handwriting is straightforward, looks like it will be easy to read. It's written on both sides of each page, so twelve pages of writing." He stopped and blew out a long, loud breath, then paused for a moment, speaking away from the phone.

"My wife Sue is here. She wants to be in on the action."

"Fine with us," Nick said. "Before you start, do you have a protective covering you can put the letter and the envelope into after you've read it? It's important to preserve it properly."

"He does," said a female voice.

"Ok. Here goes." Peter cleared his throat and began to read.

'My name is Julie Montgomery, born Julie McAlister. I was born in 1917 in Glasgow. This is an account of the history of

my youngest brother, Brodie McAlister. The facts I am about to relate are already known to my sister Helen. We agreed we should never speak of them, but I have always believed sometime in the future there would be justice for Brodie, so I am writing down this story in the hope that one day, someone will deliver the justice Helen and I failed to achieve for him.'

"Sounds like this will be quite a story," Peter said. "Yes, I'll keep going. She's flapping at me here."

"So are we," Zelah whispered.

'After the death of our mother, Grace McAlister, at the hands of our father and his subsequent hanging for her murder,'

He paused again for an audible intake of breath.

'Helen, Brodie and I were placed in an orphanage. Our elder brothers, Malcolm and Lewis were deemed to be sufficiently mature to look after themselves. The early years were not too bad. But, then we were moved. The next orphanage was a terrible place. I will not go into detail here. It is too painful and the memories still give me the occasional nightmare. Helen stayed there for just one year. She tried to protect Brodie as much as she could. He was just eleven when we were moved. Helen left when she turned seventeen, in 1932. I did what I could for Brodie. I left the place in 1934 and went to live with Helen. We had both suffered unspeakable treatment, including starvation and beatings. One nun in particular, Sister Mary Veronica, was as evil a woman as you will ever meet. She took Brodie under her wing. We hoped she would be kind to him. But her intentions were not kindness, nor indeed anything good. She liked the children to fight and in Brodie she found a boxer. He grew tall and strong, looking older than his years. Helen and I visited him whenever we could, although we were often refused

access to him. On occasion we saw him covered in bruises, with his eyes blackened. This went on for almost three years. Helen met her Jim and together they tried to get Brodie out, to live with them, but the church refused. They convinced the authorities Brodie had what they called behavioural problems, making him a danger to himself and others, and the best place for him was with them. The evidence, we discovered, came from Sister Mary Veronica, who described herself as his carer. No-one ever asked Brodie if this was true.

'In late 1937 as Brodie approached his seventeenth birthday, no-one would be able to prevent him from leaving the orphanage. The fights were becoming intensely vicious and the damage greater. I do not know how the orphanage allowed this to go unchecked. Some details came out at the enquiry, but I will say more on that subject later.

'Just before Brodie's birthday the nun arranged for Brodie to take on another boy a year or so younger than himself, David Laird. David was not a bad boy. But they both knew that they had to put everything into it. Brodie told me that on the day it happened he hadn't wanted to fight. He was scared. He told her he wasn't going to fight. She threatened to have him transferred to a mental institution if he didn't go through with it. The outcome was, David Laird died.

'Brodie ran. He came to Helen and Jim. He swore he had not intended to hit David so hard, but the boy fell, unconscious. The following day, the news came of David's death and a warrant had been issued for Brodie's arrest. The nun had told the authorities Brodie had beaten the boy mercilessly and she hadn't had the strength to pull them apart. Brodie swore to us this was a lie, and we believed him. Helen and I went to see the nun. The meeting convinced us the woman was unbalanced.

The look in her eyes when she talked about her expectation of Brodie being hanged for murder just like his father was something I will never forget. She relished the prospect and we had no doubt she would do her utmost to achieve her aim.

'We decided we should get him as far away as possible. The police had already searched Helen and Jim's house. They had sent Brodie out just in time and he wandered the streets of Glasgow for hours. He took shelter in a local hall where a trade union hosted a talk by a man recruiting volunteers to travel to Spain to join the fight against the Fascists. When he came home Brodie loved the idea, it excited him. He could leave Scotland, go away for some time, then come back later, when the fuss had settled down and moved on. We could not dissuade him. He was so naïve; he thought this would be an adventure. He had met up with another lad, Michael McGregor, a wee bit older than himself. They planned to leave after the New Year.

'In early January Brodie and Michael left Glasgow and I went with them. Helen and Jim couldn't go, as the police were still keeping an eye them. The boys had an address in London, where they were provided with papers. Brodie gave his name as Lewis Malcolm Stewart and his age as eighteen. No-one questioned him. We found accommodation in Paddington and waited. Another young man joined us, Harry from Chiswick, a cheery chap and the three boys formed a friendship. Two days later the message came. The boys reported to Waterloo station and met up with a group of men of varying ages. Some of them I didn't like the look of and I tried again to persuade Brodie not to go. But what could I offer him as an alternative? He promised to get a message to Helen or to me to say he had arrived. We agreed a Spanish phrase on a postcard we bought in a shop outside the station.

'He was cheery when he set off. I hugged him and cried. Then I went back to Scotland. We never saw or heard from him for over a year.

'The enquiry took place and, because of the evidence given by the nun, a case of murder was declared and Brodie became a wanted man. We tried to tell the Sheriff's people of the concern we had about the nun, but they would not listen. After all, we ourselves were the children of a murderer. Who would listen to us, let alone believe what we said? They said our brother must have inherited the lust for giving out a beating from our father. I could no longer pray, but I thought about Brodie every day.

'At the end of 1938, the postcard arrived, sent from London. We were overjoyed and looked forward to his return. But he never came and we never heard from him again. As I write this account I do not know if my brother is alive or dead. I have read stories of the men and women of the International Brigade. The end was not good, the fight being lost in Spain. I tried to find out what might have happened when the survivors returned but no-one has ever told me what happened to my brother. And when the war broke out there was no longer a way to ask questions.

'My hope is that, one day, someone will read this account and discover what happened to our beautiful Brodie. He deserves justice.'

Chapter 27

Peter Montgomery stopped and for several moments there was silence at both ends of the phone. Then he said," Give me a moment please. My wife is crying and I think I am, too."

"We'll call back in ten minutes," Nick said.

"Well, that confirms it, doesn't it," Jude said. "Poor Brodie."

"It confirms nothing," Maggie replied sharply.

Jude's eyes widened. "I don't understand, you just heard the account from Julie. She was there, she confirmed he was used and abused."

"Maggie's right," Nick said.

Jude threw her hands up in a gesture of amazement. "I don't understand you people. Did we just hear the same thing, or did I dream it?"

"Just calm down," Zelah intervened. "I agree with them, a harrowing account, but we have to come at this from a genealogical investigative direction. A member of Brodie's family wrote it. She did experience the horror of the orphanage, but we don't yet know when the nun lived there. She may have arrived after Julie left, so Julie had no direct experience with her. Julie loved her brother, and as a family member she's bound to have believed him. Look, Jude, ask yourself this. How do you know Brodie McAlister didn't willingly take part in the alleged organised fighting?"

Jude opened her mouth, hesitated and closed it again. She still looked mutinous, but not quite so certain. She bit her bottom lip.

"Halo and horns," Maggie said.

"What does that mean?"

"It's one way of describing how we react to people, based on what we hear and who's saying it," Maggie replied. "Social media excels at it. The horns are allocated to people who don't make a favourable impression, like Sister Mary Veronica. What's the evidence, though? She gave a version of events to the Fatal Accident Enquiry hearing, putting Brodie firmly in the category of developing psychopath. Yet Julie's version says the nun was both instigator and perpetrator, based on Brodie's telling, based on her and Helen's subsequent visit with him. Next question, why was Brodie so keen to go to Spain, to fight in a war he most likely knew nothing about? Could it have been an opportunity to exercise his murderous personality? Did the thought of legal killing excite him? Again, we only have Julie's explanation. You've allocated him the halo, because of what his family said about him, and because of what we've learned about the orphanage, but there's no independent evidence, is there? Think about it."

Jude sank back in her chair. "I don't want him to be the bad guy. There is independent evidence of terrible atrocities at the orphanage."

"Fair comment. However, before we can definitively say he deserves the halo, we need corroboration. That's where the next piece of the puzzle slots in. Zelah is going back to Scotland to visit the two remaining people who were in the orphanage with Brodie, and we must hope they have something useful to substantiate one side or the other."

"We must call Peter back, don't forget," Nick interrupted. "He'll be waiting for us." He dialled the call and Peter answered on the first ring.

"How are you folks planning to use this information?" he asked. "Sue and me, well, we're dumbfounded by all of this. Never expected it, you know. I mean, I always thought Grandma Julie's letter would be about a family scandal, but not on this scale."

"Your relative in Scotland, Julie's sister's descendant and our client, wants to know what happened to Brodie, so letting her know about this will be the first step. After that, we'll keep on researching and maybe we can find out what happened to him," Nick replied.

"Why 'maybe'?" Peter's wife asked.

Zelah held up her hand to speak next. "There are a lot of records about the volunteers returning to their home countries, but Brodie, in whatever name he used, isn't on any of the lists. But he also wasn't a casualty in the final months of the battles. Some, not many, just a handful, decided to stay on to fight beside the remains of the Spanish army. He might have been one of those, or he might have escaped to France and stayed there. For now, it's all speculation." She paused for a moment and looked at the others. "May I suggest something on the hoof here, as my colleagues are all on this call? Once we've spoken to our client, we'll put you in touch with her and she can keep you up to date on progress."

The others all nodded. "They all agree here. Ok with you, Peter and Sue?"

"Fine with us, thanks. So, we can expect a call?"

"I'm returning to Scotland and I can update the client. When she has agreed, I'll email you her details and she can call you."

"We'll look forward to it," Sue said. "We have a son the age as Brodie when he left. It's a real scary thought, isn't it?"

"Indeed," Nick said, thinking about Max. "Right, we'll get on now."

"Good luck," Peter replied.

Zelah jumped up. "I'm about to call the homes now, see if I can travel up to meet with the contemporaries. I'll do it before you both head off." She went to leave the room, but froze. "Oops," she said under her breath.

"Head off where? Who's going off?" Maggie asked, looking at Nick. "Are you and Stella planning a trip?"

Nick closed his eyes and scowled, just as Jack walked into the room.

"You aren't going anywhere, are you, Jack? You know it's too soon for you and Max to be thinking about foreign travel," Maggie said.

"No. Who's done it?" he replied. He looked at Nick. "Zelah," Nick muttered. "Woman can't keep anything to herself."

"Someone needs to explain to me what's going on," Maggie said, standing up and putting her hands flat on the table. "Now."

"It's you who's going," Jack said. "You and Jude are going to Spain. It's Bob's idea, but he talked to all of us to check if we agreed. And we do."

The colour in Maggie's cheeks had risen to a deep red as Jack had spoken. She turned around to face him. "So, you've all decided what's best for me?"

Jack folded his arms. A muscle in his neck visibly pulsed, but he didn't back down. "Mum, you've lost your perspective. You didn't even realise how tense you've been lately, how snappy and rude. I told you, I'm fed up with being treated like a baby. Your colleagues have your back, but you don't have theirs."

Maggie's breath came in short, jerky bursts. She felt tears welling up and couldn't stop them. She put her hands up to either side of her head, and Jack stepped back, seemingly expecting another outburst, but instead she sat back down.

"Have I been such a monster?"

"No, you've not been a monster," Jude said. "But you've not been with us. I know, we did the trip to London, et cetera, but you've gone deep within yourself. It's like you're trying, but a fog has come down and it isn't lifting. Is that unfair?"

"No," Maggie whispered. "It's not, but why the hell would going to Spain help?"

"Context," Nick said. "Your energy is so low. It's been getting weaker, but now it's almost invisible. Bob's thought if you just stay here, waiting, you'll go under." He walked around the table and sat beside her, taking her hands in his. "We'll all take care of each other, do our best to ensure no harm comes to any of us. Spain is the next logical step, now we know Brodie did volunteer. We can get through the outstanding research, find out about Brodie's progress to Spain and when he arrived there. There's plenty of documentary evidence. We'll discuss it all, put together a plan for you both to follow. I've drawn up some options. You can do this."

"I'll think about it, OK? That's the best I can say for now."

"That's good enough," Jude replied. "Come on, let's make some tea and start talking." She took Maggie by the arm and pulled her up.

"How are we supposed to get there? Are there flights, even? I thought Covid still didn't allow for plane travel to Spain."

"We're going to take Bob's camper van. Road trip," Jude said, her eyes lighting up. "It'll be fun." She gave Jack's arm a quick squeeze as they left the room.

Zelah, who had used the kitchen to make her calls, had just finished. "Sorry. I dropped the ball there. We were supposed to wait for Bob. Where is he?"

"No idea," Maggie said.

"Something's going down." Jack had followed them into the kitchen and began to rummage in the fridge. "He'll get in touch."

But Maggie heard nothing from him. After an evening of discussion and planning, she went to bed at midnight, exhausted and not happy to be woken up by Bob trying to creep into bed.

"What time is it?" she muttered.

"Just after three," he whispered.

"Why are you so late?"

"Developments. I'll explain in the morning."

She sat up. "Explain now."

"OK. Helen Redland is dead. Strangled and dumped in the Usk."

Maggie thought for a moment. "Good," she said. "I'm not sorry. Her being gone makes us all safer. Is Max OK?"

"Yes, he's fine. Bit distressed and worked up. He had to identify her, as there isn't any family."

"Well, that's an end to her story. Who did it?"

"We don't know, yet. That's what I'll be working on tomorrow. Make that today. I need to sleep."

Maggie lay down again, feeling no guilt at her reaction. Helen Redland had been a monster and, in her opinion, the world would be a better place without the woman in it. Bob would find out who had been responsible, but she didn't care too much, as long as it wasn't Max, which she thought not possible anyway, as he had been with Bob and Joe all day. She could go to Spain with more confidence and less concern. She fell asleep again within minutes. Bob, however, lay awake for some time. No need to tell Maggie, but his list of potential suspects for Helen Redland's demise had four names on it. Two of them were Nick Howell and Zelah Trevear. The next twenty-four hours were likely to be uncomfortable.

Chapter 28

Bob was already in the kitchen when Maggie joined him mid-morning. She had been awake for half an hour already, thinking about how to approach the trip to Spain, still angry he hadn't spoken to her before discussing and deciding with her colleagues, family and friend, but accepting the way she had behaved had worried her family and friend, and now Bob had the added burden of a murder on his plate. She had no interest in starting an argument she had no hope of winning and anyway, she hadn't yet rebuilt a sufficient store of energy. In fact, she still felt as if she were running on fumes so confronting Bob for the sake of a confrontation would only make matters worse.

They found themselves performing a strange dance ritual around each other, not looking directly, not touching, keeping a just-too-far distance for each one to show awareness of the other's potential to snap and attack. Maggie gave in first.

"Oh, let's just sit down and talk to each other. I can't be doing with this."

Bob muttered, "Works for me. What time are the others due?"

"Not sure," she said, accepting his peace offering of a mug of coffee and a hot croissant. "Nick should be here soon and I heard Jude humming in the bathroom. Zelah's going back to Scotland this morning." She glanced at her watch. "She's on the plane by now She's back tomorrow evening."

His head snapped up from his mug. "What's she doing in Scotland? Why did she go back so soon?"

"There's one available flight today. Tomorrow she's going to visit a couple of survivors of the orphanage. We're trying to understand about Brodie McAlister and his time there and more about his personality. Why are you so keen to know?"

"I need to talk to her and to Nick." He put the mug down, sat back and folded his arms. Maggie stared at him, puzzled, until realisation hit like a body blow, jerking her head upwards.

"You cannot be serious!"

He leaned forward. "Can you sit there and tell me with one hundred percent certainty – one hundred percent – neither Nick nor Zelah has a reason for wanting to see off Helen Redland?"

Maggie opened her mouth, but knew no reassurance from her would be sufficient and anyway, she couldn't possibly give such reassurance.

"I can't say with a hundred percent assurance I didn't have a reason for wanting to see off Helen Redland. Don't ask me about my colleagues."

They were still staring at each other a minute later when Jude entered the kitchen, whistling happily, until she saw them. "Whoa! What's going on here? The Mexican Border Wall is rising across the table." She paused, then walked further forward and said to Maggie," Is this because of Spain?"

"No, it's because Bob thinks one of my colleagues could have murdered Helen Redland."

"Oh. Well … could they?"

Maggie jumped up. "You're taking his side."

"I'm not taking any side. Sit down, Maggot." Jude barked out, not politely, and Maggie sat, scowling.

Jude put her hands on her hips "First of all, he would have had a reason for such a suggestion. He is a senior police detective, isn't he, so perhaps listen instead of just reacting, which you've been doing too frequently lately." She turned to Bob. "When did she die?"

"Between six and midnight yesterday. Strangled and thrown into the river."

"Well," Jude mused, "from what Maggie told me it couldn't have happened to a nicer person. And I'm guessing, Maggot, you don't care if she's dead." Maggie raised her eyebrows in a '*you think?* 'signal.

"I guess Max is OK?"

"He's fine, sort of. He was stressed but he coped."

"OK, so Nick stayed here until about six thirty, then he left to meet Stella. Zelah went off to her flat mid-afternoon and booked a flight to Edinburgh, where she is now. She's due back this evening, I believe?" Jude explained to Bob.

Maggie nodded.

The front door opening created a momentary distraction and Bob jumped up in response to Nick's call of 'hello' from the hallway. "Stay here, both of you," he growled and went out to join Nick. They both disappeared into the office, with the door firmly slammed shut by Bob.

"Nick wouldn't harm a fly, in fact, he always tries to catch them and let them out, even the wasps," Maggie remonstrated.

"Tell me, Maggie, if you were in his shoes and she'd been trying to manipulate Jack, what would you be capable of?"

Maggie flashed a glower at Jude, but didn't respond. Who truly knew what a person could do in such a situation? Of course she couldn't speak for either Nick or Zelah and this was unfair on Bob, caught in the centre here. He had a job to do and she knew he would do it, without fear or favour. Her best bet was to trust him and her friends, and keep out of the way of his investigations.

"We can talk about the trip to Spain, if you like," Jude said dropping down into Bob's vacated chair. "I thought it'd be controversial, but it's a doddle in comparison to murder. What are you thinking? Have you had time to think? Are you up for it?"

Maggie hesitated, then made a slow nod. Before going to bed she had thought about little else. Jack's start date for university wasn't for another three weeks. She had worked out how many hours it would take to get there, how they would manage if there were no official campsites open and myriad practical considerations.

"We need a plan. Journey time, ferries, routes, campsites, food and drink."

"Who we meet when we get there, what we need to see and find out," Jude interrupted.

"A lot to do. When are we thinking of going? I presume you've worked that out too?"

"I have. I've already looked at the ferries for the day after tomorrow and I've found an open campsite not too far from Gandesa. I've looked at the mileage and I think we can get there in two days, sharing the driving. We can have three days in Catalonia, then two-and-a-bit days back. A week in all. And," she held up her hand. "Before you say anything, everyone else is agreed they can cope without us, which will be calmer with Helen Redland no longer lurking in the background. What do you say?"

"That's quick," Maggie replied.

"So? What's holding us up?"

Maggie thought about it. "We need Zelah's info from Scotland, if there is anything useful from her visit."

"We'll get it later today. Come on, let's think about what we can get out of a visit to Spain. We'll factor in the results of Martin's searches and Zelah's info, with what Peter in Canada read out. Should give us a rounded picture of Brodie and give us some leads on what to look for when we get out there. What do you say?"

"What do I say? I say I feel like I'm being managed."

"Look, can't you just accept you're in a hole from which you cannot extricate yourself without help and you're stressed and anxious. Real life is messy, Maggot," Jude said, leaning forward, elbows on the table. "But this is an opportunity. We can have some fun, learn some stuff, we hope about what happened to Brodie and … we'll have plenty of time on the journey to reflect on what's happening to us, personally. We both need this."

"OK, OK," Maggie conceded. "I suppose …" She didn't get any further as the office door opened and Nick and Bob came back into the kitchen.

"We're going in to the station for Nick and Stella to give a formal statement," Bob said.

“We’re fine with it,” Nick said, not giving either Maggie or Jude a chance to comment. “I suspect neither of you cares Helen is dead any more than Stella and I do, but it’s important for Bob to carry out his investigation to the letter of the law. We’ll be back later.”

They left the house, Bob not looking at Maggie nor saying anything to her.

Chapter 29

First thing Monday morning, Zelah set out for the first retirement home, having made a brief call on Lolly Sadler to update her.

Lolly had been delighted to hear about the contact with Julie's family and had read through a copy of Julie's declaration. Zelah had also brought a copy of the photograph Nick had found in the collection in the US. Lolly stared at it for several minutes. Deciding the time had come to discuss expenses, Zelah spoke up to introduce the idea of Maggie going to Spain to do further research on what might have happened to Brodie.

"Well, I suppose it's inevitable, now we know he went over there. I'll need an estimate, mind you."

"I thought we could split the cost," Zelah replied.

"That sounds reasonable. Let me know what it's likely to be. Now, do you have anything further about whatever else is on the postcard?"

"No, not yet. Perhaps I can find out about the man Julie mentions in the statement, Harry from East London. If I can get a name it might be possible to track down his descendants and learn if they have anything he left behind from his time in Spain, always assuming of course he got back."

Lolly nodded. "And what about these two elderly folks you're visiting now?"

"Don't hold out too much hope," Zelah replied. "They're in their nineties and in retirement homes. One's a dementia care home. The managers of both say they're willing to talk with social distancing but I don't know if that's about the children's home, or if they'd just like a chat with someone they haven't met before. I'll let you know, whatever."

Lolly grinned. "Thank you. I must say, you've made amazing progress. I didn't expect anything back from you for a week at least."

Zelah stood and picked up her bag. "There's four of us working on it," she said. "And we have some experience already of Spain and the Civil War. Right, I'll be off. I'll call you tomorrow."

**

The two retirement homes weren't too far apart, on the outskirts of Edinburgh towards the coast. The first home sat on the sea front, with a direct view of the sea, on private land, the garden backing onto the beach, with tables, chairs and benches. She could imagine in the summer it would be a pleasant place for the residents to sit and eat, chat and gaze out over a blue sea. Today, it was overcast and breezy and Zelah pulled her overcoat around her shoulders. As she parked the hired car and put on her mask, a strong gust off the sea caught her as she moved into its direct path and she had to pause a moment to keep her balance. Not a day for the frail and wobbly to be outside, she mused.

The manager greeted her at the entrance, a brisk, stout woman with iron grey hair resilient against the wind, wearing a tartan-based uniform. She checked Zelah's temperature then ushered her in and took her coat, pulling it off her shoulders, which would otherwise have annoyed Zelah had she not just been blasted by heat of the intensity of a tropical zone. She felt her forehead going red within seconds and sweat began to run down the sides of her ears.

"She's waiting for you," the woman said, walking down a short corridor towards the back of the building. "She's excited about your visit."

"Does she understand what I'm going to talk to her about?"

"Yes, she does. Here we are. Be careful, now. She's ninety-one and quite frail."

As the door opened, Zelah momentarily stopped in her tracks, staring at the view of the North Sea through a set of full-length windows with a door leading out onto the garden, until a voice interrupted her.

"Lovely, isn't it? Makes this place less boring. Thank you, Miss Roberts, you can scoot now."

The manager flashed Zelah a quick grin and closed the door.

"She's not so bad. She takes excellent care of those of us hanging on here."

If Zelah had expected a frail lady with a lace shawl and thick stockings, nothing could have been further away and her excitement and anticipation rose as she realised this was no memory deficient old biddy. The woman who rose to greet her was around her own height, straight and slim, dressed in cargo pants and a beautiful paisley sweater that hugged a figure still boasting a defined waistline. The haircut, short and sharp, was coloured a becoming platinum silver.

Zelah looked at the extended hand which pulled back with a snort and "Forgot, not allowed to shake, and you need to keep six feet away from me and not touch anything. And we have to talk through these bloody masks." The hands bore the usual wrinkles and brown age spots, but the nails were manicured with a blood red varnish.

Zelah sat on a chair on the opposite side of the room. "How are you keeping, Mrs McShane?"

"Please call me Mary, I'm taking as much care of myself as I can," Mary Cameron McShane said, having spotted Zelah's inspection of the nails. "Nice colour, isn't it?"

"Lovely. Not subtle," Zelah replied, grinning. "My kind of colour."

A woman in uniform entered with a mug of coffee for Mary who took it and said, "Down to business then. You're here about the orphanage. Terrible place. What do you want to know, Mrs Trevear?"

"You haven't asked *why* I want to know."

"I don't care," Mary replied. "I am anticipating you're going to tell me anyway."

Zelah bit her lip. "It's about the orphanage, yes, but it's also about another child, whom I'm hoping you'll remember. His name is Brodie McAlister."

As she said the name the woman's head jerked with a sharp, audible breath. "Now there's a name I haven't heard in many moons, over eighty years ago in fact. Why are you asking now?"

Zelah decided to pitch straight into the story, keeping nothing back. She revealed what they knew, what they hoped to achieve and why she had made this visit.

Mary McShane sat back, folded her arms and said, "So you want my impression of Brodie?"

"Yes, I do. You do remember him?"

"Of course I remember him. I remember Julie, too. I don't remember Helen, but I must have been too young when she left. Julie was a sweet girl. But Brodie now. When I first came across Brodie I thought he was a monster."

"Why?"

"For a start he was so tall for his age, I had to bend my head back onto my neck to see him. The age difference didn't help either, him being fifteen, me just eight or nine. He always followed the she-devil around – that's what we called Sister Mary Veronica. That woman had as much compassion and kindness as Torquemada. Brodie was her acolyte, so it seemed. But then, one day I had cried because another child had taken my toy, the only one I had, a teddy bear. I can't remember its name now, but I had brought it from home when my mother took me to the orphanage and it was the only thing I had to remind me of my home. Brodie found me. I expected a slap and an order to shut up, but instead he gave me a hug, told me to dry my tears and come with him. We found the thief, who took one look at Brodie and threw my bear at me. Brodie put the word out no-one should ever try to take my toy again. From that day on I adored him. I was broken hearted when I learned he had run away."

"You didn't see the fight?" Zelah asked.

"No, I could never watch. It scared me in case someone hurt him badly. They never did, but I couldn't watch. Sometimes, she used to make us watch, but I closed my eyes, listened to the sound of the punches and the grunts and cries. I had nightmares about those sounds for years after I left. My husband organised therapy for me, which helped, but I still remember, sometimes," Mary closed her eyes and took a long, deep breath.

"A terrible place," Zelah murmured.

"You can't imagine," Mary replied, shaking her head. "I had to stay there for another few months until a family member came and took me away. I can't tell you how secretly pleased I felt when I heard that a car hit the she-devil and killed her, some years later. I've never admitted that before."

"How often did the fights take place?"

"About once a month. The boys lived in fear of being chosen to go up against Brodie. Now, when I look back on it, I believe Brodie went easy on most of them. Maybe he had told them to take a dive, even. She used to stand on the side watching, smiling. She had thin lips and a long quivering nose, like a rat." Mary stood up and walked around to the back of the chair, leaning heavily on it. "I haven't been reminded of this for some time."

"Then let's not talk about the fighting. Just one more question, if that's OK. What kind of boy was David Laird?"

"Och, he was a big lad, bit slow on the uptake if you know what I mean. He hadn't been with us long. I don't think there was any harm in him and he wasn't a natural fighter."

"Did anyone ever ask any of the children about the fights, after David died?"

"Not a one. Mind you, we wouldn't have answered if they had. We were too scared of her and we truly thought no-one would believe us if we said a holy woman encouraged boys to beat the life out of each other."

Zelah nodded. "Sister Mary Veronica was the epitome of evil, from what you're telling me."

Mary nodded and returned to her seat.

"What will you do now, Mrs Trevear? Will you find out what happened to Brodie?"

"We'll do our best. My colleague is going to Spain in a day or so, to see find evidence of what happened there."

"I'd like to know, please, if you do find out. He was a good boy and he was my friend. My best friend for a while."

"Of course. I'll come back up. I'm off to see another of the children now, Alexander Smith. Do you remember him?"

Mary's face creased up in thought for a moment, then she hit her hand on her trouser leg. "Of course, little Xandy. He's younger than me, I remember. He's still going, then?"

"He's in a dementia care home," Zelah said, standing up. "I'm not expecting anything useful from him."

"That's sad. I've still got my marbles, even though my hips have long since left the building."

Zelah laughed. "You're doing well, Mary. I see you have a laptop," she said, glancing over at the desk.

"I like to keep up with the world. I'm writing a book."

"Your life story?"

"Hell no, too boring. It's a murder mystery set in an old people's home. Not based on anyone here, of course." She winked at Zelah.

"I'll look forward to reading it when you publish."

"I'll walk with you to the door," Mary said. She picked up two walking sticks from behind the chair and they set off down the corridor.

At the door Zelah nodded and said, "Thank you. This has been helpful. I'll let you know what we find."

"Be sure you do, Mrs Trevear. Good luck to you."

Chapter 30

If the visit to Mary McShane had been a pleasure, her meeting with Alexander Smith had been a nightmare and left her angry and frustrated. The home sat at the lower end of the comfort scale. Alexander's room felt cold and miserable, spartanly furnished with no personal photographs or mementos of any kind and smelled of stale cabbage and lack of personal hygiene. Zelah began frowning as she walked into the hallway.

A manager, to whom she had lied about being a distant relative, his only surviving one, accompanied her to the room. Alexander lay on a single bed with a tatty quilt faded with age covering his legs. White faced and trembling, and, she thought, defensive, wincing as if he were about to be slapped. His collars and cuffs were frayed and his trousers displayed bare ankle. He stared vacantly at Zelah, peering through bloodshot watery eyes.

"Does he wear glasses?" Zelah asked.

"Yes, but he loses them, leaves them everywhere," the manager snapped, frowning. "Lost your glasses again, Mr Smith," she shouted at him.

"Hardly surprising. What effort do you make to keep them around his neck? Chains and ribbons not available in Scotland?"

The woman sniffed and didn't reply. Zelah could feel hackles rising and took a deep breath to keep herself in check. "Who's his next of kin been up to now?"

"His social worker. He never married so there's no children or grandchildren and he doesn't have siblings."

"Because he grew up in an orphanage," Zelah snapped. "Before I leave I want the name of the social worker. He looks ill. Are you taking proper care of him?"

The woman shrugged. "End stage prostate cancer. Nothing to be done." She sounded as if she was talking about some boring everyday event. Zelah's face reddened and a vein pulsed in her neck. Fighting to keep control of her fists, she pulled up a chair close to the bed.

The manager reacted instantly. "Move back please, you can't get close. Social distancing." Zelah reluctantly scraped the chair back.

"My name is Zelah, and I'm your third cousin once removed," she began, for the sake of the manager who had seated herself six feet behind them. "I've just come from speaking to Mary McShane. You knew her as Mary Cameron. Do you remember her?"

Alexander Smith stared at her. She waited a few moments. "Mary lived at the orphanage too. She remembers you. She used to call you Xandy." Zelah thought she saw momentary flash of recognition. "How about another boy at the orphanage, called Brodie McAlister. Do you remember him, or David Laird?"

Nothing. He smiled and said in a reedy voice. "What's your name?"

"Zelah. My name is Zelah. I want to ask you about Brodie McAlister. Do you remember Brodie? He took care of you, kept you from being hurt by the bigger boys."

He smiled again.

Zelah sighed. "Oh well, never mind Xandy. I'll come back another day."

"You won't get any more from him. He hardly talks these days," the manager said, standing up and starting to walk towards the door.

Zelah went to stand and taking one pitying glance at the bent, shrunken, declining man on the bed she prepared to walk away.

"A terrible fight they had, indeed it was."

She spun around again and sat on the chair again. "Yes, Xandy, terrible wasn't it. You saw it, didn't you?"

He nodded and began to speak, staring over her shoulder, in a low faltering voice with a pause between each few words. "Aye. The she-devil making them hit … again and again and again. Davey fell. Brodie tried to pick him up … but she wouldn't let him. Davey wasnae moving. She said he was dead, Brodie had killed him. Brodie ran off. But Davey did get up. She took him away and … I followed them." He raised a hand and with effort tapped the side of his nose. "I saw what she did, but I never told. She'd have done me, too." A tear appeared in one eye. "Poor wee Davey. She did for him … I saw it. Brodie never came back. Where is he? Is he coming to see me?"

"May be, Xandy. Mary may come to see you. Would you like that?"

He nodded. "Pretty wee thing, she is. Nice girl. She's my friend too. Is she here?"

"She's close by," Zelah said. "Thank you, Xandy. Would you like me to come again?"

"Who are you?"

"Zelah. I'm Zelah, your cousin. I'm leaving now, but I'll be back." She said this with an ominous look at the manager. "I'll get the name of that social worker now, and the telephone number."

Outside in her car, Zelah made the call. After ten minutes of non-stop back and forth opinion she ordered him to find another home, for which she would pay the fees in full and move Xandy as close as possible to Mary McShane's home. "I have never seen or felt anything so depressing," she paused and shook her head. "I'll expect it to be sorted out by tomorrow. Message me the names of alternative homes and some pictures."

He had argued with her, she had no right to insist the man moved, being just a very distant relative who up to now had taken no interest in Alexander Smith's care. Zelah had threatened him with a lawsuit for neglect and informed him her lawyer would be in touch to draw up a contract for payment. In the end he had capitulated, but insisted he talk to his manager and director before he took any action as they would want proof of her relationship to Mr Smith. She suggested he do so there and then, which he refused, it being Sunday and they were not to be disturbed for anything less than an extreme crisis. She should consider herself lucky to have caught him, he explained, as he happened to be the on-call emergency social worker.

"Bloody jobsworth," she muttered as she drove away, thinking this gave her chance to draw up a family tree, should they look into it too closely. She didn't think they would, as her funding of the move would cost them nothing. They already knew Alexander had no assets or anything of value for a scammer. And, from what she had seen, he wasn't long for the world, probably no more than a matter of months, if not weeks.

She made another call and was heading to the airport when she swerved and pulled over to the side of the road, ignoring the road rage gesture from the car behind her.

"Tosser," she yelled back with an equally contemptuous gesture, and took out her phone.

Having made more calls she turned the car around and headed back to Edinburgh and her hotel.

Chapter 31

Maggie put the phone down.

"That was Zelah. She's not coming back today, or tomorrow."

Jude looked up from Nick's desk. "I guessed. Fill me in, won't you?"

Maggie explained Zelah was off on a mission, to rescue Alexander Smith from his hideously unpleasant care home and have him moved to a comfortable and happier place.

"It's incredible the man has survived. Zelah says after he left the orphanage he had to fend for himself with no family or support. Of course it went badly. He got into trouble, had a couple of spells in jail, couldn't hold down a job. He became an alcoholic and ultimately homeless, living on the streets. He entered the home about five years ago. Zelah's says it's a dump and, given no-one's ever given a hoot about him since he was tossed out of the orphanage at seventeen, the least she can do is to make the end of his life comfortable and caring."

"Does she do this often?"

"No. Just every now and then she sees an injustice and weighs in. This time she's pretended to be a relative." Maggie huffed as Jude laughed. "Good for her. She knows how to get things done, doesn't she."

"Reluctantly, yes. When they check her out they'll find she's more than able to pay for a new care home, but sometimes she drives very close to the edge of the law."

Jude considered. "Well, she's trying to do good for a man who, by the sound of it, has never had anyone do anything for him and been badly let down by '*the system*'." She frowned. "Too many slip through the cracks, so I won't worry about her white lie to move him out of a bad place. Anyway, what's the news?"

Maggie took Jude through the two meetings. The emerging picture was of Brodie McAlister being an acolyte of the nun, but hating it and her. He wanted to get away to live with his sisters, but the orphanage prevented him.

"And, crucially, he didn't kill David Laird. Alexander Smith recalled the boy got up after Brodie ran, but something else happened. Zelah said he didn't say what, just the nun '*did for him*'. She said he recalled being frightened at the prospect she might do for him too, if he told anyone. Mary McShane confirmed no-one spoke to her, or to any of the children during the Sheriff's enquiry, as far as she knew."

"Has Zelah told Lolly Sadler?"

"Yes, she called her back and passed the news on."

"So, where does this leave us now? Do you feel better about the trip to Spain?"

"I guess so."

"You still don't sound convinced," Jude said. "What will help?"

Maggie thought about it and drummed her fingers on the table. "There's too much going on. It's like a jigsaw puzzle. The frame is there, but the inside is just a series of unlinked islands and without an overhead view it's impossible to see where each section fits."

"That's how you do a jigsaw puzzle?" Jude said with a grin.

"I did a lot of them during lockdown," Maggie pouted. "Yes, that was my method and it worked for me. So, I'd like us to pause and get together for an update. That's you, me, Nick, Zelah and Bob. Yes, that's what comes next. I feel adrift at the moment, so much has happened it's hard to process. If I can get a grip on the broader perspective, how everything is linking together, which areas are still outstanding, then I think I'll be comfortable in setting off in a day or so."

"Not easy if Zelah is staying in Scotland. Can we include her by video?"

"I guess we'll have to. Let's pack it in for today. I don't know if Nick's coming back here, but Bob will come home, although I don't know when. Let's see if we can arrange something for later today, or early tomorrow, then you and I can set off late afternoon tomorrow, in time to get the overnight ferry to France. OK?"

Jude nodded. "I'll let the guy in Spain know it's a tentative plan and I'll firm up the arrangements, not book anything, but be ready, assuming it all works out. Why don't you make a list of what we know and what we don't know, so we can make follow-up plans for when we're in Spain?"

"OK. Tell me the route you're thinking we'll follow."

Jude reach across the table to a paper map, which she unfolded to show the whole of France and the north of Spain. She traced her finger along the route as she explained. "Well, down to Portsmouth tomorrow, for the overnight to St Malo, then down the west coast of France, past Bordeaux, then into the Pyrenees. It's not motorway from there, but we can get past Pau then over the border, here. Maybe we can stop somewhere overnight near the border. We're self-sufficient in all things for the journey so we can stop anywhere, when we get fed up with driving."

"Those roads in the Pyrenees are steep and winding. They're going to increase the journey time, and they can be daunting if you haven't driven them before in a big vehicle."

"Have you? Driven them before?"

Maggie nodded. "I did it last summer, Bob insisted if I were to be allowed to drive his motorhome I had to learn every whistle and bell, so we went down to Andorra for a couple of days on our trip to the Dordogne. I had to drive around the mountain passes. I did fine. I'll do that section."

"I hoped you say that. I'm fine on long, straight roads, but the goat tracks were worrying me. It is the quickest route, I agree".

Maggie continued to stare at the map. She had already calculated what they would have to take with them, both personal and for eating, drinking and general living in the van for five days. She reached across the table, picked up her notepad and a pen and began to write lists. Jude watched for a moment, a gentle smile on her lips, and quietly walked away.

Jude busied herself worked out routes and timings and booked the ferry crossing with a cabin. They could sleep overnight, as well as eat an evening meal and breakfast before setting off. Maggie, when consulted, insisted they have a cabin with a window.

"I suffer with seasickness, so I need a view."

They had elected to return from Caen, with an evening Channel crossing, to bring them home late evening one week later. Jude took up whistling around the house. Maggie was circumspect, not only because of some continuing anxiety about being away but also because this would be a mammoth journey in a short period of time. However, she didn't want to dampen Jude's enthusiasm, so she said nothing as Jude chatted away about various proposals.

By the end of the day they had a complete working plan. Maggie felt ready to set off, now she could see the 'big picture 'but still wanted the meeting with Nick, Zelah and Bob to ensure they had covered every eventuality and detail. After calling and re-calling, Jude had arranged it for nine the following morning.

Late afternoon, Zelah called Maggie to confirm she wouldn't be returning before they set off. Talks with social services were slow and frustrating, but she had dug her heels in. She planned to visit three dementia care homes and select one. Then came the final battle to move Alexander into the home she decided would be best suited for him. Lolly would accompany her. They had made another quick visit to Alexander. Lolly had been allowed to look in through the window, and having been equally disgusted by the living conditions, had agreed with Zelah she would make weekly visits to the old man. The final message of the evening came again from Zelah, in the form of a text just before eleven.

'Have Ruby's response. Message almost intact. Interesting! More on the call'

"Well, she could have given us a tad more detail," Maggie grumbled to Bob who had just arrived home.

"She's off the hook personally for Helen Redland's death," Bob replied wearily as he slumped down onto the settee.

Maggie went to sit beside him and put an arm around his neck. "Sorry, how's it going?"

"It isn't," he replied, yawning. "Time of death is now after seven in the evening, which lets Zelah and Nick out. Helen Redland was seen walking along the river front close to the theatre around six, towards the footbridge but then there's nothing. I've got someone looking into the tide times, to work out where she went in. If she was walking at six and dead by seven, allowing time to meet someone, argue and be strangled, it must have happened close to the Transporter Bridge. But why did she walk from town? It doesn't make sense."

"Any more clues?"

"She made two calls, to two burner phones. I can speculate on who they went to, but no proof."

"I'm guessing one is Emer McCarthy Miller," Maggie said.

"Yes, she had spare phones and SIM cards in her bedsit, their way of keeping in touch. Pre-arranged coded messages."

"Will Emer know she's dead, do you think?"

"Not yet, I hope. But by tomorrow she will. I need to sleep. How's your plan going?"

"We're sorted. Leaving tomorrow late afternoon for Portsmouth. Jude's got the arrangements in hand. I will need you to take me through all the whistles and bells, and check the van's ready, though. Will you have time in the morning?"

"I should be back in at eight, but you and I can check it all out before then. You comfortable still with driving?"

"Are you kidding! The thing practically drives itself. You won't be on the call at nine?"

"Sorry, no." He heaved himself up from the settee. "Come on, let's go. Last night together for a week."

Maggie paused. "We've done well together, haven't we?"

In response he leaned in and kissed her. "Perfect."

Chapter 32

When Nick arrived the following morning, Maggie had already drawn up two lists, one of what they knew and had discovered so far, the second of outstanding issues, some in the UK, others to be followed up in Spain. She was impatient to hear what Zelah had heard from Ruby at the lab, as whatever the postcard contained could alter both their journey to Spain and their overall perception of the entire project.

Bob had left early, after taking Maggie through all details of the camper van. He had bought it the previous year and they had taken it to France, the latest model with every possible gadget and widget including solar panels to recharge the electrics, which meant they wouldn't have to worry about finding a re-charging point on their way to Spain. Since their visit to France the previous summer there had been little opportunity to use it. They took a short drive with Maggie at the wheel until she felt comfortable and accustomed to the lightness and ease of the driving.

Jude gave an impressive whistle when she saw it. "This is something else. I've driven these all over the States but nothing as smooth as this. We're going to have fun."

Maggie still had a flutter of nervousness about being away, knowing Emer McCarthy Miller could already be in the country. She knew she had to clamp it down, but it gnawed at her and wouldn't go away. She had slept uneasily the previous night, waking Bob, thrashing around and shouting.

"What was that about? You're sweating."

"Terrible dream," she muttered. "Emer had Zelah by the throat, pulling her backwards towards the edge of a cliff. I shouted 'no'! but I couldn't move, the way you can't in dreams, and they fell backwards over the edge. That's when I woke up."

He hugged her close. "We're taking every precaution; we'll find her."

"I know you will, but please make it soon."

**

Maggie had sent Zelah a copy of the lists and when she called at nine thirty she jumped straight into a discussion of the 'outstanding 'list.

"We need to discuss the postcard first, because what it says changes some of what we know, and tells us where to go next," Zelah began.

"Let's have it, then," Maggie said. "Zelah, do we still need to get to Spain?"

"Absolutely you do. You'll understand why now."

She gave a short cough, then read out loud. "Ruby has reconstructed the full message and the postmark details. It's postmarked at the beginning of December 1938, from London. It says: '*Lo siento mucho Helen. Harry posting and has my little book. Am well and staying for now*'. It's signed with the initial 'B'."

No-one spoke as they digested the meanings in the message. Maggie sat back for a moment, then said, "Zelah, are you certain it says, '*for now* ', not just '*now* ?"

"Definitely. He intended to return at some point, is my interpretation. Something stopped him. You should find out about where he might have been in Catalonia, if he stayed."

Maggie nodded. "Then, there's Harry. Nick, didn't Julie's statement mention him?"

"Yes, she wrote about 'Harry from Chiswick'. We can find out about him. But, the '*little book*'? Could it be a diary?"

"Could he have written one, do we think?" Maggie asked. "That would be something. But if there is one, why did Harry not pass it on, because Lolly has never mentioned it."

"I spoke to her last night," Zelah said. "She's going back up into the attic in her mother's house to check out the unopened boxes. I'll let you know if she finds it, or anything else."

"I can work on Harry from Chiswick whilst you're away," Nick said. "I'll check out the returners list and speak to your man Martin, see if we can find out anything else about him. If he can give us family name and an age, I'll look at the 1939 England and Wales war register. Unless Harry volunteered before the compiling of the register, his name should be there."

"Which does change the focus for Spain," Maggie mused. "Jude, we'll need to concentrate on where Brodie might have gone back to and what could have happened to him." She paused, steepling her fingers on her chin. "Bob told me and I read that some International Brigaders, who married in Spain, stayed with their new families. We can get a view from the people we meet out there."

"Is there anything else?" Zelah asked. "I'm meeting Lolly to start viewing care homes."

"When are you back?" Maggie asked.

"Can't say yet. I had a call from Stephen. The atmosphere started tense and isn't improving much. It could be time to knock some heads together, so I may fly to Dublin from here. Anyway, whatever, I won't see you before you go, so good luck and let us know whatever you find."

"Will do, and Zelah …" Maggie began.

"What?"

"Be careful. She's here by now, looking for you."

Zelah snorted, said goodbye and the call ended.

"Right, time to get going," Maggie said. "Nick, if you're OK with doing the research, Jude and I can crack on with getting ready to leave. We'll be heading off after lunch."

"Fine with me," Nick replied.

Chapter 33

Maggie and Jude journeyed down to the south coast of England in good time, with less traffic on the road due to the high number of people now working from home. They reached the port of Portsmouth on time and rolled onto the ferry. Maggie breathed a sigh of relief on hearing the announcement that the trip was expected to be smooth. After dinner they returned to their cabin, where Jude took up a book to read again about the final days of the Civil War.

Maggie slept surprisingly well. When she woke the sun was already above the horizon and they were an hour off St Malo harbour. Just before eight they set off through the streets of the ancient walled town, in the direction of Rennes. They talked infrequently on the first leg of the journey, as Maggie concentrated on driving the van and customising herself to driving on the opposite side of the road. After a couple of hours they stopped for a break in a village south of Nantes, and sat in the sunshine in the main square, drinking coffee and eating freshly baked croissants from the local patisserie. Jude took over driving and they headed to the outskirts of Bordeaux, for their next stop.

The weather improved as they headed further south and although the end of September was approaching, the temperature had reach thirty degrees at midday. The scenery had been spectacular for most of the journey and the two women had allowed themselves to forget the outside world and relax with conversation unrelated to their lives and enjoy the journey. By the time they stopped Maggie felt more relaxed than she had done for the past weeks.

Now it was decision time regarding their direction and Maggie had no hesitation in opting for the shorter route through the mountains, as opposed to the longer way around Toulouse.

After an early straightforward run, the mountains came into view, the Pyrenees looming jagged and snow-capped in the distance. They stopped briefly in Pau when the first stars became visible in a deepening blue sky, and pushed on, but as the sky darkened further they accepted that their ambitious plan to reach and cross the Spanish border before nightfall would have to be abandoned. Maggie drove on for another half an hour before they found a suitable night stop, which still left five hours of driving to Gandesa, including crossing the high border.

"If we can be up early, we can be in Gandesa around midday or just after," Jude said, her head bent low over a giant map she had laid out on the dining table.

"That's what the satnav says," Maggie replied. "Come on, let's eat then sleep. I'm exhausted. I haven't driven so far for over a year."

"I'll check on news, see if Nick managed to contact Martin and if there's info for us," Jude replied, switching on her tablet. "Yes, an email. Oh, nothing yet. He's contacted Martin who's on it. Says we can expect something tomorrow. That's disappointing."

"No, he needs time," Maggie replied, yawning. "It'll take concentration to go through lists and files. I'm going to sleep. I'll set an alarm for six thirty. That OK for you?"

"Fine. I'll send a message to the guys in Gandesa, let them know what time we'll be there. We need a plan for tomorrow."

"First thing, get up the mountain road into Spain. Then we can start talking about plans," Maggie replied.

Jude looked puzzled.

"You'll see," Maggie replied.

Chapter 34

Jude's knuckles had gone through the white, gripping stage and now she could no longer feel her hands, as Maggie swung the van carefully around another hairpin bend and Jude peeked over at the thousand foot drop immediately beside her door, with just a foot-high metal barrier separating her from eternity.

"Almost there," Maggie said, holding back the grin. "I've done this as carefully as I can, Worm. If I go any slower we'll start rolling backwards."

Jude swallowed. "It's not just the swinging around and the drop. It's the lunatics who keep overtaking us."

Maggie laughed. "They'll be locals. They could do this in thick fog. They get fed up with vans like this crawling up the road."

Ten minutes later they reached the top of the pass. They crossed the border with a wave through from the customs and police on duty, and stopped on the Spanish side, where Jude jumped out and put her hands on her knees, taking deep breaths.

They were at a viewing point and Maggie walked to the back of the van to look at the view on the Spanish side. She zipped up her sweater and shivered as she gazed down the descending road at distant snow-capped mountains. The countryside here was bare rock and grass stretching for inconceivable miles. They were just one of two vehicles, the second being a car on the opposite side of the road close to a narrow track leading up to a summit. She guessed the driver had walked up for a better view. In another time, another life, she would have done the same, driven on by an urge to reach the highest point. There was such a sense of freedom to stand higher than everything around yourself, see all horizons. But not today; they had a schedule to maintain.

Jude had managed to stand upright now, still breathing deeply. Maggie went into the van, made a flask of steaming hot coffee and handed one out to Jude, who drank with a shaking hand.

"For me, it's seasickness," Maggie said. "The final part will be easier. The road isn't so steep going down. Come on, climb back in. Can you drive when we get onto a flatter straighter road? My arms are aching."

Jude nodded.

An hour later they stopped and changed seats. Jude's face had returned to her normal pink glow and she happily took the wheel for the final leg of the journey into Gandesa, where they arrived shortly after midday.

The modest, plain town was as Maggie remembered from her previous visit with Bob, quiet and business-like. The campsite sat on the outskirts towards the wide valley heading down towards Gandesa. Apart from their van, there were just other three vehicles: a couple of German and Dutch vacationers and an Italian family. Maggie parked the van and hooked up the electrics and water. Neither felt like driving back into the town, so they ordered a taxi to the main square where they took a seat at a café serving drinks outside and waited for their Spanish contacts to arrive. They had both discarded sweaters and as the sense of relief set in at the journey being over, they sat back and relaxed in the warmth of the afternoon sun filtering down through the tree canopy bordering the square on three sides. Windows were open in the apartments above the array of shops, offices, salons and cafes in the square. Two tables were occupied, one with a young couple both engrossed in their mobile phones. At the other, three grizzled men played cards. They occasionally gave out a laugh, a shout of mock protest or a comment, all in rapid Catalan. They were dressed in workers 'clothes, with short sleeved shirts, heavily tanned with barely a head of hair between the three. In the background, muted sounds of televisions and radios, chattering and the occasional call of people leaning from their open windows were the only sounds, apart from the constant lively twittering of birds in the trees. The warmth was heavy and Maggie felt the weight in her eyelids as she gave in to the compulsion to close them and let her mind wander free.

A sharp poke in the arm jerked her head up.

"Here they are, wake up!" Jude whispered as a car drove into the square and parked close to them. Maggie shook herself and looked around, as a man and a woman emerged from a smart black Mercedes. Jude waved. They waved back and headed in the direction of the café.

The woman was around Maggie's height, with copious black hair tied back in a pony tail. She wore shorts and tee shirt and hiking boots. The man, a little taller, was also dark-haired but with a darker skin, the colour of someone who worked outdoors. They both walked with a lively gait. They approached Maggie and Jude and the woman went to kiss a cheek, but pulled back.

"Sorry, I keep forgetting. Social distancing!" Her voice was low and melodic with no trace of an accent, but when the waiter arrived to take their order she responded in fluent Catalan.

"Good to meet you, face-to-face," Maggie began. "I don't know how much Joan told you about our client. Jude briefed him, but the picture has changed with extra information since we set out. And I've been wrapped up in research, so I'd like to get up to date on how you can help us."

"Of course," the woman replied as the waiter returned with two espressos. "I'm Louise Faraday and this is my partner, Miguel. I work officially as a holiday tour guide, but I also help out with an organisation promoting tours for people interested in the International Brigades and the historic places here in Catalonia. Miguel is an archaeologist. His English is OK, but he may need some help if we get technical." She smiled at him. "He's worked on some of the excavations happening from time to time around Gandesa. There are multiple unexcavated mass graves, here and around Spain. We're hoping to organise another one next year."

"Joan told us a little about your background, Louise. I understand your grandfather was a Brigader? So how do you come to be living in Catalonia, and speak the language so fluently?"

"That's right. My grandad came here in 1937, full of youth and enthusiasm and hope. He met my grandma here and he fell in love with the place. When he had to leave in 1938 they arranged a route out for Grandma. She was called Lluisa. I'm named after her. Grandad loved Catalonia and always wanted to come back, which wasn't possible until Franco died, in 1975. Once the transition to a democracy began my grandparents came back to live here and my dad came with them. He met my Mum, got married and here I am."

"Have you always lived here?" Jude asked.

"Always. I was born in Gandesa and my family lives here. Grandma was so thrilled to be home. She lost family members during the Civil War, and afterwards, being a republican. You know the history?"

Jude nodded.

"Some survived and got through the following years. Now, I have a nice big extended family. I've been brought up tri-lingual. Grandad talked to me about the brigade, told me stories about the battles and his comrades. He was pleased when Spain decided not to 'forget'."

"We have a friend in Wales," Maggie said. "She's the great granddaughter of a Brigader. And we met a survivor last time we visited, that's my partner and me. He died last year, sadly, here in Gandesa in the retirement home."

Louise sat up. "What was his name?"

"He was Lluis Portels. He was a village boy, who gave us vital information to help us to trace the story of our Brigader's wife and child."

"I remember him," Miguel cut in. "A spirited chap."

Maggie smiled and nodded.

"Would you like to bring us up to date with your latest information?" Louise asked, bringing a notebook and pad from her satchel. "You have two days here, I think? We need to know what to plan, to make the most of the time, and if we can help you discover what happened to your guy."

Between them Maggie and Jude summarised the story, with Louise nodding and making notes.

"What we found out as we were travelling, is the additional wording from the postcard. Brodie, or Lewis Stewart, as he was known, went to Barcelona but decided not to return home." She handed over a copy of the postcard from the file, which Louise took, read and passed on to Miguel. Maggie could see they were both frowning.

"Is there a problem?" she asked.

"Not as such," Louise replied. "But, once the Brigades were gone, it was left to the Spanish and Catalan volunteers to fight the Fascists and they were losing. The Brigades kept records whilst they were here, but once they left…" she shrugged. "There are few records. And now there's no-one left around these parts, to directly recall what happened. We have personal stories, and we know there were Brigaders who chose to stay on. But there aren't any official records."

"We know," Jude said, stifling a yawn. "We do have some records, and we know Brodie fought at the Ebro battle in September '38, the final one the Brigaders took part in. In fact, as he arrived at the beginning of 1938, this was the only area of Spain he knew, so if he returned, this was where he would have come to."

Louise nodded to Jude. "You're tired, I can see. It's been a long journey for you. We need some time to look through what records we have, see if there's anything might connect to this boy. How about we meet up again tomorrow morning? We might have something for you."

"We could do with a rest," Maggie said. "So that's OK for us. Here again? What time?"

"Let's say ten, tomorrow morning," Louise replied. She and Miguel stood. "We'll leave you now. Have a comfortable rest and we'll see you tomorrow."

When they had driven away Maggie paid the waiter as Jude organised a taxi to the campsite. When they arrived back Maggie organised a meal and they decided on an early night. It was still warm enough to sit outside the van and listen to the cicadas as the sun set and the first stars appeared.

"Are you thinking what I'm thinking?" Jude asked.

"I saw the look pass between them, if that's what you mean," Maggie replied. "This could turn out to be an unproductive move on our part. It sounds like there's minimal information."

"Well, we get to see some local sites. We'll get a feel of what happened here, maybe."

"But I suspect we'll be going home with little to show for the trip."

Jude yawned again, setting Maggie off. "I've had it. I'm going to read myself to sleep. Don't give up yet, Maggot. We've just arrived. Be hopeful. Tomorrow may bring something unexpected."

"I hope you're right," Maggie replied. "But they'll have to pull a big fat rabbit out of a tiny hat. Let's see what tomorrow brings."

Chapter 35

A text arrived as Maggie and Jude were breakfasting in the van at eight the following morning, from Louise.

'We have someone to speak to this morning, may be a lead for you. Can we change our meeting time to around midday?'

"If there's information, then I'm OK with that," Maggie said. "How shall we use the time?"

Jude put down her bowl of cereal. "I'd like to see Corbera, if that's OK with you. And there's a museum. Could we get there, too?"

"Yes to both. Let's get a taxi, though. Corbera's steep. We can be dropped off at the entrance to the old town, then afterwards we can walk to the museum. It's not too far and it's downhill." She checked her watch. "What time does Corbera open to the public? I'm presuming you've checked."

"Yep. At ten. Yesterday's taxi chap said to give him a call if we need a lift anywhere else. I have his number."

"You and he were chatty yesterday."

"He asked why we were here and I told him part of the story. Needless to say, he had family on one side and an opinion about keeping the memory alive. He was in favour, so we may even get special rates."

"You have a knack of convincing people to do the right thing," Maggie chuckled. "Give him a call. It's only ten or fifteen minutes from here, so if he picks us up just before ten, we'll be there in good time."

When the taxi arrived Jude sat up front with Jordi, the driver and again chatted away to him as they travelled towards Corbera. At the entrance, Maggie could tell Jude was making arrangements.

"He'll be outside the museum at a quarter to twelve. He's keen to know what I think of the ruin."

"Sure he isn't keen on more than that?"

"The man has a wife and six children, Maggot. He's a dyed-in-the-wool republican. His great grandfather was shot by the Fascists. He wants us to find our boy."

"Sorry." After a minute with her coffee Maggie said, "I've noticed lately you've been calling Brodie McAlister '*our boy*'. This is a client, Worm, and it's looking like a case where we may not reach a definitive answer."

The rays of the morning sun were now touching the front window of the van and across the dining table. Jude sat back and put up her hand to shield her eyes. "I'll have to move from here in a minute and we should be getting ready."

"Deflecting, much?"

Jude leaned over to one side to avoid the direct sunlight. "I don't know the answer. I do feel strongly about this boy. Before you say it, I know he would be almost a hundred years old now, but his only life story is as a teenager. That's all I can see, a young boy, preyed upon, running, terrified, without happier choices. And ultimately, paying a high price. The highest price."

"Not too far from your own story?"

"No. That's not how I see it. And yes, I am invested, beyond where I should be. It's become emotional." She looked away. "How do you stay detached? You must see more stories like this one?"

"Hmm. Good question. Sometimes I feel a strong empathy, and a need to know. But I always remember the client, it's their story, not mine. I can walk away from whatever is the truth. They can't and I've seen people traumatised by what they've found out. You know, in some ways, and this is going to sound bizarre, it's what attracts me to this job and keeps me enthused. We're all attached to our ancestors and our past, whatever it was. We are who we are, because of what they were. We're invested. Of course, there are people who aren't interested, but as we get older, and realise looming on the horizon is that time when we'll become the past, we develop a thirst to know, or some of us do. Anyway, that's philosophical discussion of the day over and done." She reached out her hand and put it over Jude's. "Worm, if you become too invested in a story like this, there's every chance it won't end well and you'll suffer for it."

Jude squeezed Maggie's hand. "I can live with it. I know it's all history, but they were real people and in this case, I do feel an emotional connection. Don't ask me why." She pulled her hand away and stood. "Let's get ready, shall we. I'm looking forward to seeing Corbera."

As she walked away to the tiny bathroom and shower, Maggie thought, '*Corbera's not going to be a happy experience for you, either*'. Still, there was nothing she could do or say to separate Jude from her fascination with the history. Like a computer game of virtual reality, Jude had dived headfirst into a world that existed in her imagination. This morning, reality would take over.

Chapter 36

Jude's excited prattling dissolved into a grim silence as they entered the shattered streets of Corbera d'Ebre and started the climb to the top of the hill. At the summit they visited the massive, now glass-roofed church, then began the walk around what was left of the streets.

It was as Maggie remembered. Some areas razed to the ground, others retaining the smashed skeletons of buildings, human dwellings as they had been before three days of intense bombing by the German Luftwaffe had left the village a smoking ruin. Maggie left it to Jude to set the pace, giving her time to stop and absorb what she was experiencing. Despite having seen it before, Maggie was still moved by remains tying the broken bricks to people. In some houses, the internal framework of wooden joints now pointed up to the sky like dead, rotten flower stalks; in others, the remains of a fractured staircase, a bath hanging from a ceiling, kitchens where once intimate family gatherings would have taken place. Now all just disintegrating rubble.

As they reached the end of the second street and the border of the old town, where a lone olive tree stood, Jude put her head on Maggie's shoulder, tears running down her face.

"The bombing lasted three days, non-stop. Do we know how many died here?"

"I can't remember precisely. I know that as it began the villagers grabbed what they could of their personal possessions and ran. They rebuilt the town at the bottom of the hill and left this as a memorial."

"Target practice," Jude said. "Hitler's air force used this village as a practice run for bombing raids for the bigger war he was relishing."

Maggie wandered away from the tree to the edge of the hillside, with its view of the fertile land in the valley and the mountains, joined a minute later by Jude.

"You're right. It's accepted history now that for Hitler, Spain provided military strategy and target practice. It served him well."

"Let's get down to the museum," Maggie said. "Enough of this."

**

An hour later, as they waited outside the museum for Jordi to arrive in his taxi, Jude hadn't spoken since they had left the building.

"Thoughts?" Maggie said.

"The museum's interesting, fascinating, but the wreckage of the old village grinds the true picture into your head."

"And your heart," Maggie replied, checking her watch. "We're meeting Louise and Miguel in ten minutes. Ah, here's Jordi now. I've been thinking about everything we know, and I have an idea of where we should go next. Not now," she said. "When we meet up with them, all of us together. I want their opinion." She got into the taxi and before Jude could take up a conversation with an eager Jordi Maggie said, "Did you tell them about Claire Lewis?"

Jude blushed. “No. I was embarrassed to explain over the phone. You never know how people are going to take it and how they might change their view of you. Is it so important?”

“I think it’s crucial,” Maggie replied.

Chapter 37

Nick clapped his hands together and gave himself a high five. He would have shouted too, but he had no-one in the house to celebrate with him what he had discovered during the morning.

The day had begun with a text from Maggie telling him and Zelah they were going to visit Corbera d'Ebre and its museum, then meeting up again with the Spanish contacts who might have some news for them. Well, he had some news for Maggie and Jude. He had not only found the identity of 'Harry from Chiswick', but had located him and discovered his family still lived in the house from which Harry had departed for Spain, back in 1938.

The initial news had come from Martin, who had come through with Harry's full name. He had been Henry Michael Summers, aged twenty-three, from Chiswick, profession Painter and Decorator. Harry was single then. It confirmed he had arrived in Spain on 15th January 1938, the same day as Brodie Mc Alister, alias Lewis Stewart. There were no further notes on Harry's conduct, but it did have a black-and-white face portrait, of a handsome lad with a full head of straw-blond looking hair, a square face and a bold stare. Martin confirmed Harry had survived the conflict and returned to London in December 1938 with a group of more surviving Brigaders. He had forwarded the web location of the information on the Trust's website and suggested ways

Nick might try to trace Harry. Not that Nick needed help with that, but he expressed his gratitude for the thought.

Armed with the full name, age and location, he found Harry on the 1939 War Register, living at 24 Somerset Avenue in Chiswick with his mother and father, Michael and Queenie, and Elsie Summers. Both Harry and Elsie had a marital status of 'married 'and were the same age. This meant Harry and Elsie had married in the nine months since his return. He checked it out and found the marriage in June 1939. Moving on from there, he learned Harry had enlisted in the British Army.

Then followed a tragic discovery. Harry Summers had been killed on the sixth of June 1944, on the Normandy beaches, leaving Elsie a widow with one young child, a boy named Michael after Harry's father, born in June 1940.

His next online destinations were Ancestry and the London Metropolitan Archives, where he knew there were polling records. He found these starting in 1948. Both Michael and Queenie were still at the address, with Elsie also still present. Over the following years Michael and Queenie disappeared from the electoral role and when he checked he found they had died in 1955 and 1957. But Elsie and young Michael stayed on. And the icing on the cake, he had just found Michael Summers Junior still lived at the family home.

As he sat pondering what to do next, Nick heard the front door and a call of' hello?'. Bob put his head around the office door, nodded at Nick and asked him how the research was going. Nick thought Bob didn't really want to know. His grey face and his drooping eyelids told of another night without sleep. So, he gave the briefest of highlights. Bob suggested before carrying on he should speak to Zelah and Maggie, giving Nick the opportunity to ask if Bob had spoken to Zelah yet.

"Yes, just in brief yesterday. Quick update, she's no longer of interest. Time of death has been confirmed at around 7pm, when Zelah was on the flight to Scotland. Right, I'm off to sleep." He closed the door, then opened it again. "Did you know Zelah's going to Ireland, not coming back here?"

"Sort of. She said she was thinking about it."

"She's worried about the McCarthy Miller woman. There's still no trace of her. Zelah's decided to be with the families in Cork. I think she's going to electrify the fences, barricade them all in."

Nick grimaced. "Can't say I blame her. I'll set up a call. See you later."

He knew Maggie and Jude would be meeting with the Spanish genealogists and he didn't know where Zelah was or what she was doing, so he texted them both to check they would be free for a video call later on, telling them he had traced Harry but wanted to get their input into how he should proceed. Answers from both came back within the hour. Zelah would fly out to Cork the following morning. Maggie and Jude were both delighted with the news and keen to hear more. They would also have news to share. He set up the call for six o'clock, forwarded the link, then decided to take a look at ongoing Maze projects. There had been two enquiries he hadn't dealt with for a couple of days. One requested a full history and a book, for Zelah. Another was a brick wall case, right up Maggie's street. He got down to working up a response with an estimate for both. Business could not be neglected.

But, in the back of his mind remained the concern about Emer McCarthy Miller, for all of them. The worrisome thoughts grew as rising resentment began to interfere with his calculations, causing him to stop and start until he could no longer continue. Nick was not prone to fits of anger or temper, but this had become too much for any of them to suffer much longer. He was worried, not just for Zelah and Maggie and their families, but for his family, Stella and Max. For them, this waiting was becoming unbearable. He almost wished the woman would show her hand. Anticipation of what she might do had become excruciating as they waited. Whatever it was, he hoped it would happen soon.

Chapter 38

Zelah had just dropped Lolly Sadler at home and was heading to the airport, after looking at another dementia retirement home, when Nick's message arrived with the link for the video call. This time, she and Lolly had agreed that what they had just seen would be perfect for Xandy Smith. Not just clean, bright and welcoming, the walls were covered with photos and mementos, all themed to events in the history of the residents. There were weekly events planned. They had timed their visit at lunchtime, not the most popular with staff, but Zelah wanted to see the food being served. It both looked and smelled good. The available room was on the ground floor. No access to the outside, but bright, well-furnished and en suite. Also part of the package was a physical care facility for end-of-life residents, into which Zelah had been able to discuss moving Xandy when the time came. They were both confident Zandy would be well cared for here in his final months and hopeful he might start speaking again.

After final financial discussions with the home manager, Zelah put the arrangements in Lolly's hands. She had turned out to be a capable woman, in no way afraid of dealing with social services representatives, in fact looking forward to dealing with them on Xandy's behalf and she admitted she had developed a fondness for him. Zelah felt confident she could head off to Ireland.

She had checked in with Stephen again before breakfast and he reported a quieter but still tense atmosphere. He looked forward to her arrival.

She reached Cork at five and arrived at Rosscarbery in time for the video call. Having briefly greeted everyone and taken note of the variety of glum expressions, she headed to the office and locked herself in, then joined the call.

Nick, Maggie and Jude were chatting about Catalonia, with Jude describing the museum visit.

"Welcome, Zelah. Good flight?" Nick asked.

Zelah grunted. "I've been here ten minutes and I've had enough already. It's like walking into a wild west stand-off."

"They're nervous, I guess," Maggie said. "There's been no sign of Emer here and from what you're saying, not there either. The longer this takes, the jumpier we'll all be."

"My earlier thought," Nick added. "I won't be sorry when she makes her move. It has to be soon, she must know Helen and Sherry are out of the picture and she must be running out of resources, so she has to expose herself by going into shops and supermarkets, surely? What's she living off if she doesn't take the risk?"

"Road kill and dead cats," Zelah said. "Wouldn't surprise me."

They all laughed, which broke the tension that had built up as they discussed Emer McCarthy Miller.

"No, she's a girl who's used to luxury," Maggie said. "But, Nick makes a reasonable point. Anyway, how's it going with Xandy Smith?"

"Sorted. He'll move soon. The arrangements are underway and the paperwork's all done. Lolly Sadler's taking over the details. Shall I start?"

"Why not?" Maggie said.

"I haven't a lot more to report, anyway. Lolly is pleased with our progress. She accepts Brodie went to Spain, hence your visit. I've agreed with her we'll pick up most of the cost of the trip, as she's going out of her way for Mary and Xandy. Fair exchange. She's starting unpacking her mother's final couple of boxes, but no sign of the diary, notebook, whatever it is, yet. That's it from me."

Nick took over. "My news is I've traced Harry. He was Harry Summers, from Chiswick. When he returned from Spain he went back to his parents' house, married a girl called Elsie within the year, enlisted in the army in 1939, fortunately for us after the war register was compiled, then died on D-Day, but not before producing an heir in 1940. And the heir, who's called Michael, and his grandson Justin Summers, still live in the family home. My next step is to approach Michael and Justin, and I want your input on how I do this."

"That's brilliant, Nick," Maggie said. "Have you found an email or phone, or Messenger address for him?"

"Not yet, but I'll keep looking. If I can't find any of those, there are just two choices, doorstepping them or writing to them and asking for an appointment."

"Doorstep them," Zelah said. "If you write and ask for an appointment and they ignore it, we'll never get to speak to them."

"If Michael is still there, he'll be in his late seventies and likely wary," Maggie protested. "These days no-one likes being cold called and if a stranger turns up on the doorstep any member of the family is quite likely to shut the door in Nick's face."

"Compromise," Nick replied. "How about I go up to London tomorrow, check either Michael or Justin is at home. I can put a note through the door saying who I am and a bit about Maze and the project, plus my phone number and see if anyone bites. Whatever method we choose carries risk, so let's try to lessen it by approaching quietly."

"And you are the best person for the quiet approach. I agree with Nick, and Jude is nodding."

"OK, if that's what you all think," Zelah said.

"We do," Maggie replied. "Now, our turn and we have a story to tell. I'll hand over to Jude here. It's all coming together."

Chapter 39

"When we reached the café," Jude began, "Louise and Miguel were waiting for us and we could tell they had something to share, but Maggie insisted I tell them about Claire Lewis and how Maze came to be involved in the project, because it wasn't just Lolly Sadler. It also involved the part of the message about Charlie."

"How did they take that?" Zelah asked.

"As you'd expect, I suppose. Louise frowned and pressed her lips together. She's clearly of the opinion anything beyond the everyday ordinary must have a sensible, normal explanation. She snorted at the idea of a medium. However, Miguel didn't. She went to say something either sarcastic or downright rude, judging by her expression, but he caught her arm and told her to be quiet and listen. I think he forgot I could understand. She wasn't happy, but she folded her arms and sat back."

Maggie took over. "I told them I had already heard about Charlie, on the previous visit Bob and I made to Lluis Portels, but had forgotten. When Claire told us what she did, Bob remembered. Again, I didn't link it to Lolly Sadler's story … no, that's not right. I did, but I didn't give it significance until we arrived here and started to look at the war sites again. Miguel mentioned an archaeological dig he'd been part of, when the archaeologists found Charlie, and this morning, going around the museum, I realised the significance."

"Which is what?" Zelah demanded. "Hurry up, I have a family feud to get into."

"Somehow, Charlie and Brodie are connected. By this time Miguel was nodding his head and looking excited. He spoke to Louise."

"He said to her, in Spanish '*that could fit with the story we have*'," Jude interjected. "Then, she began to look interested. Well, less sceptical."

Maggie took up the story again. "They've found someone, a man whose father had been conscripted into the Republican army at seventeen, in the dying months of the war. He's from La Fatarella, the village close to where Charlie the skeleton was unearthed. They had put the word out British genealogists were looking for a young lad who fought with the International Brigades and left, but might have returned here and rejoined the brigade for the final battle of the Ebro, in November 1938. A contact told them this man had a story worth listening to. So, they're taking us to see him tomorrow afternoon."

"And before we meet him, we're going to the excavation of the trench and pill box, the site of Charlie's skeletal remains," Jude said.

"Excellent, sounds like we all have a plan. Sorry, have to go. Can we speak again this time tomorrow?" Zelah asked.

They all agreed and Nick said he would set up the call and send out the details.

"She's got her hands full," Jude said to Maggie when the call had finished.

"I'm not surprised it's breaking down in Ireland," Maggie replied. "Too much bad history between Michelle,

Gerry and Mischa. But … perhaps it won't hurt them to have a meltdown. Get some things out in the open."

Jude smiled but didn't comment further.

She and Maggie returned to the campsite. Two of the vans had gone. They sat outdoors with beers as the sun set over the mountains behind their site.

"Dinner?" Maggie said after a short period of silent contemplation.

"I'll cook," Jude replied. "I'm so glad we don't have to dress up and find a restaurant. This is bliss, isn't it? Eating outdoors, warm and casual. And an exciting day coming up." She stood and headed into the van, saying over her shoulder to Maggie, "I'm glad we came. If we are going to get a result, hearing it in person will be spectacular."

"Maybe," Maggie replied. "There's no happy ever after, Jude. It's most likely he died and that's what we're going to hear."

"But it will be an ending. Not knowing is worse." She stepped up into the van and Maggie could hear her humming away as she opened and closed the fridge and cupboards, found some chicken and vegetables, and began to sing as she chopped and put water on to boil.

Maggie sat back and closed her eyes. She could acknowledge she was less stressed since they left Wales and travelled here. Tomorrow might be both traumatic and upsetting, but not for personal reasons. At a distance she could see how Jack had grown up, into a young man who needed space. Alice would be next. So much had happened since the day she met Zelah in the library in Newport and, she reflected, she wouldn't change a moment of it, nor did she regret any of it since, despite the traumas. Her life was fulfilling and exciting. No, she wouldn't change anything. They had survived and would get through this. She stretched out on the lounger and went to pick up her beer, when her phone rang. She checked if it was someone she wanted to speak to, being of a mind to ignore it, but it was Bob, who had said he would only call if absolutely necessary. With a slight knot in her stomach she answered the call.

As he began to speak she sat upright, her expression changing from puzzled to horror, just as Jude put her head around the open van door and stopped in mid-question.

"I'll call you back. We'll discuss it ... five minutes."

Jude jumped down. "What is it, what's happened? Is it Jack, Alice?"

"Sit down," Maggie said.

Jude stood in the doorway, bolt upright. "Tell me. Who's hurt? I'm here for you."

"It's me who's here for you," Maggie replied. "James Martinez has just left our house. He's demanding to know where you and I are. And he wants his money back. Jude, what have you done?"

Chapter 40

When Maggie woke the following morning to the smell of fresh brewed coffee she found Jude already awake and sitting outside the van, stretched out, luxuriating in the rising sun.

After the revelation of the previous evening, which had begun with Jude walking off and not returning for half an hour, during which Maggie went from being angry to terrified, to deciding not to go running off after her friend but to finish cooking dinner and wait for her return, they had settled down to talk.

"Yes, I took him for everything he had," Jude replied to Maggie's question about the money. "When you said he'd come looking for me I was horrified, but when you followed it with him wanting his money back, I knew that's what he'd really come for, not for me. He'll damage me if he can, but he wants the money. Well," she said, sitting up, "he's not getting it."

"From what Bob told me, after you'd stormed off, the timeline you gave me for leaving New York and arriving in Cwmbran doesn't match with what he told Bob."

Jude's cheeks reddened. "No, I guess I was a little vague. I took more time around Europe than I might have said."

"You're prevaricating. Truth, please, if we're to get out of this."

"I spent time setting up bank accounts in a couple of EU countries, and depositing cash."

"How much cash?"

"A hundred thousand euros."

Maggie opened her mouth, closed it again, twice, then breathed deeply in and out.

"He shot me and he beat me," Jude said, in the face of Maggie's silence. "He owed me."

"Morally, yes, I agree. Legally, I think you are in deep shit. You must have known he would come after you."

Jude shrugged, then frowned. "I'm assuming Bob didn't tell him where we are?"

"What kind of idiot do you think he is? Of course he didn't tell him. But this does put him in an egregious position."

Jude sighed. "Yes, I see that. Look Maggot, I'm not going to apologise for what I've done to James, but I am sorry you've become involved in my mess." She stood up. "I'm tired. I need to sleep, and I hope, do some thinking. Change of plan coming up for me."

With that she left Maggie and went to her sleeping cubicle. During the night Maggie thought she heard Jude walking around, inside and outside, but didn't try to join her. Best left to her own thoughts, she decided. They could talk again in the morning.

Now, in the early morning sunlight Jude looked surprisingly relaxed with her feet stretched out and her face, bearing her designer sunglasses, tipped up towards the sun. Maggie took her coffee outside and joined her friend.

"Lovely morning, again. You look … what's the word I'm looking for? Laid back."

"I guess I am, thank you. I did a lot of thinking in the night."

"Want to share?"

"Not yet. I'd like to get through today's plan, visit the site and meet the contact. We're here for your project, that's the priority today. If James even finds out where we are, he won't get here for at least a day yet."

"Bob has told him to come back in a couple of days when I – not you, he didn't even admit you'd been with us – will be back. Which gives us a couple of days, including the journey home, to decide how to deal with what might happen next."

Jude gave Maggie an appraising stare and the beginning of a smile, but didn't comment, giving Maggie a hint of an idea of what might be on Jude's mind. But, she decided, the project was paramount and they were in for what she anticipated would be a momentous day. Focus on that for now. Jude's problems would have to wait until later.

**

The campsite being situated on the road towards La Fatarella, Maggie and Jude were ready and waiting when Louise and Miguel arrived in a land rover. They had been told to dress for the outdoors and some rough terrain, so all four were sporting walking books and shorts, but just with a shirt or t-shirt as the weather promised to be hot again.

The journey to the village took a little over half an hour, passing farms and smallholdings across the countryside. Thanks to the climate there were plentiful fruit and vegetables growing, mostly for personal consumption judging by the size of the plots. Maggie noticed a few farm animals, just the occasional donkey tethered close to a farmhouse, and goats.

The countryside undulated gently, but always within the shadow of the mountain ranges that had played so vital a part in the battle of the Ebro: the Serra de La Fatarella, the Serra de Pandols and in the background the Serra de Cavalls.

They passed the ancient town where they were later to meet the contact and headed out into the country, towards the ridge of the Serra de La Fatarella, coming to a stop at the foot of a huge wind turbine. Jude had earlier expressed dismay at the way in which these massive structures were spread randomly around the countryside. "Concrete sticks, shoved into the earth in the name of progress," she said as they drove along the minor road.

"Better than electricity pylons," Louise replied. "Although I agree they don't blend in well."

Jude snorted as she left the car and reeled at the blast of hot air that smacked into her face.

"Where are we?" Maggie asked. "What are we going to see here?" Looking around, she could see a copse of trees on the head of the ridge, just ahead of them, and spectacular views of the surrounding countryside.

"We're going into that small wood," Miguel replied. "There's a memorial there to the International Brigade. This is where they held the final defensive line which ensured the remaining army could reach the crossing point of the Ebro up at Flix, about twenty kilometres from here. Then, we're going down into an excavated trench, the one where we found the remains of the skeleton now called 'Charlie'. There's also a restored concrete … I forget its name in English."

"A pillbox," Louise said. "The Fascists destroyed many in the final assault on this part of the line and the roof collapsed, killing everyone inside. Then the Guardia Civil destroyed the rest in the late 1940s. The Maquis had been sleeping in them at night and leaving coded messages for other groups. It's been restored now to how it would have been in 1938."

"Then, we might be about to see what Brodie experienced," Jude said.

"Don't get your hopes up yet," Maggie replied.

Chapter 41

Miguel led the way into the wood and along a narrow path, walking in single file. Bracken and grasses had grown up here during the summer, but were now dying back. The hum of the wind turbine provided the background noise, together with the haunting sound of swaying branches that formed a thick canopy above their heads, as the occasional puff of wind passed through them.

They skirted around the edge of the wood, then went back towards the boundary of trees marking the back of the wood. In a clearing stood a rough hewn stone, around a metre high, with a bronze plaque at its smooth front, picturing two combatants, one with a grenade, the second with a rifle. Miguel translated the inscription.

"It says '*fifteenth International Brigade, La Fatarella, battle of the Ebro 1938*'. Then the words lower are '*in memory of the combatants of the fifteenth brigade defenders of liberty*'. By this time, the brigade was called the Mixed Brigade. The Internationals remaining were those who had elected to stay, or who came back. The majority were local, mostly older men and young boys."

"Does anyone know how many non-Catalan or non-Spanish fighters were with the brigade at that final battle, Miguel?" Jude asked.

He shrugged and shook his head. "There are hardly any records at this time. Only stories of those who survived."

"There weren't many of those, were there?" Maggie said.

"No. But later you will meet the son of one survivor." He looked around. "You know, we have a picture of what this place looked like in 1938. There were just two trees. This," he swept his arm around the copse, "has grown up since. We understand some tried to run up over this ground when they could see it was too late, but they were shot and fell here."

Maggie looked around. "I'd ask you what happened to their remains, although I think I know the answer."

Miguel nodded. "There will be some here, still. The Fascists had no respect for their enemies. They might have dug a hole and thrown them all in together, but more likely they were just left and the nature has grown around them."

The light dappling through the canopy fell for a moment onto the plaque and as it rippled across the surface it seemed the faces of the soldiers were moving, their lips muttering, maybe a prayer, Maggie thought.

"Let's go," Louise said, breaking the solemn mood that had descended with the dappling beams and wrapped itself around them. She marched off from the wood and across a hundred or so metres of open land, then stopped.

"This is the ditch, this is where the archaeologists found Charlie." She jumped down and they followed. The ditch followed a zig-zag path, with corner positions where the defenders could crouch down. It ended in the reconstructed 'fort', a concrete pillbox. Halfway along the ditch Louise stopped.

"He lay here, in this corner, on his back, one arm raised above his head. This would have been his defending and firing position."

"I've read the archaeology book," Jude said. "They think he stood up to throw a grenade but was either too slow, or something went wrong and it exploded in his hand."

"Once the Fascists had overrun the trench they took what they wanted from him, his helmet and his gun," Maggie added, staring at the muddy floor, "and just covered him up with dirt when they filled in the trench. Nothing to identify who he might have been."

For half a minute they all stared down, then Miguel broke the silence. "He would have died quickly, there was great force in the explosion," he said, still staring. "The team checked everything he had to try to identify him, but nothing personal survived. There was a blank white sheet of paper, perhaps for a letter he never got to write."

"Where is he now?" Maggie asked. "I heard of a dispute about who should investigate his remains further and he ended up on a shelf somewhere."

"As far as I know he's still there," Louise answered.

"That's disgusting," Jude spat out. "The man deserves a funeral, a proper burial. Leaving him like that is as bad as what the Fascists did to him." Maggie could see a tear running down her friend's cheek. Jude knelt down and brushed her hand over the earth, then jumped up. "Let's carry on, then."

They walked in single file around the zigzags of the trench and into the pillbox. The contrast was arresting, cold and dark and, Maggie thought, horribly oppressive with its solid grey walls with their bullet scars still visible where snipers had fired into the pillbox, and its low overhead ceiling of concrete. An intense burst of claustrophobia overwhelmed her. She had to get out, leaving Jude staring through the thin slit in the wall facing the downward sweep of the hillside towards the village.

Louise and Miguel said they would wait at the top of the trench, then walk them back through the trees to the car. Maggie waited a couple of minutes, but Jude didn't come out, so she poked her head in, to find Jude standing stock still, staring through the slit.

"You OK?" Maggie asked when Jude didn't move or look around.

"I thought I felt them, coming up the hill," she muttered. "Tanks. I imagined a vibration up through my feet, I knew they'd be here soon." She looked around. "Am I going mad?"

Maggie gave her a quick hug. "We've said often enough traumatic events can leave an impression and this must have been overwhelmingly traumatising for anyone manning this bunker. Come on, let's go. The others are waiting."

For a second Jude frowned, glancing around. Then she followed Maggie out of the pillbox. They reached the edge of the trees as Miguel led the way back, again in single file, with Jude bringing up the rear. Halfway through, in the most thickly shrouded area, Maggie realised she could no longer hear Jude's footsteps and turned around. Jude had stopped again, but this time, gazing around the carpet of greenery, bending to smooth her hand with gentle strokes along the grass as it swayed around her. Maggie walked back to her. "What now?"

In reply, Jude nodded her head towards the path behind them. Maggie looked, but saw nothing and said so.

"Miguel said others were killed here, back then when there were no trees, and just left to rot, in shallow holes. I can't call them graves."

"Why do you say that?" Maggie whispered.

"We're being observed," Jude replied. "Don't ask me what I mean, because I can't explain. Just that. A feeling, of being observed, as we pass by."

Maggie glanced around, feeling nothing herself, but anxious to leave now. "Come on, nothing we can see or do here."

Jude nodded and followed her to the car. No-one spoke as they set off. Miguel watched Jude as they drove towards La Fatarella, giving her a questioning look, but not asking questions. As they reached the village he broke her silent contemplation, saying, "I think the English word is 'moving', is it right?"

Jude nodded. "Did they all die, in the trench and pill box," a momentary pause, then "or up on the ridge?" Maggie looked over at her.

"Yes, we think so. We also think there were bodies left on the ridge. They are likely to still be there, skeletons like Charlie. Maybe one day they will be found, do you think?"

Jude gave him a piercing look, smiled and acknowledged his unspoken meaning with a brief inclination of her head.

Chapter 42

Nick sat in his car, leaning back as far as he could, watching the house in Somerset Avenue, Chiswick, in which there appeared to be no sign of life. Unlike the well-kept narrow frontages along the avenue, the Summers' house was a rubbish tip. He had walked up and down when he arrived and, as well as the overspilling bags of refuse he noted that the curtains, still drawn at eleven in the morning were so threadbare they had no colour remaining. The window frames were rotting and the paint on the front door worn to bare wood, with the two numbers indicating the address hanging sideways. This was not promising.

As he contemplated whether he should take up Zelah's suggestion of doorstepping the inhabitants, the front door opened and a man walked out into the street. He looked to be in his twenties, shaved head, neck tattooed with what looked like a swastika and biceps bulging beneath the nylon tracksuit jacket. Nick had just decided you shouldn't judge by appearances when a neighbour emerged from a house a few doors along, took one look at the tracksuited man and scowled, receiving in return a two-fingered gesture, plus an insult Nick couldn't hear but had no difficulty lip reading, followed by spitting in the neighbour's direction. Very not promising. Nick had an urge to start the engine and scurry back to the M4, just a short distance away, in the direction of Wales.

The front door of number twenty-four opened again and an older man appeared, glanced up and down the street and threw another bag of refuse on top of the pile under the window. This man looked to be in his seventies or older. Could this be Michael Summers? Summoning up his courage, Nick decided to approach. He jumped from the car before he could change his mind and reached the door just as the man turned to re-enter the house.

"Excuse me, are you Michael Summers, your father was Harry Summers?" He spoke with his best smile.

The man turned around, rheumy eyes peering suspiciously at Nick. "Who wants to know?"

Nick handed the man his card, which he took and read. "So what if I am. What you want? Have I won something?"

"No, Mr Summers." Nick had to think fast, to stop the man becoming angry at the lack of a prize. "Your father had a document, a diary possibly, given to him when he returned from Spain. I'm representing a client who is related to the man who wrote the diary. We hoped it might still be in your family's possession."

"Don't know nothing about no diary. And my dad wasn't in Spain. He was in the landings in France in '44. Died there."

"It was the Spanish Civil War, Mr Summers. Your father volunteered. He went to Spain to fight against the Fascists just before the start of World War Two."

"What Fascists?"

Nick resisted the urge to roll his eyes. "The uprising led by General Franco, supported by Hitler and Mussolini."

"Don't know nothing about that. We beat Hitler, but I reckon he would have done sommat about all these bleeding Pakis."

Nick turned and walked away. No diary was worth this.

"Oi, where you going? Is it worth anything, this diary?"

"No," Nick shouted over his shoulder.

"Only, some bloke come here when I was a nipper. Collected something he said my dad had kept for him."

Nick stopped, steeling himself to turn around again. "When was that, Mr Summers?"

"I would have been about ten, so 1950-ish, I reckon. Said he wanted his book."

"He wanted '*his*' book, not collecting it for someone else?"

"Nah, he said his book. My Mum got it for him. He was right chipper, gave me a shilling."

"Did he say his name? Do you remember anything else about him?"

The man shrugged. "Nah. Had a funny accent, though, I remember that."

"Thanks," Nick said. The door slammed shut as Nick walked away. As he reached his car he saw the grandson Justin approaching. No need for him to know Nick had been talking to his grandfather. He started the car and drove off before the younger man reached his house, shaking his head once again. The man who had volunteered to go to Spain to fight against Fascism had a great grandson with a swastika tattooed on his neck. '*Humans*," he muttered as he joined the M4 motorway. '*We never learn*'."

An hour into the journey he stopped at a service station and sent a message to Maggie. He had been puzzling about who the man who collected the diary could have been, given they were certain Brodie McAlister had died in Spain. Her reply told him she and Jude had just visited the site of Charlie's demise and were about to visit the son of a Civil War survivor family who might have some news of interest to their inquiry. She suggested they arrange a call once Nick reached home and she and Jude were free. She ended her text with: *'interesting, and agree puzzling. Feeling case is more complicated than we thought. Speak later'*.

For the remainder of the journey Nick worked his way through a number of ideas, dismissing most of them as either impractical or far-fetched, but deciding on new lines of enquiry to check. In his mind this case was growing and spreading tentacles and he suspected the outcome would surprise all of them, if any one of his outlandish ideas proved to be correct.

Chapter 43

"The man we are going to meet is called Andreu Carles. He has some concerns about talking to you," Miguel said as they entered the village and found a parking space. "Many of the old people, especially those who went through the early days of the Franco regime, don't want to remember it. Times then were terrible for republicans, even more so for Catalans."

"I believe it was brutal," Jude said.

Louise nodded. "Franco wasn't satisfied with winning. He wanted to exterminate as many republicans who supported and fought for the Republic as could be found and disposed of. Rule of law was dispensed with. He wanted to make his revenge was so terrible no-one would ever think of rising up against him. One of his Ministers, a man called Serrano Suñer, hated Catalans because of their desire for independence, claimed it was an 'illness'. Franco banned our language. Work was scarce. People starved to death in the years following the end of the Republic."

Maggie and Jude walked behind Louise and Miguel into the house of Andreu Carles, in a short street on the outskirts of the village of La Fatarella. A straight dark windowless corridor led to the back of the house, leading on the right to a sitting room overlooking over a spacious courtyard garden. The doors leading out onto the courtyard had been opened, letting in a light, fresh breeze. Maggie and Jude were ushered into armchairs opposite the worn settee on which their hosts sat. Louise and Miguel leaned against the wall behind the settee.

The hosts, one man and one woman, were both in their seventies, Maggie judged. The man's leathery face told of years of exposure to the Catalan sun. Maggie thought he wasn't above five and a half feet tall. The woman, dressed in black, stared at them with amused curiosity.

Through Louise interpreting he welcomed them to his home and offered tea and cake, which they accepted. The woman, who hadn't been introduced, stood. She, too was short, but she radiated energy, although she ambled on buckled legs. Louise and Miguel made small-talk in Catalan until she returned and the drinks and cake were served.

The man put down his cup. "How can I be of help to you?" he said in Spanish.

Miguel summarised the reason for their visit. Maggie occasionally recognised some of the words, places and names, at which the man nodded.

"Ask your questions," he said, nodding, when Miguel had finished.

Maggie explained again they wanted to confirm whether or not Brodie McAlister had returned to La Fatarella to support the brigade and take part in the final battle, where they believed he died. If this man could clarify anything about a young foreigner on that final day, the fourth of November 1938, they would be grateful, although they weren't hopeful. "Does it mean anything to you? Your father was around the same age as the boy we're looking for. Did he tell you anything about that day?"

He spent a moment looking at Maggie, then at Jude, then back to Maggie. "What would you do with such information, if I could provide it?"

"We're here on behalf of his family. They never saw him again and now his descendants would like to know what happened to him. That's all. There's nothing I am keeping from you. It's a family quest."

"I will trust what you say." For a second his wife put her hand on his arm and squeezed, but he shook her off.

"My father was one of the scarce lucky ones who escaped. He found the body of the foreign boy. He brought it back to his own mother, here in La Fatarella."

Maggie drew a sharp breath, then exhaled. "That was admirable of him, and incredibly brave." Then she frowned. "Why him? Why not other Catalans?"

The man shrugged. "Because they were all dead. He still had a sliver of breath."

Maggie's mouth dropped open some seconds of confusion as she took in what she had heard.

"Not dead?"

"Close to death, shot three times, including a bullet in his head. When my father came across him, after the Fascist troops had moved on, he was not conscious, but breathing, just. After dark my father carried him back to this house. My grandmother nursed him here. He became conscious for short periods, but the wounds were too serious. She thought he would die within a few hours. He muttered a great deal, which frightened my grandmother. As well as the soldiers, there were townspeople who were willing to report her to the authorities, so she kept him in the cellar. She called him Lluis."

"Why?" Jude asked, sharply.

"It was the name of her eldest son, who had died in the fighting and it sounded like his muttering. He said names, said his name was Lluis, but she couldn't understand other foreign words. He kept repeating a Spanish phrase ..."

"*Lo siento mucho,*" Maggie interrupted.

The man nodded. "How do you know?"

"Those were the words on a postcard he arranged to be sent home to his sister, Helen, in Scotland, if this really is him."

"Ah, 'Helen'. My grandmother thought his wits had gone with the bullet. To her, it sounded like '*heli* 'which is Catalan for helium, the gas. Then the soldiers came, asking for her eldest son, my uncle Lluis. She told them he died, he had developed typhoid."

"Did they search the house?" Maggie asked.

"No," he replied. "They weren't interested in a dead body, especially a contagious one."

"A courageous woman. So, when Lluis, or Brodie, died, was he buried as her son?"

"She told them that's what had happened. They accepted it and left."

"And what about your father? Were they not interested in him?"

"She told them he was just fourteen, and hadn't taken part in the fighting, nor the youngest one, who was twelve. She was terrified for them. Franco's men were known to take away young men and boys, even if they hadn't been in the

Republican army, if they were part of a family with an active soldier, like my uncle Lluis. But, luck stayed with her. They left her alone. They were looking for men who had fought, at this time. They didn't come back for the boys."

Maggie nodded. "So, Brodie McAlister is buried here under the name Lluis Carles. Can we see the grave?"

"If you wish," he replied, his face set like stone. "Please don't speak about any of this outside my house."

"Of course not. I hope to tell our client how the story ends, that's all. I assure you we'll be discreet."

She stood up and turned to nod at Louise and Miguel that it was time to leave. They moved towards the door, but Jude didn't move. "Come on," Maggie whispered.

Instead, Jude turned to the old man and said, in Spanish, "There's something I'd like to check with you, Señor Carles."

"Excuse me, I did not know you spoke our language."

"I realise that. You said about your mother's message to the soldiers '*she told them that's what had happened*'."

A smile spread across his face, revealing bright strong teeth and lighting up his eyes and he nodded, but his wife sat up, her breath shortening and audible, and whispered something to him. Again, he brushed her off.

"You have understood, Señora. That is what she said."

"But it's not what happened?" Jude asked.

"No. He did not die. He recovered. He left this house two months after he arrived here. His wounds had healed, although he was weak. The bullets had gone through and out. His luck stayed with him also."

"Where did he go?" Maggie asked when Jude had translated. "What else do you know?"

The man shrugged. "My family heard no more from him. He might be dead a few kilometres from here. He might have been captured, or he might have reached Barcelona, where there was still resistance and people who would help him to find his way to France. I cannot tell you what I do not know."

"You can't, or you won't?" Jude demanded.

"I cannot, because this is all I know. I did not intend to tell you so much. You have said you will be discreet."

Maggie nodded. "And I will keep my promise. Come on, Jude, there's nothing else for us here."

Jude stood up. She looked at the old man and said "Andreu, I thank you for all of us. Secrets are not easy to keep for a lifetime. You have my respect. We'll leave now. I thank you and your wife for your hospitality."

As they walked out into the sunshine, blindingly bright after the dark house, Miguel said to Jude, "You did that well, thank you." Louise gave her a quick hug.

"What did you say?" Maggie asked. "It was something he appreciated." Jude told her and Maggie squeezed her arm.

They ambled into to the centre of the small town, warm, empty and silent in the afternoon lunch break.

Maggie had been deep in thought, not noticing what the others were discussing. Jude touched her arm and she jumped. "Sorry, miles away."

"Not surprising. What now? Back to the campsite?"

"I think so. This changes everything. I need to speak to Nick following his visit this morning. Then, time for review and consideration."

"Could it have been Brodie who collected the diary?" Jude asked.

"That's top of our list of what we have to find next," Maggie replied.

Chapter 44

When he reached Maggie's house, Nick went straight to the office and began to research each of his speculative ideas.

As he had expected, most of them he shut down without lengthy exploration, but there was one for which he couldn't find an outcome. Nick was not a person given to wild imaginings, but this idea, although wild for him, was accompanied by an itch in his head.

Within the hour, he had found the answer, but was it significant? That would depend on what Maggie had to say when they organised their call later. For now, he had done what he could. He began to write up his notes from the morning visit, waiting for the message to come through with details of the call. He knew it wouldn't happen for some time, as Zelah had gone to Cork to discuss further security with the firm she had been hired and not likely to be free a few hours.

He sat back in his chair, allowing his mind to wander across some crazy ideas and realised he might have a chance to consolidate his earlier discovery. Logging on again, he checked whether electoral registration details were available in Scotland for the post war years and found them for Glasgow, for the years 1957 – 1962. He entered a name and began a search.

Within seconds the results appeared and his stomach rolled with excitement as he saw the names listed. Next, he needed to further investigate the names, to find out if any significant dates matched, in particular a date of birth. Just one did, the same person on multiple entries, all at the same address. This was astounding news. He was sufficiently excited to try a call to Maggie, but she didn't respond. Sighing, he set his mind to having to wait until she and Jude had completed whatever they were doing.

After kicking his heels for a further hour, the message arrived with the log-in details of the call for six o'clock. Zelah would also be joining them. Another hour to wait. Nick made himself a sandwich and went out to sit in the garden to make the most of the remaining afternoon sunshine. As he watched the sun go down over the mountain he gave Stella a quick call to update her and let her know he would be home later, then tried Max, but he didn't answer. He wondered where the boy might be. Their relationship was, in Nick's opinion, improving, but he had noticed lately Max was still withdrawn. He thought there might have been some easing of tension after the death of Helen Redland, but Max seemed untouched by that. Nick's ability to 'perceive' enerty gave him the advantage of realising Max's low vitality. Or was a disadvantage? He couldn't decide if he should speak or not. Would Max view such an attempt to discuss something so personal as intrusive? He was desperate to get closer to his son, but didn't want his attempts to be rebuffed and push them further apart.

Bob's voice called to him from the house, that Maggie was on the call and they were waiting for him to join. He jumped up, grinning when he realised the outcome of his musings and considerations was that he had fallen asleep.

Maggie, Jude and Zelah were chatting about the weather in their locations, as Nick joined them. In Ireland it was raining; in Spain they were enjoying a warm outdoor evening, again.

"Apologies. I got caught up in some thoughts. Your garden has a soporific effect on me."

"It sends me to sleep," Zelah said, with a piercing grin into the camera.

Nick smiled. "Fair enough. Anyway, I have some fascinating news."

"As do we," Jude said. "Can we start, please? I can't wait to tell you all about this."

She took them through the day, with a quick summary of their visit to the battle site, then, in greater detail, the meeting with Andreu Carles, ending with the news of Brodie McAlister, aka Lewis Stewart, leaving the town of La Fatarella alive. If she had expected shock and awe, however, she was surprised and disappointed it wasn't forthcoming. "Come on, guys. You can't tell me you're not excited to hear that?"

"I'm delighted to hear it," Nick replied, "because it validates what I've found out today." He gave them a run-down on his trip to Chiswick and the encounter with Michael Summers, with the news that the diary had been held at the house, but had been collected around 1950.

"If the miserable git's memory is good, and the man who turned up did say 'my diary' or whatever, emphasis on the '*my*', then we can make a fair guess that Brodie McAlister managed to get home," Zelah said.

"Better than that," Nick said. "On the journey back I gave some thought to ideas around the supposition he did return. How did he manage to evade the authorities? What were his options? I have some interesting results from the searches I carried out when I got back." He sat back and Zelah leaned forward.

"If I could reach down this camera I'd shake you! What have you found?"

"Two things. No, three; or is it four? Let me go back a little." He caught sight of Zelah's expression, swallowed and speeded up. "I guessed that, if he got home, he might go to Scotland, or he might try to find help from people he knew in Spain. He may have tried Harry Summers, I don't know. But what I did find is that he enlisted in the army in 1939. He isn't on the War register, so he must have done so before it was compiled in the September of that year. Did he try to contact his family in Scotland? I believe he did. We'll never know who, unless something turns up in Lolly's papers, but we know the information never reached Julie in Canada. However, there were another two brothers, Malcolm and Lewis. Perhaps he tried to find either or both of them. And that's where I found the first interesting news. Malcolm was living in Glasgow and was called up. But Lewis? Here's where it's a watershed. Lewis died, in 1936. I don't know what of, yet; I've sent for his death certificate. However, I found from available records that Lewis never married, that he'd been in and out of trouble, and was, at one point, a vagrant. Brodie knew about that."

"How do you know?" Maggie asked.

"I said he enlisted, ahead of being called up, which he would never have been, because the name under which he enlisted was … Lewis Edward McAlister."

"A man who was already dead," Zelah said. "Well, nice work, Nick. But are you certain it's him?"

"Yes, I am, quite sure. When he signed up he had to give his date of birth. I checked and the date of birth he gave was of the real Lewis McAlister, born in 1913 and the middle name of the real Lewis was Edward. It's him."

Jude spoke first. "Well, this had been a day. Case turned completely on its head. What do we do now?"

"We report back to Lolly Sadler," Maggie said. "Nick, can you call her in the morning. And we should keep digging. We might still find out what happened to him after the war."

"I have some news on that front, too," Nick said.

Zelah rolled her eyes, which Nick either ignored or didn't notice.

"I started checking available electoral registers for the main Scottish cities. I found entries in Glasgow, of a Lewis E McAlister, living at an address consistently from 1956 to 1962."

"Helen must have known," Maggie interrupted. "She couldn't have been living so close and not known."

"Maybe. The final piece of news is that I found his death. He died in 2011, in Glasgow, but that's all I know. Entries only become public fifty years after the death, so I'll have to wait until Monday to find out if there's any further available information when I call the registrar's office."

“It’s enough for now,” Maggie replied. “With some digging we can find out where he’s buried; oops, pardon the pun.”

“If he wasn’t cremated,” Zelah added. “I agree, it’s satisfactory for now. Lolly Sadler will be shocked, and her prissy sister may well spontaneously combust, but, it’s a super outcome for us.”

“And on that note, let’s leave it there,” Maggie said. “I’m exhausted and we’ve up to twenty hours of driving starting tomorrow.”

“Agreed,” Nick said. “I’m taking some time out tomorrow. A nice, quiet Sunday. Have a safe trip and I’ll let you know how the conversation goes with Lolly tomorrow.”

They all logged off and Nick let Bob know he would be back in the morning to make the call to Lolly, before heading off to join Stella for an evening drink and a meal.

Over dinner he told her he was looking forward to making the call the following day, and he expected the client would be shocked, but hopefully pleased.

As it turned out, Lolly Sadler made the call the following morning, and Nick, when it ended, was left in a state of shock.

Chapter 45

Lolly Sadler had collected Mary McShane, at the door at ten precisely, and made the ten-minute drive to the home where Xandy Smith was now happily ensconced, chatting en route about how they would approach the introduction of Mary to a man who hadn't had visitors, or any distraction for several years. They decided that, as he was unlikely to remember Lolly, they would both join him, introduce themselves, then Lolly would go to sit by the window, to be out of his range of vision but still able to hear whatever conversation ensued.

"Remember, Mary, his mind wanders. And he hasn't been used to conversing in the past several years. He isn't like you."

"Can't shut me up, you mean?"

Lolly glanced across and saw Mary laughing. "Something like that, yes."

"Don't worry, I'll be gentle with him. If he doesn't talk, my gabbing will be enough for both of us."

When they arrived, Xandy had been washed and dressed and had had his breakfast. He sat propped up in a wheelchair at a coffee table in his room, with a carer taking him through some photographs of the royal family, at which he smiled happily.

"Xandy, your visitors are here," the girl said in a sing-song voice Lolly thought sounded like someone talking to a child, but then again, he was child-like, so she smiled and thanked the girl.

They pulled up chairs and sat as close as they were allowed to Xandy, who gazed at them with polite but baffled interest.

"Do you remember me, Xandy?" No response. "I'm Lolly. I came to see you last week. Today, I've brought a friend. This is Mary. Mary Cameron." Mary sat forward. His face lit up.

"Little Mary! She's a pretty wee lass. Is she coming to see me? I don't like those masks. Take it off."

Mary bit her lip, glanced at Lolly, and put a smile on. "I'm Mary, Xandy. We were together when we were children. Here, look at this picture."

From her bag she pulled an envelope, took out a faded photograph and put it within his reach. Xandy bent his head down until his nose almost touched the paper. Then, he stabbed at it. "Mary Cameron!" he said, pointing to a girl.

"Yes, Xandy. What do you remember about her?"

He didn't react, so Mary began to point out others on the picture and he followed with smiling interest. He sat back, frowning. "No Brodie there."

"No," Mary said. "This picture is taken after he left. This was in 1938. That's over eighty years ago. We're ancient now, aren't we? Ancient as the dinosaurs."

"Is he coming to see me? Is Brodie boy coming? I haven't seen him for a while now."

"I don't know about Brodie," Mary replied gently. "What about …"

He interrupted her. "He brings me grapes. I like Brodie boy."

Lolly turned around and shot a bewildered look at Mary, who shrugged back surprise. "That's nice of him," she said. "Would you like us to bring grapes, Xandy?"

"No. I'll wait on Brodie boy."

Lolly thought it was pointless trying to tell him Brodie was long gone. His head had gone back down onto the picture of the rows of children, moving slightly, nodding occasionally. Mary sat back and left him to it.

Lolly went back to looking out of the window. She would bring the visit to an end, soon. Mary looked tired; this had upset her. In the car park two cars pulled up, families visiting on a Sunday. One held two adults who looked as if they were arguing about who should enter first. The other, a man with a carrier bag. All likely visiting relatives who had, however reluctantly, been committed to this home when they could no longer be cared for by their families. Lolly grimaced and hoped this would never happen to her. But you never knew. A beeping on her phone with an incoming message distracted her. It was from Nick, who wanted to speak to her and asked when would be convenient. As she began to type out her reply, footsteps in the corridor stopped close by. The manager put her head round the door.

"I'm sorry to interrupt, but there's another person here to see Mr Smith. He isn't a relative, and I've explained he can't come in. One of you must leave now. Mr Smith should only have one visitor at a time, but I allowed you both because of the seriousness of his condition."

"I'll go," Lolly said. "I'll find out who this man is." She walked down the corridor, where the man with the carrier bag stood outside the front door. As she joined him he said, "I didn't realise Xandy would have so many visitors."

"I'm not a relative but I've brought a friend from his past. Who are you?"

He hesitated a moment. "I'm related to another friend from his past. I've been visiting him in his previous home. I was shocked to find today he's been moved. I know how ill he is. Look, he likes grapes. Would you give him this?" He held out the bag towards her.

"I don't think that's allowed here. Why don't you go around to the window? He can see you from there. I'll come with you."

The man nodded and she led him around. As they reached the room, the man knocked on the slightly ajar window, and Xandy looked up. When he saw who it was, a wide grin appeared on his face.

"Brodie boy! Did you bring grapes?"

The man nodded, his eyes flicking to and from Lolly, Mary and Xandy. Without Xandy's shout Lolly thought the man would have retreated, but Xandy was waving a shaking hand in welcome, so he leaned further across the sill.

"I'll just leave these for now and come back later," he said, smiling and holding up the bag.

Mary stood up. "Oh no you won't. There's something about you, like someone I should know. Who are you?"

The man's eyebrows shot up at her brusqueness and he stared at her, unspeaking. Then he said:

"I'm Brodie McAlister. Who are you?"

Chapter 46

For Maggie and Jude dinner had been a quiet affair. After the discoveries of the day Maggie wanted to spend time considering what they should concentrate on next and was keen to start the journey home the following day as early as possible. However, Jude's usual cheery eagerness to discuss potential actions was absent, as she repeatedly went to speak but stopped, tapping her index finger against her lips which moved in silent inner conversation, all the time sinking further down into her chair as the evening sky darkened the space between her and Maggie.

"What is it, Worm?" Maggie said, when she couldn't wait it out any longer and had lit candles on and around the table. "If you run your fingers through your hair any harder it's going to stay looking like a Mohican."

"Decision time," Jude replied.

"Want to talk about it?"

Jude thought for a moment. "Let's open another bottle of wine. I need it."

"Not for me. With the drive home looming tomorrow I won't do well over the mountain passes with a hangover. If this is about facing James when you get back …"

"No, not that. It's more about …" She stopped, emptied the dregs of the wine in the currently open bottle into her and Maggie's glasses, took a deep mouthful, tossed it back. "About whether or not I come back at all."

"Hmm. Does that shock me? Honestly, no. I've been watching how you've immersed yourself into this place. You love it here, don't you?"

Jude sat up and put the glass back down on the table. "You could see that? Yes, you're right, Maggot. I've felt connected to this place from the moment we sat down in the town square and waited for Louise and Miguel. And I'm kind of excited, about what I could do here."

Maggie nodded. "Jude, please think about the bigger picture. Is it just about avoiding your husband? If so, is this the best response? He might keep hunting, find you here."

Jude said, "I don't want to see him again, that's true. But if I didn't feel so strongly about staying, I'd have no hesitation coming back with you. Look, there are things I haven't told you. He won't find me. I have a US passport in another name." She waved away Maggie's incoming protest. "I know, it's illegal. And criminal. It was just to get out of the country without him being able to find my name on a flight manifesto. I fixed it up before I left the States, courtesy of a couple of the women at the refuge. They may have been in hiding, but they'd picked up some useful contacts." She grinned, taking a hairband off her wrist and tying back the now wild cascade of hair. "I'll have to disguise myself. The hair will go, and change colour, redhead maybe? I'm planning to hire a place in the countryside, not too far from town. I'm thinking, goats …"

Maggie burst out laughing. "Are you serious?"

Jude's eyes were wide with few blinks, as she leaned forward and held out her hand across the table. "Totally. I'll make a commendable farmer. Thank you for not being cross with me."

"How do you know I'm not cross?"

"Because I've seen you when you are. You hold forth with impressive clarity. And I'm sorry to leave you to face the drive home alone. I'll miss you. You've been a wonderful friend these past two weeks."

Maggie squeezed the outstretched hand. "Apart from goats, what will you do?"

"I'd like to help Louise and Miguel, I think. What I've learned about the Civil War era here has changed me. I'd like to be a part of commemorating the memories, of the International Brigaders who came here, and died. I don't know how yet, but I need a quick solution, because as of tomorrow I'll be homeless."

"They're coming to say goodbye in the morning. You can tell them then, and I won't be surprised if they have any number of suggestions to get you started. They're lovely people." She yawned then stood up. "Right, I'm off to bed. This has been quite a day and it's not going to calm down when I'm home. But the more I think about your false passport, you must get rid of it, burn it, whatever. You did use your UK passport to come here, didn't you?"

"Of course. Like I said, it was just to get out of the US without him being able to stop me."

"Good. Because if you want to stay in Spain you have to act quickly, and totally legally, with your UK identity."

"Why?"

"You haven't kept up with Brexit, have you?"

"Not really, no. I thought I'd be able to stay."

Maggie shook her head. "You'll have to establish residency before the thirty-first of December with your UK citizenship in your own name. Then, I suggest you get a good lawyer. At least you have the money … hang on, you did set up your bank accounts with your own name, please tell me you did."

"Yes, I did."

"Then it's possible, if he finds you, he'll use legal means to get his money back, regardless of what he did to you."

Jude tapped the side of her nose. "Bring it on. I didn't just cut and run. I have some interesting information about how he got his hands on some of that money. His salary didn't come close." She leaned forward and took Maggie's hand. "Try not to worry, Maggot. I can look after myself."

Maggie grimaced. "I'll be keeping in close touch."

"Good, me too and just one other thing. You have to keep me up to date on the story of Brodie McAlister. If I'm not mistaken, there will be more surprises. Instinct tells me it's not over yet."

"Agreed. I also have a gut feeling some shocks are in store. Of course I'll keep in touch. You'll need a new phone, though."

"I've thought of that." She raised her glass, Maggie picked up hers and clinked them together. "To solving your case, whatever the solution turns out to be."

Chapter 47

Nick, being an 'early bird', had finished breakfast on the terrace at Stella's house and had packed up his bag to head over to the office, when his phone rang. Seeing Lolly's name, he answered the call.

Five minutes later Stella found him still sitting, staring at the table, moving his head slightly, as if trying to work something out. She touched his arm and when she got no reaction, poked his shoulder.

"Earth to Nick Howell, come in please." Still no reaction. She walked around to face him and sat down, picked up a mug and banged three times, which got his attention. When she saw his face she immediately thought: '*bad news*'. "What's happened, love? Who was on the phone?"

Now he looked up at her. "The client, Lolly Sadler. She and Mary McShane are visiting Alexander Smith. Another visitor turned up. He introduced himself as Brodie McAlister."

"What!" Stella gasped. "That can't be possible. Can it?"

"No, not the original, he'd be a hundred years old. This man is saying he's the son of Lewis Edward McAlister, or the man known by that name."

"Wow." Stella tipped her head to one side. "So, given what you found out yesterday, is it possible this man could be Brodie Junior? And if it is, does he know who his father really was?"

"I don't know," he replied. "When Lolly told him who she was, he became agitated, didn't want to speak to her and tried to leave. She manged to calm him down, told him there was no cause for panic, because we already knew some of the story."

"Did she elaborate on how much?"

"No, because we haven't had time to tell her all of it, yet. I'm trying to think what to do next. I said I'd call her back in ten minutes. Where do I start?"

"Nick," Stella said decisively, "you're the one who needs to stop panicking. I would suggest you call her back, tell her there's a lot more information to come from Maggie's visit to Spain and she should share what she can with this man. Provided, I would say, he agrees to share with her, and with all of you. Perhaps she could arrange a date to meet with him, when one of you could get there with her."

Nick nodded. "Yes, yes." He glanced at his watch. "Maggie and Jude will be leaving Catalonia any minute. I should call them before they set off, tell them about this and make arrangements for us all to speak at leisure later, with Zelah too."

Stella stood up, then said," I would suggest you ask her to ask him if he has the diary. Just that. If he says 'yes', that should confirm who he is and make it easier for you all to meet, if he will agree to a meeting."

Nick called as she finished speaking and Lolly answered immediately. He relayed the message then waited whilst she spoke to Brodie, biting his lips as he heard the question being asked, but not the response. He had started to rock back and forward in his chair when Lolly came back to him.

"He says 'yes 'to both questions. He will meet us on Wednesday; he wants a couple of days to think everything through and he's going to check out Maze. And he's astounded we know about the diary, but yes again, he has it."

Nick exhaled a puff of breath. "Please get a location and time from him, Lolly. Can you also reassure him there's nothing to worry about, not from our side."

"I'll walk to the car with him now. Xandy's agitated, too. Best we talk away from him."

"Thank you," Nick said.

He rang Maggie immediately, surprised to find her already a couple of hours into the journey. She explained there had been a change of plan, not one that affected Maze, but she would be heading straight home and hoping to catch an earlier ferry. She reassured him it was nothing to worry about, but she wanted to get the journey started and promised she would call him once she reached the French motorway and if his news wasn't important it could wait, then ended the call before he could add more.

"Something's happened out there, too," he said. "She didn't say what, but she says nothing bad or worrying, just a change, so I won't worry. Right, I'm going over to the office to organise a call later and let Zelah know what's going on, and get going on writing up all of this new stuff. Maggie's hoping she can reach Cherbourg or close by late this evening then get the first ferry over to Southampton, to be home by late afternoon tomorrow."

At the office, he called Zelah in Ireland. She didn't express the shock he'd expected. "This one's turning out to have more twists and turns than our Maze logo," she said. "Who is he, in truth?"

"Good question. My feeling is he's related to the McAlister family, but beyond that I'm not prepared to speculate."

"But of course you have an idea?"

"As do you, Zelah, but you'd prefer not to speculate, either. Can you get to Glasgow on Wednesday?"

"Shouldn't be a problem. The atmosphere here is improving. We've gone from arctic to chilly, enough for me to step back for a couple of days."

"Are you developing diplomacy skills, my friend?"

"Hell, no! I just stop them from physically attacking each other, Gerry and Mischa that is, aided and abetted by Stephen. He's a gem. Michelle keeps out of the way; cowardice in the face of conflict is still her primal reaction. Anyway, what are you going to do now?"

"I should reply to a prospective client who has a relative he believes was a major player in the Chartist movement and the riots in Newport, although I must say I've never heard of the man he's named. I'll do some research. And I'll take a look at another case which might be interesting."

"And what about Maggie? What's happened in Spain?"

"I don't know what the latest thing is, but she's going to call when she's on a clear straight road. They're hurrying back."

"Whatever. If there's anything else I need to know call me. If not, let me know when Lolly gives you the date and time of the meeting on Wednesday. Over and out."

Chapter 48

Having decided to take the mountain route home, Maggie crossed the border into France at midday, and headed for the motorways taking her back up to the port of Cherbourg. She had booked a crossing for the following morning at six. By the time she reached the outskirts of the town and found the camping she had booked for an overnight stay, she feared she would fall asleep at the wheel and would need a neck brace for a week to recover from the stiffness and pain.

She had spoken to both Nick and Zelah again as she travelled and they had brought her up to date on the latest events of the Brodie McAlister story. Although she winced at the prospect of having to fly to Scotland the day after she reached home, she resigned herself to it being necessary. She also told them about Jude staying in Spain, at which Zelah expressed outrage that Jude had left Maggie to make the journey alone.

"I'm fine with it. It was the right thing for her. I, on the other hand, am going to look like the hunchback of Notre Dame for a few days after this, even though the van is a comfortable drive. Anyway, I must go, to have any chance of finding the camping before it closes at midnight."

Having slept well and suffered none of the usual queasy effects of a sea crossing, she arrived back home in the late afternoon, pleased and relieved to find the house empty, which would allow her a couple of hours sleep before either Bob or Jack arrived, but decided to nap on the settee rather than go to bed. She stretched out her shoulders, winced and flopped down.

What seemed like a couple of seconds later, but glancing at the clock on wall and seeing three hours had passed, she sat up, groaned with the pain in her shoulders in muscles that seemed to have solidified whilst she slept, with pain intensifying by the second. Her throat also felt like she had swallowed a lump of sandpaper. She limped into the kitchen and flipped the switch on the kettle, to find nothing happened. This was the last straw; swearing profusely at whoever had allowed this to happen and done nothing about it, she went out to the van, muttering and grumping, opened the side locker where the toolbox was kept and took out a couple of screwdrivers. Back in the kitchen she began to attack the plug. Bob chose this moment to arrive home. He saw her and moved in to give her a hug, but took a step back at the expression on the face turned that responded to his greeting.

"Glad to have you back. What are you doing?"

"Kettle's not working."

"I know. It packed up this morning. I've bought another one." He stood back to reveal the bag he'd put down on the table. Maggie gave him a wry grin. "OK. Forgiven." She moved towards him to return the hug when they both leapt apart at the sound of several short rings on the doorbell.

"You expecting anyone?"

"No," he replied. "But … hang on. I know who this might be and it's not good. Wait here."

Maggie stood leaning on the sink. Whoever it was, was about to get an earful if they were here to complain about something. She wasn't in the mood to be polite.

Bob reappeared, with what Maggie recognised as his warning look, followed by a man. Tall, dark and handsome, film star looks, quite stunningly so. But, there was something about his smile – oily – and the way he looked at her, which put her on her guard.

He held out his hand to her and said "Hi, there." She was instantly alert. The accent gave it away.

"My name is …"

"I know who you are," she said. "James Martinez, the wife abuser." She turned to Bob. "Show this man out."

James Martinez took a step back, put his palms up in a gesture of appeasement. "Whoa, there. I don't know what my wife told you, but I can assure you I am no abuser. Look, I can understand you and she have been friends since your schooldays, and you want to help her, and that's good. But, there's a lot you don't know. Please hear me out."

"Let me think about that." Two second pause. "No. I don't think I will. Leave, now."

He took a step toward here. "Look, lady …"

She raised her hand and Bob stepped in. "Put it down, love. It's dangerous."

Maggie glanced down at her hand and saw the screwdriver, which was now pointed at James's chest. "What? It's just a screwdriver!"

"Not the way you're holding it," Bob replied and reached out to take it from her.

"I wouldn't have stabbed him," she said to Bob, with a rapid wink. "Although, he did shoot Jude, so perhaps he has a concealed weapon."

James tried to laugh, to show his disbelief at the idea, but his lips lost the fight.

"Tell me where she is and I'll leave."

"She's in Europe."

"Oh really. And where precisely in Europe?"

"No idea. I dropped her off in France. She could be anywhere by now. She's planning to travel. For at least two years, to get over the trauma of having been beaten, shot and abused by you. Now, get out of my house and never, I repeat, never, come back here."

He stood for a moment looking at her, then at Bob, then laughed again. "You're a fool if you believe a word she said."

"I believe every word she said. I don't believe anything coming out of your mouth. Bob?"

"Come along, Mr Martinez. I don't want to have to arrest you."

Bob's tone told James Martinez this was not a joke. He walked to the door, then turned around.

"I'll find her. She stole from me. And if you helped her…"

"Good luck to you proving she took anything that wasn't hers. A lot of money, was it? Good that, on a policeman's salary. And don't threaten me. Bye bye."

She gave him a cheeky wave and he left. Bob returned, smiling. "Wasn't that interesting …" Before he could say more Maggie groaned as her legs buckled and she fell into his arms. He led her into the sitting room and onto the settee, then poured her a large brandy and sat beside her.

"He won't be coming back," he said, taking her free hand as the glass tinkled against her teeth. "Maggie, are you sure he doesn't have some right to the money she's taken?"

She put a hand up. "Of course I can't be a hundred percent sure. I guess some of what she took was his but, she did tell me more stories about her time with him and some of that money, although she didn't exactly say so, is probably related to bribery. He's a monster and if he's broke, well, good. Anyway, he can't be totally broke or he wouldn't have had the ready cash to travel over here and stalk her, would he."

"True, but it doesn't make what she's done honest or legal."

"No, just morally OK, for me, anyway." She leaned into him. "I know about being left stranded without a penny. But I didn't deserve it. He does."

"Fair enough. I'm not going to say anything and I don't think he'll ask us for help to find her. Too much to reveal about their past together. I'll keep a check on him." They sat for a moment, then Bob said "I don't think he'll stop looking for her, though. He can use police contacts in France and Spain. I'm thinking you know how to contact her?"

"Of course. I'll have to let her know he's been here, but I think she can be reasonably sure he can't find her. I'll warn her to lay low for a couple of weeks, see as few people as possible. Louise and Miguel will help with that."

"So, you had a good outcome, and my van is in one piece. Well done."

"Brodie McAlister managed to get home, yes, but now this man has turned up in Scotland saying he's Brodie McAlister. It's puzzling, but we'll know in a couple of days." She stopped and yawned. "God, I'm tired. Where's Jack? Is he back this evening?"

Bob glanced at his watch. "Yes, should be here any time. You need to sleep, but eat first. I'll get something ready. Ah, here he is." He got up and called out to Jack, who came in and threw himself on Maggie. She pushed him off, laughing. "Good to see you too, son. How's it been this past week?"

"Fine. Bob can cook a bit and he's been teaching me some basics. Just two weeks to go now. I've got my place in a hall of residence."

Maggie supressed another yawn. "That's great. It's the best choice for your first year. Pull me up. My legs are wobbly from driving for hours. Come on, the chef is at work in the kitchen. Let's join him and I'll tell you all about Spain. Then, I'm looking forward to sleeping in a proper bed for many, many hours."

She managed to get through the meal before staggering upstairs and falling into bed, her sleepy thoughts being that the case should be over soon and the mystery of Brodie McAlister solved.

Bob went to check on her a couple of hours later to find her gently snoring. He sat by the side of the bed and gently pulled a few wisps of hair away from her eyes. Maggie didn't move. He had come home specifically to give her a piece of news, but the arrival of James Martinez had put paid to that, and he saw the depth of her exhaustion, so additional worrying news on top of a long, tiring and stressful day would not have gone down well. He decided to wait until the following morning, to break it to her that Emer McCarthy Miller had been spotted in Dublin.

Unfortunately, the information hadn't reached the Garda in time to pick her up. Emer was on the loose again, but the surprising news was that, instead of heading for Cork, she had made enquiries about a ferry to Wales. He had already told Zelah and Nick, and asked them to leave Maggie sleep. They were all going to need fierce concentration and alertness.

Before going to bed he checked all of the windows and doors and put the burglar alarm on. They had to take vital precautions, now. He was confident it would be over soon, but had to admit to himself he was beyond worried about their safety. Emer would not hesitate to remove any one of them who stood in the way of whatever she wanted.

Which he knew was, first and foremost, Zelah and everything she had. Everyone else would just be collateral damage to Emer McCarthy Miller.

Chapter 49

When Maggie awoke she put her hand to her head and groaned, either the result of the travelling, or of confronting James Martinez, or of the triple brandy she had drunk. Most likely all three. With one hand on each side of her skull, she pressed hard to stop it bursting open to relieve the pressure. The smell of fresh coffee from somewhere in the house tempted her to shuffle out of bed and, still groaning, head down to the kitchen, where Bob and Jack were seated at the table.

"Coffee and painkillers, in that order, please," she muttered as she joined them. No-one moved. She had closed her eyes as she sat but now opened them again. "What?"

Bob poured her a mugful. "Jack, get the painkillers, will you, son? I'll find some tranquillisers. She's going to need both."

She peered up at him. "Something to tell me?"

Jack reappeared and she swallowed the pills with the hot coffee, wincing as the liquid burned her throat. "OK. Out with it."

"It's not great news. Emer McCarthy Miller is known to have been in Ireland."

She nodded her head, carefully. "Does Zelah know?"

"Yes, she does. But that's not all. She was looking for information on ferries to Wales. We think she may be coming here."

"Before or after Cork?"

"We don't know that, either. She disappeared before the Gardai reached her."

"Great," Maggie muttered. "So what are we supposed to do here?"

"Be very, very careful. Keep all of the doors and windows locked and watch out for anyone unusual being around. We did manage to get some CCTV so at the moment she has short dark hair and looks to have put on a load of weight, but that's a disguise. Look, she's not subtle, that we know. She's unlikely to creep up on you. More likely to try to lure you somewhere. Just, watch out, OK?"

"OK. Well, I'm still going to Scotland this evening. Jack, do you want to come with me?"

"Um, no thanks. I'll be staying with Max and Joe until you get back. It's safe there."

Maggie looked at Bob, who nodded. "He'll be fine there. They can't go out for a couple of days, but they can get in a heap of supplies to keep them going. I'll stay here. And if anything breaks tomorrow, I'll make sure to keep you in the loop."

"Bob, who do you think is the most vulnerable, who she'd go for first?"

He sat back and folded his arms. "That's a good question. I still think it's Zelah and she'll be with you in Scotland. She's got the house at Rosscarbery well covered. There's a barbed wire fence been installed. And if it wasn't illegal, she'd have electrified it. She has extra security, night vision, everything. I don't think Emer will get close without alerting them."

"But it was her home. She knows the countryside well."

"Let's just get on with our lives," Jack said. "Whatever is going to happen, will be soon. The sooner the better, as far as I'm concerned." He stood up and left them.

"He's right," Maggie said. "We can't just sit here and wait. Right, time for a shower to hopefully give me some energy, then I'll speak to Zelah and Nick, before I book my flight." She paused for a moment. "Bob, when you said she might try to lure us in, what did you mean? How could she possibly do that?"

"I don't know. I'm mega-suspicious of anything unusual. I'm going to work now. They know about this and I've got plenty of leeway if anything needs following up. You go and get human. I'll see you later. I'm taking Jack down to the flat, and you to the airport. No arguments."

"None coming your way."

Maggie had hoped to begin some deeper investigation into the case involving the alleged Chartist rioter, but couldn't concentrate. Before starting she had arranged a quick teleconference with Zelah and Nick. Zelah would leave Cork at midday to fly to Edinburgh. She told Maggie she had booked a suite at a hotel with a sitting room as well as two bedrooms.

"We need somewhere to talk privately with Lolly and the so-called Brodie McAlister. He's mentioned a café, but I don't think that's good enough."

"Fine with me," Maggie said. "I'm knackered and if I don't have to leave the hotel, so much the better."

"I've asked Lolly to bring Mary McShane, if she wants to join in, which I suspect she will."

"Do you have a plan for how you're going to handle the conversation?" Nick asked.

"No," Zelah replied. "We should let him lead. He's the one with the information. We have the questions."

"I just hope he turns up," Maggie said.

"Well, if he doesn't, I hope he realises we'll hunt him down. We haven't come this far to be left at the altar now."

"Nick, what about you? What are you doing?" Maggie asked, ignoring wanting to tell Zelah she had no intention of staying in Scotland any longer than necessary and expected to be home on Thursday, with the case tied up, Brodie McAlister's appearance notwithstanding.

"Stella and I are keeping indoors," he replied. "But I'm worried about Max. I thought his mood might lift, now Helen Redland is out of his life but that's not happening. I'll go down to the flat to talk to him. He may not want to listen to me, but I have to keep trying."

"They're safe there. They have Joe keeping an eye on them."

Maggie and Zelah arranged to meet at the hotel later and the call ended. Being still too restless to concentrate on work, Maggie went into the garden with a notepad and pen and started on a list of questions for Brodie McAlister.

An hour later she had written a full page and was shocked when Bob arrived to take her to the airport. She rushed to pack a case for the two night stay and they headed off to Bristol.

On the journey she told him about Nick's ongoing concern for Max.

"I noticed he's been preoccupied. I'll drop by and have a word, too. Maybe it's because his part is done and he's wondering what to do with his life, now this chapter is ending."

"I hope so," Maggie replied, getting out of the car. "Keep an eye on Jack, too. Make sure he knows they are not to leave the flat. See you on Thursday."

**

Once the plane had taken off, Maggie slept, waking when the steward nudged her arm to ask her to put on her seat belt for landing. She had intended to call Jude from the airport, but there hadn't been enough time. Bob had given her a new phone and she had texted Jude the number. A quick text had told her friend about James Martinez and Jude assured Maggie she would make plans to be sure that, if he turned up, he would get neither information nor answers from Louise and Miguel. They had never heard of Judith Crawley Winters. Sarah Smith, lately arrived in the area, would not be mentioned.

She and Zelah dined on room service. Brodie McAlister had confirmed he would come to the hotel the following morning at ten. Mary McShane would most definitely be attending with Lolly. '*Wouldn't dream of missing it*', she had replied to the invitation. The scene was set. The following day should bring the final answers to Maggie's list of questions, and reveal the remaining history of the original Brodie McAlister.

Maggie slept surprising well, having put her worries about Emer McCarthy Miller aside. The main thing still troubling her, was Bob's statement about Emer luring someone to meet with her. She couldn't understand how it might happen, given everything they knew, but a niggling worm somewhere in her brain told her they had missed something. As she drifted off to sleep there was a small comment someone had said that didn't make sense, but tiredness got the better of her. She let herself sleep; she needed all of her energy to concentrate on the meeting tomorrow and whatever it was could wait until she was home again.

Chapter 50

"Oh, hell! What's she doing here?"

Zelah's voice travelled around the lobby and Lolly Sadler grimaced as she approached Maggie and Zelah in the foyer.

"Sorry," she muttered as she reached them. Mary McShane frowned and shook her head as the third member of the group scowled at Zelah.

"You must be Maggie Gilbert," Lolly said, holding out her hand. "Let me introduce you. Mary Cameron McShane, who knew both Brodie and Xandy Smith at the children's home." Mary held out her hand and Maggie took it with a smile. "And my sister, Michaela Wilson." Again Maggie held out her hand, but received nothing back. Lolly's sister kept a tight grip on her handbag, which she had raised up to her chest. They stood in silence, waiting for someone to break the ice.

"Why are you here, Mrs Wilson? You made it clear you wanted nothing to do with this family search." Zelah's tone was ominously gritted, but this time she kept her voice down.

Michaela Wilson sniffed. "I don't believe a word of this. You have set this up to embarrass my family. I knew you for what you are the minute I set eyes on you – a schemer, trying to take money from my sister." The woman had made no attempt to keep her voice low. As she spoke her eyes darted around the foyer and her lips pursed in triumph when she saw people had stopped to watch. "You are conducting what the newspapers call a scam. I am here to expose you. I have called the newspapers and I happen to know one of them is here already." Again she glanced around at her audience, and nodded.

"Oh God," Maggie muttered under her breath. Zelah had remained calm, which Maggie knew was not a good sign and an explosion of volcanic proportions might erupt any moment But that would cause even greater interest and if Brodie McAlister arrived right now, he would likely turn tail and run away. Maggie was about to try something soothing when Mary McShane, who had been standing behind the sisters, walked forward, preventing Maggie from stepping in by placing herself in front of Michaela Wilson, and banging her stick on the floor. Michaela Wilson, finding this unknown person standing well within her discomfort zone, tried to take a step back, but Lolly blocked her in.

"I know you, Michaela Wilson," Mary began in a low voice. A few of the onlookers tried to move forward to hear her, but a look from Zelah persuaded them to stay where they were.

"My husband, the late Ronald McShane – ah, I see you know his name, as do some of the people here, I can see from their raised eyebrows –once dealt with you, did he not? I was there, in the court. I heard the whole case and in my opinion you were lucky to get away with a fine. You are a nosy, troublemaking, vicious, interfering old hag. A hateful and hate filled woman. Zelah Trevear is the wife of a famous artist and with the wealth to blow you out of the water, which she will have no hesitation in doing and you will end up in court, yet again, I have no doubt. Now, get your nasty backside out of this hotel and do not come near these people again. What your sister now does with you is up to her."

Michaela Wilson had gone from angry red-faced to white and shaking. Whoever Ronald McShane was, the mention of his name had had the effect Mary intended. "Move. Now," Mary said.

The woman bit her lips, but turned to face Lolly. "You'll regret this."

"No, I will not. But you will, Michaela. Never come to my house again. As far as I am concerned, we may be sisters, but I don't want any contact with you. Ever."

Michaela's eyes widened. Lolly stood firm, unblinking. Maggie had moved around to the side and could see Michaela Wilson's hands were squeezing dents in her bag. She glanced around for some ally to come to her rescue, perhaps, Maggie thought, a member of the press she had contacted. No-one moved. They all looked away, as she caught each person's eye. She looked down at the floor, then, in a sudden, violent movement, pushed Lolly out of the way and ran towards and out of the hotel entrance.

After a few minutes' silence, people began to slip away, some muttering to each other.

"Come on, let's go up to the suite," Maggie said. "We need to get attention away from us, so Brodie McAlister won't be noticed when he arrives." She could see one woman still looking keenly at her. Was she the reporter? Maggie took Zelah by the arm and marched her towards the lifts, Lolly and Mary following.

Once they were in the lift, Lolly sagged against the wall. "I am so sorry—" she began. Zelah held up a hand. "No, don't apologise. Mary struck a fine blow." Turning to Mary she said, "I don't know who your husband was, but I'm guessing a judge?" Mary nodded. "And a well-known one at that," Zelah added. Again, Mary nodded.

"What did she do?" Maggie couldn't help asking.

"I don't know," Lolly replied in a high, unsteady voice, shaking her head. "That's the first I've heard about whatever it was. I always thought her so upright and moral. I don't know what came over her."

"It doesn't matter," Mary said firmly. "I'll tell you later," she added to Lolly, to Maggie's disappointment. She made a mental note to search for a public account when she was home.

They reached the suite and flopped down into the settees and armchairs. Maggie made cups of tea and coffee and handed round the pastries supplied by the hotel, all eaten and drunk in silence.

After five minutes Zelah said, "Right, Maggie has a list of questions, but my suggestion is we just ask him for the story, then let him talk. Agreed?" They all nodded. As she finished speaking there were three sharp raps on the door. "Are we ready?" Again, nods all round. "I'll let him in, then."

Maggie thought she had had no preconceptions of what he might look like, but the man in the doorway was nothing like she could have imagined. Having seen the photo of the original Brodie as a young adult, she could see no resemblance and wondered if he could be who he was claiming to be, or was this a trick of some devious kind.

Zelah ushered him in, gave him a cup of coffee as he sat perched on the edge of a seat, politely nodding at Maggie and Zelah as they were introduced.

"We thought you might like to start by telling us—" Zelah began but Maggie, who had been digging into her briefcase, interrupted her.

"I thought you might like to see this," she said, sliding across the table the photograph taken of Brodie McAlister in Spain, leaning against a tree, with his beret sat slanting on his head. As the man took it and gazed at it, he smiled. Then Maggie knew.

Chapter 51

"Mr McAlister, you can keep that, if you would like it."

He looked up at her. "I would love that, thank you, Maggie. I have nothing of him at this age. I have a few photos of his army days, but nothing from Spain. He was so young, wasn't he?"

"He lied about his age," Maggie replied. The man nodded. "And his name," he added. "He told me everything on his deathbed. I think this is what you all want to know?"

"Please, Brodie," Lolly said. "We've brought what little we have. Mary can tell you about the orphanage and the fight with David Laird. I have Helen's postcard and a copy of the letter written by her sister Julie and Maggie and Zelah have the outcome of their research. So, would you like to begin? Perhaps you can tell us how you came to know your dad wasn't who he pretended to be?"

He coughed, put down the photograph and nodded.

"I found out in the final days of his life. Until then, I had no idea. He had a birth certificate, you see, the original for Lewis Edward McAlister in 1913."

"Original?" Zelah asked.

"Yes. I'll get to that."

Zelah nodded and sat back.

"I'm thinking you all know about the murder of Grace McAlister by her husband and what happened to the five children? Of course you do. Well, my dad, Brodie, was the youngest and he went into a children's home with his sisters Helen and Julie. Do I need to tell you about his time there?"

"No, you don't," Lolly said, reaching out and putting a hand on his arm. "We know all we need to know from Mary, and she has more she can tell you"

"Thank you. When David Laird died, Brodie ran, to Helen. He stayed with her and James and Julie for several weeks, a couple of times just avoiding being caught by the police who guessed he would have gone there and came back a number of times in the hope of finding him. But, it wasn't long before Helen accepted he couldn't stay there forever. One night, whilst he walked around the town to avoid the police, he was freezing cold – all this happened in December '37 –he saw a light in a building and walked in. It was a recruiting meeting for Spain. There were just a handful of listeners, but it was warm and they offered him tea and biscuits, so he stayed. He watched the film, listened to the speaker. He became convinced the Republic was on the point of victory. Another young lad there was equally enthused and together they decided to sign up and go down to London. When he got back and told Helen and James and Julie, they were horrified, but they couldn't dissuade him. He had to be in London for the first week of January, so after Christmas and the New Year, Julie travelled with him and the other lad to London. They were given identity papers, told the drill, and a couple of days later they set off with a group of men, all purporting to be going to Paris for a wild weekend." He stopped, put his hand inside his jacket and pulled out an envelope. "This is the diary he wrote, which he did for Helen and Julie. He knew they were working to exonerate him from blame. He thought they would want to know what he had been doing in Spain. You're all welcome to read it. But I have to tell you, it doesn't make easy reading."

"He went to Spain at a time when the Republic was losing its fight against the Fascists," Maggie said.

Brodie nodded. "You see, what he found when he got there, after a horrendous journey over the mountains in freezing cold and snow, was not what he had expected. They were given some training, and then sent into battle within a couple of weeks. He found himself in close fighting with Fascist troops, the majority Germans and Italians. Some of what he saw scarred him for life. But there were some positives, the best part being, he felt like he had a family. The men and women of the International Brigade all looked after each other. Brits, Americans, Canadians, others from around the world. They educated him too, in politics, and in Communism, but the context was different then. As time went on he saw some of the friends he made wounded or killed. Others deserted, including the lad he had travelled with. He had one friend he stuck with, called Harry, from London."

"Harry Summers," Maggie said.

"Yes. He gave the diary to Harry, and the postcard. So, when the Spanish Prime Minister decided to send the international troops home, Dad decided he had to return to Scotland. But he was terrified. He hadn't heard from Helen or Julie. He didn't know what had happened to the case against him. He still believed he had killed David Laird and would hang for it, like his father before him. The night before he and Harry were due to leave Barcelona to make their way through France and back to England, he gave the diary and the postcard to Harry, asked him to post the card and, when it was safe, send the diary to Helen. Then, he sneaked off and returned to the village where the Brigaders had been stationed, a town called La Fatarella."

He stopped and took a deep draught of water and drew in a breath. "He had picked up a few words of the Catalan language. There were a few others who had stayed on, Germans and Italians and a few others for whom it would have been certain death to try to return to their own countries. They were preparing for the final battle of the Ebro. Do you know the story?"

"Yes," Lolly said. "I've been reading up on it. The main army needed to get back across the river, up at Flix, around twenty-five miles away, but the Fascist army advanced fast. There were around a thousand fighters, called the fifteenth International Brigade, but the majority were local men and boys, who dug into trenches above La Fatarella to hold off Franco's troops and allow the main army of around twenty-five thousand to cross the river into safer territory."

Maggie took over. "Yes. It was suicide. They knew they'd be outnumbered and overwhelmed, but they fought with everything they had to delay the Fascists and they succeeded, though about five hundred of them died. We learned in Spain that most of those are still in the trenches on the facing ridge from where the skeleton called 'Charlie' was found." She paused, shook her head.

"My father was there," Brodie said. "He saw a man who had, in the weeks of his return, come to be his friend and father-figure, blown up by a grenade and die. That may have even been Charlie, but we'll never know. Then he was shot, up on the ridge, by a German soldier and he passed out, his last thought being he had reached his time to die, too. But, he didn't. Someone found him barely breathing, and took him to the village. A family, headed by an old lady, hid him and cared for him, until he could leave, in January 1939. He got back to England, sick and in a bad way with pneumonia, but he had reached home. If I knew who they were, I would go there and get down on my knees and thank them myself. But, too late now."

"It's not too late, Brodie. We were there last week. We know who they are."

Chapter 52

"My colleague and I travelled to Catalonia last week," Maggie said. "We met the son of the man, or rather the boy, who found Brodie and took him back to his own mother. You know, officially, he's buried in the cemetery there, under the name of her eldest son, who had gone missing in action and was never found."

"He was never able to thank them," Brodie said. "He collapsed in London and spent months in hospital, almost died again. He reckoned he led a charmed life."

"Why couldn't he thank them himself?" Zelah asked.

"Because he could barely remember what had happened, or where he had been. Of course, you'll know it wasn't safe for any Brigader to go back to Spain until after Franco died. The man's determination on vengeance lasted throughout his vile life."

Maggie nodded. "We had a similar case a couple of years ago. Our man didn't go back for more than forty years, and when he did, he found it all too emotional."

"So what happened after he recovered?" Zelah asked.

"He had nowhere to go, except back to Scotland, which was too frightening for him. He was homeless for a couple of months, in London, a terrible experience, so much so he decided to take a risk and find out what had happened to his family. He went back to Glasgow to find his two older brothers, Malcolm and Lewis." He stopped and his shoulders sagged. "He desperately wanted to see Helen and Julie, but after watching and seeing a police visit to Helen's house, thought it was still too dangerous, for them and for him. Anyway, he couldn't find Malcolm. So, he looked for Lewis. That's when he found out Lewis was dead. He had died in 1936, a homeless drunk, killed in a knife fight in Glasgow, at the age of twenty-three. No-one had even tried to find any family. They must have presumed he didn't have any. They buried him in a pauper's grave, unmarked. My father said it was the first time he cried."

Again he paused, taking another drink, with shaking hands.

"He was lost, thought this was the end. He didn't know what to do or where to go. There was just one choice. Helen's home. He went there and staked it out, but found the place empty. He was dismayed, thinking they might have moved, but by a stroke of luck, overheard neighbours talking and realised they were away on a holiday, Helen and James, and Julie with them. So, he broke in. He stayed there for two days, exploring the house, looking for ideas about what he could do. In the study he found a box of family papers, including all of the McAlister's birth, marriage and death certificates which didn't include Lewis's death. And it came to him that if they didn't know Lewis was dead, if no-one knew, then could he become Lewis? He felt sure his brother wouldn't have minded. He remembered Lewis as a gentle soul, in no way capable of coping with being put out of his family home. I'm thinking when Helen left the orphanage, she would have looked for Lewis, but had not found him. So he took the birth certificate, returned the house as he'd found it, and he told me, with an aching heart and tears, he left them and Scotland."

Maggie could see a glistening in his eyes. "Do you want to stop, Brodie?"

"No. I need to tell you everything. I've been carrying this for too many years. He made his way back to London, found a job in a kitchen, and when war was declared, in 1939, he saw his way forward. He signed up, went into the army and stayed there for the next fifteen years. He got through the war unscathed. That McAlister luck again." He smiled.

"Anyway, he was stationed in Germany for most of the time, then the Far East. He left the army in the mid-1950s. He decided he could risk coming back home. He'd gone to find Harry Summers on one of his home leave periods, only to discover Harry had been killed on the Normandy beaches in '44. But he did get back his diary, and because Harry hadn't had chance to send it on, he realised Helen and Julie didn't know what had happened to him. That was when he made another fateful decision. He would not find them to tell them he had survived, in case he compromised them with the law. I need a quick break."

They had been so mesmerised listening to Brodie's story it took a second to take in what had asked for. Maggie jumped up first. "Of course. What would you like?" She glanced at her watch. "Wow, it's almost midday. Should we have something to eat? We can organise some sandwiches, or something, couldn't we Zelah?"

"Already done," Zelah replied. "I guessed this would take some time. It should be here any minute. Brodie, I assumed you'd like something?"

He nodded. "I'm not expected home. Where's the bathroom?"

Maggie pointed him to a door to the immediate right of the entrance. Once he was out of the room Mary sat back in her chair. "There's something else, you know. Something important to come."

"What makes you say that?" Lolly asked.

"A combination of instinct and observing men over a long lifetime. There's just a slight hesitancy. He's working up to something."

A knock on the door announced the arrival of the room service lunch and as Brodie returned from the bathroom they helped themselves and chatted. Mary wanted to talk about the children's home, but Maggie saw Brodie make a quick reply, then move to speak to Lolly. '*Mary's right,* 'she thought. He's avoiding her. '*Let's hope whatever it is, he's going to tell us'*.

Once they were all done, Zelah asked if he was ready to carry on and Brodie nodded. "Almost done now, but something important you need to know." Mary raised her eyebrows, but kept silent.

"Dad left the army in the mid-fifties. He had no home to return to, so he set himself up first in London, then, when he felt more comfortable, he moved up to Glasgow. He had trained as an engineer in the army and made a career for himself. Something happened then and he couldn't bear being in the UK any longer so in the early '60s he emigrated to Australia. He met my Mum and they had me. No more children, and I've always suspected I was an unexpected accident. Before you ask me, I don't know if my mother knew about his real identity. He was married in the name of Lewis Edward McAlister and he had the birth certificate to prove it. Mum died in the late nineties, so I couldn't ask her.

"I was in my thirties by this time, still single and living at home. When he told me after her funeral he wanted to return to Scotland, I'll admit I was shocked. We'd always believed him to be an only child with no other living relatives, who'd lost his parents at a young age, so I couldn't understand why, at his age, after such a settled life in Oz, he wanted to leave. Well, whatever, I agreed to come with him. We came back to Edinburgh in 2001. I thought he was eighty-eight, but now I know he was eighty-one. Explains why he was so sprightly for his age." He stopped, laughed abruptly and shook his head.

"He began to look for family members. That's when he found out Julie had gone to Canada, but Helen was still alive. She was eighty-six. Her Jimmy had died. Did he tell her who he was? Yes, I think he did. I have a photo I've brought with me. Take a look at this." From his jacket pocket he extracted a picture of two elderly people, sitting side by side, arm in arm, with the sea in the background. When they had all taken a look he turned it over. The caption on the back said, "*Me and my wee brother Lewis.*"

"But it should have been 'big brother 'shouldn't it?" Lolly asked.

"Maybe," he replied. "A slip, perhaps? Who knows. Helen died the following year."

"I remember her," Lolly said. "But I don't remember her brother at all. There was Malcolm, but he was quite snotty.

He didn't want to be involved with the family. I never understand why back then, but I do now."

"Helen knew Dad was Brodie, but they decided to keep up the pretence. Let's sleeping dogs lie, as the saying goes. Officially he was still wanted for unlawful killing."

"That would be why she never introduced him to us. I don't think my Mum met him, either, or if she did, she never said. Poor Grandma. She must have been so pleased to have him back, but couldn't tell anyone who he was."

"Indeed. Anyway, dad died in 2011. We thought he was an amazing ninety-eight, but in reality was ninety-one. But he was still a spritely old boy right up to his death, from liver cancer. It was a struggle for him, but he told me his story." He took a breath, his eyes closed. "I can tell you I've never had such a shock. And for a while I was angry with him."

"It must have been difficult for you," Lolly said. She put a hand on his arm. "I for one am so glad we've found each other at last, and we know about Julie, now. Her family is waiting on news, too."

"But there's more, isn't there," Mary said.

He nodded. "When he had settled down in Edinburgh he started going out at night. Wouldn't tell me anything about where or why. I got the impression there was something, or someone, he was looking for. He finally told me at the end." He turned to Mary. "It was about the orphanage, but not what you think."

"Was it about … her?"

"Yes. At this point I must ask you… do you want to know how this ends?"

"Of course," Mary replied. The others glanced at each other, puzzled, then Maggie, realising what and who they were talking about said "It's the nun, isn't it? Sister Mary Veronica."

Brodie nodded.

"Oh, God," Maggie muttered. "She died in a hit-and-run accident in the mid-nineteen fifties. Are you going to say he was at the wheel? That he killed her?"

Mary held up her hand. "I think I know the answer to that question. It's '*no*', isn't it?"

Brodie nodded. "But Sister Mary Veronica was indeed murdered, with deliberation and planning, by Xandy. Alexander Smith."

Chapter 53

"No! I guessed that's what you were going to say, but it couldn't have been deliberate." Mary would have jumped up out of her chair if her hips had allowed. Instead she sat up and shook a fist at him.

"I'm sorry," he said. His shoulders sagged and he looked at her with defeat on his face. "But it's true. Dad told me what happened when he found Xandy, who turned out to be the reason for his secret night-time wanderings around the streets, when we relocated here. He knew, you see, and he wanted to be sure Xandy was protected."

"Please continue," Zelah said, somewhat frostily. "I would like to know why the man whose fees I am paying at an expensive care home should not be turned over to the police."

Brodie jerked up, squaring up to her. "Dad found out after he left the army in the fifties and it's the reason he went to Australia. He wanted to know what had happened with the orphanage. He never said this, but I think if Xandy hadn't already done it, Dad would have. The way he spoke about her …" his voice dripped with anger and contempt. He looked across at Mary. "He knew you were OK, you'd married a young lawyer. He checked up on a couple of the others. He wanted to do something, you see. Expose the woman in some way. He was stunned when he found she'd been killed in a hit-and-run. So, he did some investigating. He knew the police would know little about her time at the orphanage, in the way he'd know, so he guessed it might have been someone who'd been subjected to her vile attention. He asked around."

"He didn't ask me," Mary interrupted.

"I can't tell you why not, because I don't know. What he did discover was, after Dad left, she was frenzied and took it out on particular victims, Xandy being top of the list. Did you know that? Did you do anything about it?" he shot at Mary.

She shook her head. "A relative came to take me away a couple of months after you left. I didn't keep up with any of the children. I was too ashamed." Lolly put a hand on her arm and felt it shaking and trembling.

"I think we should stop for a while," she said gently.

"No," Mary said. "I will need to go soon, but I want to hear the end of this story."

Brodie shrugged. "I'll make it as quick as I can. When Dad found Xandy he was already in a bad way. He'd been released from the home into the world, totally on his own, at seventeen, in 1948. Things had been hard after the war. There wasn't decent work about and Xandy fell into bad company. He spent some time in jail on and off over the next eight years. The final time he was released, in 1955 he had nowhere to go, again. He was back on the streets in Glasgow, living rough. One day, he was begging at the station and he saw her, with a crowd of well-wishers. She saw him but she didn't recognise him. Just another disgusting worthless beggar, to her." He broke off and looked at Zelah. "Did you know the church planned to give her some kind of special recognition for her work with vulnerable children?"

"No, and the thought makes me sick."

"It made Xandy sick, too, when he worked it out. She was on her way to Edinburgh to meet with the archbishop. He decided there and then she would never, ever get a reward and began to plan. He took his time, stalked her for a while, got to know her movements. He discovered that, once a week on a Wednesday evening, she went to visit a friend, another retired nun. It was late in the year and the nights were dark. On the evening in question it was also raining so no moonlight. During the day he stole a car, and waited close to the friend's house. She went in at her usual time. She always retraced her route home. He picked out the darkest and least populated spot on the route, followed her and ran her down. He told Dad he had no hesitation and no regrets. But, and of course there is a 'but', afterwards, when it was confirmed she was dead, it affected him. He had killed, crossed a line. He sank into depression and, inevitably, mental illness. When dad found him he was in an asylum. Do you know what those places were like back then?"

A groan from Mary stopped him. "Aye. I do. He wasn't the only one of the orphanage's inmates ended up in such a place."

Brodie smiled. "Dad managed to get him out. Found him somewhere to live and gave him some money. Back then, such a broken man had no help. He just had to manage himself. Then Dad went away. He'd had enough, needed to leave Scotland and the terrible memories. He spent the following forty-five years in Australia. That's where I was born. As I said, we came back after Mum died. By that time, the enquiry had begun. Dad knew he couldn't give evidence but he was determined to make sure Xandy, if he had survived, was OK. When he found Xandy he was in his seventies, wandering in his mind and barely capable of dressing and feeding himself. Dad pushed social services to get him into a home. It wasn't too bad, that first one. Dad visited him regularly. He still never told me anything about his past and I still thought he was Lewis. Then, in 2011 his cancer was diagnosed, end stage. He died six weeks later, but not before he told me his story. It took me a while to come to terms with everything he had told me. I had to bury him as Lewis Edward McAlister."

"Do you want to change that?" Maggie asked. "I don't know if it's possible, but we could find out, if you wanted to."

"No," he replied. "It would only cause trouble now. I'm ashamed to say I ignored Xandy for several years. I kept reading in the papers about the enquiry and I began to feel great anger, but I didn't know what to do. Until last year." He gave them a blissful smile. "I met a woman, a wonderful woman and we married. I told her my dad's story and she encouraged me to look for Xandy. We both suspected he had died, so I was amazed to find him in the home a few months ago." He turned again to Zelah. "I've been appalled at the place, but I didn't have the money to move him. I think I've been a thorn in the flesh of the manager of that previous place. They weren't even keeping him clean. Morag and I have supplied clothes, fruit – that's where the grapes come into it – and tried to visit him regularly. It was one hell of a shock this week when I turned up to find his room empty. I hadn't been able to go for months until the Covid restrictions were slightly relaxed. Not one of them even stopped me to tell me he had moved. I really thought he had died this time." He shivered. "I went charging off to the manager's office and yelled quite a bit. She told me he had moved and when she gave me the name of the new place, I was so puzzled. Then I went along there and met all of you. And that's it. You're up to date." He sat back in his armchair.

Chapter 54

No-one spoke as they each in their own way absorbed the story and its implications.

"So, Mrs Trevear, do you want to stop paying fees, now you know he killed the nun?" Brodie asked, gently biting his lip.

Zelah didn't reply. She glanced at the others, frowning, indecisive. She poured herself a glass of water and took a prolonged sip then asked, "Apart from us, who knows, or suspects him?"

"As far as I am aware, no-one, just me and Morag. Now, it's all of you."

"I have a question," Mary said. "How much does he remember?"

"I am quite certain he remembers none of it," Brodie answered. "His memory is poor, as is his health, you must have realised. Did they tell you he has prostate cancer?"

"Yes," Zelah replied, "although I didn't realise how close to the end he is."

"He has a Do Not Resuscitate order, which I hope has been passed on, but nothing would surprise me with that former place. Anyhow, it won't be long. Weeks, if that."

"We had to organise a Covid test before the new home would admit him," Mary said. "They're scrupulously strict. I have regular tests myself. They made an exception for me to visit him with Lolly, because of the cancer and his extreme state. He's going to die in comfort and contentment, thanks to Zelah."

As they each turned to her, Zelah said, "I want a solemn promise, a vow, that what we have learned here today never leaves this room. If that's agreed, I'll pay the fees and nothing of what he did will ever, ever be disclosed."

One by one they nodded.

"Do you have any more questions for me?" Brodie asked.

"Hundreds," Lolly said, "all of which can wait. I'd like to meet your wife, if that's OK. We're family now. And that includes you, Mary, if you'd like."

"I would, very much. But now, I'm finished for today. I need to get back to my nice home and my comfortable space and my bed." She stood up and Lolly went to help her. "No, no. I can manage. All of you listen – I may not be here for long, either. So, in case we five are never together again, I thank you all. You've done the right thing, Zelah Trevear. From what you've told me of your late husband, I believe he would have approved. Brodie, I hope we can meet again, because your dad was special to me. But, we'll see what the future holds. Lolly, I'd like to go now." She picked up her sticks and headed for the door. Brodie said a quick goodbye to Zelah and Maggie and followed them out.

Zelah flopped back onto the settee. "Another case over and done."

"Yes, that was quite something, wasn't it? I had another question but in the end I couldn't remember what it was. I expect when it comes back to me I can—"

"Damn," Zelah shouted, jumping up and running to the door. She returned ten minutes later, came back panting and grinning, holding up a notebook.

"The diary," she said. "Can't believe I forgot to ask. I've promised to take the best care of it and return it via Lolly, before we leave in the morning. Do you want to read it first?"

"Yes, please," Maggie said. She went into her bag and produced a set of gloves, took the book from Zelah and sat at the desk.

Zelah decided to call Nick to update him. As Maggie read and added the occasional comment, Zelah took Nick through the story.

"Amazing," he said. "I admit, I thought he had died in Spain and at best we'd find out how and when."

"Indeed," Zelah replied. "Any news at your end?"

"Nothing. I'm going down to the flat soon, to visit the boys, make sure they're behaving themselves and I'll check if they've run out of beer yet."

When the call finished Zelah got out her laptop and joined Maggie on the opposite side of the desk. "I'll start writing this up. You'll have to read it later and fill in the bits I've missed. Maggie? Did you hear that?"

"Sorry, sort of. This is fascinating. For a boy who grew up in a children's home without a decent education to prepare him for the world, he has an engaging writing style. I wonder if Brodie will ever publish it, or if not, give it to the Trust?"

"I don't see how he can do either," Zelah replied. "Too much deceit."

"Well, perhaps he'll find a way, one day. What did Nick say about the boys?"

"He's on his way to see them now. He thinks they're OK. He sounded fed up. This sitting around waiting isn't doing anyone any good."

"No, but there's nothing else we can do. Everyone just has to keep to the plan and smother their impatience. What time is our flight?"

"Six thirty. We have to be at the airport at five."

"Ugh. Enough of these early starts and late finishes. I'll be glad to get home."

Zelah sighed and nodded, secretly wondering who would be the first to break, if this went on any longer. The answer was closer than she could have imagined.

Chapter 55

Just before six the following morning they sat waiting for the flight to be called, each deep in thought. Having read the diary twice over, Maggie was torn. She had questions, one in particular, but they arose out of personal interest, not because of an answer required for the case notes.

Zelah had also read it through and made a copy, which she didn't reveal to either Maggie or Brodie, then arranged a courier to return the original to Lolly, the previous evening. As far as she was concerned, the case had resolved and it was time to move onto others that had come in over the past few days, which Nick had put into a holding file to await their return.

"What did you make of the end section?" Zelah said to Maggie who had closed her eyes and appeared to be asleep, giving her a nudge with her elbow. "The piece he must have written when he retrieved the diary in the 50s."

Maggie knew what she meant, but wasn't ready to talk about it yet. She needed to speak to Jude first. Then, it might make sense; or not.

Fortunately, the flight was called and she jumped up. "Come on, let's go."

"You weren't asleep at all," Zelah grumbled.

"We can talk about it later. I had nodded off, and I intend to sleep on the flight. When we're back in the office, OK?" She walked off, giving Zelah no time to argue.

**

Back in Cardiff they split up. Bob should have been there to pick Maggie up, but as she entered the terminal building a text arrived, telling her he had been held up and had arranged a car for her. Zelah had parked her own car in the long-term parking facility. They agreed to meet at the office once Zelah had reached home, unpacked and dealt with whatever personal issues awaited her.

Bob had switched off his phone. He didn't often do this when it was important for them to keep in close contact, but Maggie knew he would only have done so if something crucial meant he couldn't answer a call. Certain he would have told her if whatever it was was related to Emer McCarthy Miller, she relaxed and fell asleep again.

She arrived home just after nine, to an empty house. This was not unexpected, Bob being out of contact and Jack at the flat in Newport with Joe and Max. There was also no message from Nick, who was normally precise about informing her of his whereabouts, if they were relevant to Maze, what he was doing and when he was doing it. Again, she had no premonition of anything troubling. Zelah expected to arrive around eleven. Presumably, Nick would turn up and they could have a quick discussion to agree the final points of the case so Zelah could begin the final report.

But by eleven, there were no messages and no arrivals. And she couldn't reach any of them, by phone or internet messaging.

At midday Maggie had paced around the house a dozen times, not sure what to do next. Go to Zelah's flat? Drive over to the Manor in case Nick and Stella were there? Go down to the flat in Newport, check on Jack and Max? She ruled out the latter. She had already put herself in the firing line with Jack for being too protective. Yet, something wasn't right. She decided to go the Manor, just a five minute drive away. But the staff told her Nick and Stella had been there earlier, had received a phone call and left immediately.

"How did they seem?" she asked.

"Um, I'd say, concerned, just a bit," the receptionist replied.

"Did they say where they were going, or when they might be back, or why they were going?"

"No, they just both stood up and walked out. It is odd, now you ask."

Maggie shook her head and smiled. "Don't worry about it. It will be something about a case we're investigating at the moment. Some client demanding immediate attention." This didn't explain why Stella had gone with Nick, but she decided not to elaborate.

Back in her car the next visit would be the boys' flat. She didn't care now if she annoyed Jack.

She had just started to pull out of the car park when her phone rang. She didn't recognise the number, but under the circumstances, decided to stop and answer it.

"Hello, Maggie Gilbert speaking."

"Well, hello, Maggie Gilbert. I've been looking forward to speaking to you." The voice had a soft, lilting Irish accent.

Maggie took a deep breath to try to calm her rising panic. "Emer. Well I haven't been looking forward to speaking to you, but I suppose it has been inevitable. What do you want?"

"I want you to come to me. I'm going to give you instructions now. You must follow them."

"Why must I, Emer?"

"Oh, because you'll want to join our little group, here. There's your friends, Zelah and Nick and Nick's lovely fiancée. And there's Max, of course. And your son Jack. They're all longing to see you."

Maggie froze.

"Good, no pointless comments. Now, drive down towards Newport. Then up towards the Cathedral. Stop in a parking space. I'll know when you're there. And Maggie … don't try to call anyone, because I'll know. And I will shoot someone, a random pick. Anyway, that policeman of yours is off on a wild goose chase. He's no use to you." She laughed and the phone clicked.

Maggie got out of the car and walked around the car park, struggling to process what she'd heard. Of course her immediate instinct was to call Bob, to leave a desperate message. But Emer had said she would know. How would she know? How would she know when Maggie reached St Woolos? Was there someone else involved, who might follow her, watching her even now? She spun around, peering into the bushes and trees bordering the river and the Manor land. No-one appeared to be about, but how could she tell? No, she had to follow Emer's orders. Getting back into the car, gripping the steering wheel in a white-knuckle stranglehold, she set off.

Fifteen minutes later she reached the Cathedral and found a parking space. Another ten minutes passed. No call. She tried to hold herself tight, but her body kept breaking out into shakes. She tried to slow her breathing down, knowing she was on the point of hyperventilating, as the sound of her heartbeat thrashed in her ears. Then, the phone rang.

"What now?"

"Now just remain calm, Maggie. We haven't done it … yet."

We? What did 'we' mean? "Tell me where to go next."

"Get out of the car, and walk up to the top of the road. I think you know where you're going now, don't you?"

"The Quinn house?"

"Ten out of ten. See you in a minute. Don't take any longer, mind. Run if you have to."

She thought about something to use as a weapon, but nothing came to mind. Nothing that would counter a gun or whatever firearm Emer had. She set off at a fast pace, and broke into a run as she reached the main road. Not bothering with the crossing a hundred yards away, she dashed across the busy road, being narrowly missed by a car driven by an elderly woman who had to slam on brakes with all her might and was now likely having a heart attack, but she couldn't worry about that. Out of breath and with shaking hands Maggie dashed up the steps and pounded on the door. It was flung open, but not by Emer McCarthy Miller.

Max Howell grabbed her with one hand by the shoulder, the other hand by the hair and dragged her down the hall and into the office, where he threw her down onto the carpet. She looked up at him, in amazement, to find he had gone to stand beside Emer, who gave him a pat on the back.

"Well done, my gorgeous boy. Another one bites the dust," she said, waving not a gun but a vicious looking curved knife.

They both laughed as Maggie stood up, glanced at Zelah, Nick, Stella and Jack. Their faces were a mixture of anger and fear. The worst of all was Nick, who glared at his son with ferocious contempt. He moved forward and helped Maggie to her feet.

"It's been him all along," he said. "He's been working with her. He's had us fooled. All of us."

Chapter 56

"I don't believe it," Maggie said. "We know him now. He wouldn't have done this to us."

Emer strolled up to her, put her head to one side and observed Maggie, who stood as upright as she could despite the pain in her head from the roots Max had pulled out.

"You … know nothing." Before Maggie could think of defending herself Emer raised her free fist and punched it into Maggie's face. "Don't speak to me like that," she whispered at Maggie, who had sunk to her knees.

Maggie's head was ringing and she felt Jack move beside her. She pushed him away. "Don't give her the satisfaction. What do you want, Emer?" It cost her a lot to speak as she felt sure her head had caught fire.

"Want? From you? Nothing. You have nothing of value to give me. I'll enjoy watching you watching me hurt your son, though. In fact, I'll start now." She moved forward, raising the knife but Max caught her free arm.

"No; you promised me I could go first."

Emer paused, nodded. "Yes, my love, I did. And I shall keep my promise. Off you go." She nudged him towards Nick. Stella stepped between them. "You'll have to hurt me first, Max."

"Is it a problem for you, my love?"

"No, not at all," he said and glanced at her, smiling.

Maggie was about to shout out, but stopped. Something wasn't right. He had smiled, but it seemed to be an effort.

Then, it slipped. She stared in astonishment. The loving gaze had changed when Emer looked away. This wasn't love Maggie saw, it was disgust. Bob had taught her well as she recognised the flash of expression. And Max knew she seen it.

'*This is not what we think it is*' went through Maggie's head. But how to intervene? How to stop it? The answer came, not from her, but from a knock at the front door. They all jumped as a voice shouted through the letterbox, "Hello, security. Is there someone in there?"

Emer turned to Max and hissed, "I told you to make sure they were cancelled."

"I thought you were doing it," he countered. They were both momentarily distracted by a snort from Zelah, whose mouth had opened to make a comment, until Maggie stepped backwards onto her foot. She turned her head a fraction and muttered, "Shut up."

"I'll deal with them," Max said. "They know me. Just keep this lot quiet." Emer nodded and he left the room. The silence was intense. Emer grinned at all of them, the knife dangling from her hand. Then came the sound of a door slamming followed by Max returning to the room.

"All OK," he said. "They're just going to take a look around the back, make sure no-one's been there. We need to keep quiet for a couple of minutes." Stella went to speak, but again Maggie intervened, making a groaning noise and holding her face. After a few minutes Emer said, "Right, they'll have gone by now. All of you, move over there." She indicated the fireplace and they shuffled over. Max watched

Maggie intently, she thought trying to convey something. Delaying tactics needed.

"How did you find him, Emer? How long have you two been working together? What about Helen? Did you kill her?"

"Well, that idiot," she indicated Nick, "just sat waiting for him to turn up. I knew he had a son, so I tracked him down." She reached out and stroked his head. "We planned to take over Kennet Quinn's business and once I knew Helen was trying to do the same, I stepped in. It was so easy."

"You didn't answer my question. Did you kill Helen?"

"No, that wasn't me." She said with a loud theatrical sigh. "I told her to wait, but she had to just ignore me and go her own way. Much good it did her."

"So, tell us all, please why are we here? What do you want? Is it money?"

"Of course it's money. And revenge. For my mammy and grandpa." She waved the knife at Zelah. "She killed them."

"No, I did not," Zelah said, firmly, for the sake of her friends who remained in ignorance of her past acts. "Your mother died in prison, as did your grandfather, who had a heart attack. Maggie will tell you. She was there when it happened."

"Well, I didn't know that. But it doesn't change the fact mammy was in the madhouse because of you. We were doing fine, until you spoiled it. You must pay. What was that?" She whipped her head around to the door.

"What?" Max asked.

"A noise. I heard a noise. Did you not hear it?"

"No," he replied.

"Go and check. Open the door. I heard something."

Max strolled over to the door, seized the handle and pulled it open. He glanced out. "There's no-one here, Emer. See." He pulled the door wide and stood aside to show the empty corridor.

"I'll look for myself," she said, starting to move forward.

Max blocked her way, grabbing her arm, giving her a patronising grin. "There's no-one there. Are you getting nervous?"

She halted abruptly. "I am never nervous. You know that." She glanced over at them again, as Max appeared to close the door, but left a tiniest gap open. '*Well done*', Maggie thought. '*You know how to play her, or I hope for all our sakes that is what you're really doing.*' She gave Max a tiny nod.

"Now, about the money," she went on, trying to ensure Emer's attention focussed on her and not on the door. "What if Zelah were to give you what you want. Would you be prepared to leave us all alone?"

Emer frowned. "I might."

"Of course she won't," Zelah snapped.

"Just shut up and listen," Maggie snapped back. "Give her a chance to explain."

Zelah stared at Maggie with undisguised contempt, as Maggie walked away from the fireplace towards the window, causing Emer to turn to watch her. "Go on then, explain what you might do, Emer. I'm listening."

"You are odd, Maggie Gilbert. I tried to kill your man, I thought I'd shot him in the heart, and here you are being reasonable with me. Now, why would that be?"

"To get us out of here and away from you and I hope if you get what you want, we'll be OK. Works for all of us, doesn't it?"

Emer opened her mouth to answer, but Maggie didn't find out whatever Emer was about to say.

The door burst open, with a flash of light and a crashing bang so loud everyone grabbed their head. Emer's eyes opened wide, realising in the instant she had been betrayed, then screamed a high pitch cream of agony and collapsed on the floor.

Then the room filled with police officers, screaming at all of them to get down and stay down. They surrounded Emer's prostrate form and one knelt over her. Maggie couldn't see what they were doing, but Emer wasn't moving. Someone shook Maggie's arm and, still unable to hear anything, she looked away to shake them off, to find Bob staring at her, mouthing something and gesticulating. She waved her arms and her head, trying to explain she couldn't hear him, but as she did so the room began to return to a sharper focus and she could make out voices.

"What have you done?" she mouthed. "Is she dead?"

Bob shook his head and shouted back," Tasered. Sorry about the flashbang. It was just a minor one, to cause a disruption so we could safely neutralise her."

The others were being shepherded out of the room, except for Zelah who had broken away from the policeman trying to guide her, and walked over to Emer's body. She stood contemplating for a moment, then gave Emer a kick. Emer groaned.

"Not dead," Zelah said. "Pity," and she turned and left the room.

"Come on," Bob said, again taking hold of Maggie's arm. This time she let him guide her out of the study and into the sitting room, where Nick, Stella, Zelah and Jack were all sitting, looking disoriented and, in Jack's case green-faced. Maggie went to sit beside him and enveloped him in a shoulder crushing hug. This time he didn't object.

Max was there too, not sitting, but standing in front of the fireplace. Bob walked over to him, shook his hand and hugged him. "Well done, son. Well done."

Max shrugged. "I hope they'll all forgive me. Doesn't look like it, from what I'm seeing."

"They will when they've heard what you have to say. First, we'll need to take statements from all of you." He turned to the seated group. "Can you all make it to the Newport station? The sooner this is over, the better. I can't take part in what comes next, but you'll be in the best hands."

He walked over to Maggie, pulled her to her feet and put his hands on her shoulders. "It's over," he said quietly. "She's the final one. No more Quinns or McCarthy Millers."

"I want to know everything," she replied, "not now, but before day ends. Just one thing, though. You could have come in any time. Max let you in, didn't he?" He nodded. "So why didn't you just barge in on us right away?"

"We needed to hear her admit to a serious crime, which she did when she admitted she shot me. If she had tried to harm any of you, though, we wouldn't have hesitated. We already had enough to put her away, but admitting to attempted murder will keep her incarcerated for a longer time. You were never in any real danger."

"Not the first time you've told me that," she said, scowling at him. "I just hope it's the last."

Chapter 57

Bob didn't arrive home until it was almost dawn but Maggie had waited for him.

"You're not going to give me earache, are you?" he asked, eyeing her suspiciously as he poured a shot of whisky. "It's not going to land well if you are."

She leaned against the back of the settee and folded her arms. "No, I wasn't going to. I know you have a job to do which sometimes means keeping stuff to yourself. I wanted to ask how you are, that's why I waited up, but if you're in a grump …"

He put the glass down, walked over to her, taking her in a bear-hug impairing her breathing and whispered, "Thank you."

"That's OK," she whispered back. "Now can you please let go so I can breathe."

He released her with a smile, picked up his glass and sat on the settee. Sitting beside him she said, "So just tell me in a few words."

"It was bloody," he began. "Some of the boys are pumped up by this stuff, the excitement, you know. Not me. The operation was well carried out, we have the evidence we need now. I wasn't part of it, you know, because of you and the others. I had to wait, which was worse than being in there. When you're in it, the adrenaline takes over. Waiting is terrifying."

She rested her head on his shoulder. "Like you said, it's over. No more Quinns and McCarthy Millers. The person I'm worried about is Max."

"Me too. Did he talk to any of you afterwards?"

"No, he disappeared after we gave our statements. Do you know where he is?"

"Back in the flat. Joe's with him. Is Jack still there?"

"No, but he's planning to go down first thing. None of us talked together afterwards. I hope that'll come later. We just all needed our own space."

He nodded. "I'm knackered. I'm going to bed. There'll be plenty of time to work out what comes next, for me and for all of us. But for now, sleep."

**

When Maggie woke mid-morning, neither Bob nor Jack were in the house. It was still warm enough to open up the conservatory to the garden and she sat, in her dressing gown, coffee in hand, looking out and making a mental list of what needed doing now the weather was making an autumnal decline. She had just stood to get a notepad when a voice said, "Sorry if this is early. We wanted to talk to you, if that's OK."

"It's fine," she replied, rubbing her eyes. Nick and Stella stood in the doorway. "Come on in, help yourself to the coffee, I haven't long made it. I'll get dressed."

When she came back down ten minutes later, having pulled on the first trousers and jumper she could find, Zelah was also waiting in the conservatory. Maggie smiled.

"I expected us to get together sometime today but I didn't expect you all so soon. Four minds with a single thought."

Before she could sit down the sound of the front door opening and closing with a loud bang caused them all to turn around. Jack walked into the kitchen, saw them all and said, "Good, You're all here. Saves me asking Mum to get you together."

"I assumed you were at the flat?"

"I was, from early this morning. We had a lot to say." He threw himself into an armchair. "I can tell you the story now, if you want to hear it. Max told me everything."

"I don't want to hear it," Nick said, starting to rise out the chair, but Stella caught hold of his sweater and pulled him back into the seat. "You're going to hear it," she said in a voice that brooked no argument. He scowled at her, but threw himself back into the armchair.

"I'm going to tell you this with no interruptions and I'm not taking questions afterwards. It began last summer. Emer found him in the South of France. He was making money there, don't even ask how. When I say found him, she had hunted him down. She sold him the story about Nick abandoning him and his mother. She took him out of the place he was in – don't ask – and took him up to Normandy. She had a house there. She told him about how Zelah had stolen everything she had and killed her mother and grandfather. And now the two of them had formed Maze Investigations. According to Emer, Mum was a junior partner and … um, the stupid one."

Maggie gritted her teeth, but kept her mouth shut.

"She said she had a plan to take Zelah down, get back what she was rightly owed, and destroy Maze in the process. He was completely taken in. They became lovers, as you've gathered. She already knew about Helen and Henry Camberwell, and that Helen had moved on Kennet in order to remove him and take over his business, working with Camberwell. She planned for Max to seduce Helen, but also fed the line to Helen. She sent him over here, expecting things to move quickly, but she hadn't anticipated the pandemic. That's how she, Helen and Sherry came to be stuck in France for longer than anticipated. And it allowed time for Max to meet Nick and Stella, and Zelah and Mum, and realise he'd been duped. Anyway, he went along with the plan with Helen, but, as we know, gave her up to Bob. Emer was furious with Helen for trying to make it look like Max had killed Kennet. And apparently Helen had been in touch with Henry Camberwell after Sherry came back. Emer was livid about that, too."

"Sorry," Maggie interrupted. "I have to ask. Did Emer kill Helen?"

"No idea," he replied. "Bob will know the answer to that one. But what you were right about, was when you said he'd never do what she wanted him to do to us. He said you realised he was faking it. Was he right?"

"Yes. I finally got to put Bob's lessons about micro expressions to the test. I saw he wasn't all lovey-dovey when he looked away from her. It looked like disgust."

"It was," he said. "Anyway, she contacted him two days ago and he went straight to Joe, told him everything. Joe's cool. He reported back to Bob pronto, and with some high-ups they planned the raid. You know what went down from there." He turned to Nick. "He would never have let anything happen to any of us. He would have thrown himself in front of her."

Nick shot a confused look at him, then jumped up from his chair and ran out of the room. Maggie stood too, but Stella stopped her. "I'll go," she said quietly.

"So the villain was really the hero," Zelah said. "Who would have guessed."

Jack stood up again. "I'm off. I'm spending a couple of days at the flat. We're going to drink beer and sleep and when we're awake, lots of beer and gaming. Mum, we need to talk. I'll be back for an hour tonight." With that, he left them.

"What's that about?" Zelah asked.

Maggie shrugged. "It'll be what it will be. What are we going to do next?"

"Well, I'm going back to Ireland, release Michelle and the brat, and make sure Mischa and the boys are OK. Then, back to work. A couple of days?"

"Let's take the rest of the week off," Maggie said. "We've earned it."

"I couldn't agree more," Zelah replied.

Three Months Later

Christmas Day

By late afternoon as darkness set in and rain poured unremittingly, Jack and Alice had departed for the gaming room with their cousins and Bob had fallen asleep on the settee, giving out a noise between snoring and puffing, which Maggie found amusing. Any louder and she'd have to disturb him, but this she could cope with.

The day had been hectic, as always and she wouldn't have had it any other way. She had managed to push down her bitter resentment at her sister who had decided to stay in Spain when the first lockdown had been announced, taking it for granted Maggie would pick up responsibility for the girls.

"It's the least you owe me," Fiona had said when she called. "I can't find a flight to get back."

"I owe you nothing," Maggie had managed to get in before Fiona's abrupt departure. However she wasn't so sure about that now.

Emer McCarthy Miller had been tried and imprisoned, sentenced to life for attempted murder, with her conviction assured by the testimony of a witness – Gerry Quinn. How Bob had persuaded him to testify, Maggie had not extracted from him, despite both direct and indirect attempts to make him talk. Zelah had protested ignorance on the matter too, but Maggie had seen a few looks between Bob and Zelah which told her there were aspects of the story neither were admitting to. She had spent some time trying to work out how Zelah could be involved. It was when she recalled Bob's theory about another passenger being in the car that killed her brother-in-law Graham and she considered who it might have been, that the horror hit her that it might have been Gerry Quinn, there at the behest of his father. Had Bob blackmailed Gerry into giving evidence against Emer? But what could the connection between Emer and Gerry have been? She decided to stop thinking about it. There were some things it was best not to know.

Zelah remained in Ireland, with not just the twins and Mischa, but with Rick Mathis. He had made a short visit in December and, caught out by the sudden imposition of another lockdown, had decided to stay on. It looked like being a lengthy stay. Zelah seemed quite happy with his company, both of them being, on occasion, taciturn and grumpy, but with a deepening understanding of each other. Maggie wondered if it would lead to a permanent relationship, but for now, it was a contented friendship and Zelah hadn't had enough of those over the years since Martin's death.

Bob's shuffling interrupted her thoughts. He sat up. "Sorry, was I snoring?"

"Not much," she replied. She leaned into him as he put his arm around her shoulder and they sat looking at the blazing fire.

"What were you doing?"

"Thinking," she replied. "The world is upside down. I'm worried this lockdown is going to last months and we'll have to work by online conferencing. And I'm concerned about Jack."

"It's just a gap year," Bob said. "He's confident about going back next year. It's good for Max, too, to have a mate on hand."

"What's he going to do, when the time comes?"

"Not your problem," Bob said, squeezing her shoulder. "He and Nick are better now, thanks to Stella. It was a massive trauma for both of them. Have you heard from Nick lately?"

"No, not since the Chartist case went on hold. It'll be OK. Zelah will keep up the website; there are stories to write up and we'll get a few cases we can manage by remote research. We'll survive."

"Of course you will. Heard anything from Scotland?"

Maggie sighed. "No, not since Xandy died in October. Lolly, Mary and Brodie and his wife were the only mourners at the funeral, apart from me, Nick and Zelah watching on the video stream. And Mary's failing, too. Lolly says she seems to be giving up."

"Maybe she'd waited for you all to come along."

"How could that be?" Maggie said. "She knew nothing about us."

"Well, you keep telling me the universe is a strange place and there's a huge amount we don't know or understand," he replied. "Come on, let's make some sandwiches and whatever. Then we'll get the kids down and play some games."

"You think you can part them from their gaming?" Maggie said.

"I know how to do it," he said, smirking and standing up. "It may involve money."

In the kitchen Maggie pondered over Bob's remark about the strangeness of life. She knew he was being somewhat sarcastic, but nevertheless … Her thoughts wandered over the conversation she had finally worked up to having with Jude, earlier in the morning.

Jude had found a wonderful life in Catalonia. She, Louisa and Miguel were firm friends and the goats were both surviving and thriving. James hadn't shown up and Jude had already begun the process to legalise living in Spain. She promised Maggie she had burned the fake US passport. Between them, Zelah, Nick and Maggie had decided the case would not be publicised on the Maze website, to ensure the privacy and safety of both Jude and Brodie. "There'll be plenty of others," Zelah said. "Although this one would have been a winner. Never mind." Maggie wasn't sure she meant the last bit.

Maggie had sent Jude a copy of the final diary entry in Brodie McAlister's diary, after Zelah admitted she'd copied it.

"So, what did you think about the final entry, the piece he wrote after he retrieved the diary?" Maggie asked tentatively.

"What did you think?"

"Don't answer a question with a question. Was it … what I think it was?"

"Yes, it was. I don't understand it either. He wasn't dead."

"Maybe he was, for a flash of a second in time. Perhaps Andreu's father finding him and picking him up when he thought he detected a breath, brought him back."

"Lots of maybes," Jude said. "Honestly, Maggot, I'm not sure I want to know."

"Perhaps, Worm, there are some things it's best not to know."

"Amen to that."

Final Entry From the Diary of Brodie McAlister 1955

I am devastated to learn Harry died. After all we survived in Spain, to die on the beaches of Normandy, perhaps not far from me. I was a lucky one. I waded through blood and bodies and limbs and torsos. I survived.

In the end I am pleased he did not send my diary to Helen. He sent the postcard, so she knew I had survived the journey. But she could not know what it was like when I was there. Which is just as well, looking back.

Reading it now has brought back such memories, both joyful and dreadful. I came to love and respect those comrades, those friends, who helped me become a soldier. I saw them die, around me, next to me. Others taken prisoner and shot. No Geneva convention for Franco. I used to laugh in the war here in England when people asked why I wasn't terrified by the blitz. I told them I was Luftwaffe target practice in Spain. It must have been such a shock for Hitler when our boys threw them out of our skies. If we had had such help as Franco had! Perhaps Hitler would have thought twice. Too late now.

My diary ended in Barcelona. Now I am going to record what happened when I went back to the front. Back in '38 I could not return to Scotland. I was too frightened I would be taken and hanged. My luck had held out, perhaps it would again. So, before dawn on the morning our convoy was due to leave for France I snuck out and two days later I was with the boys in Catalonia where I joined what was left of the XVth on the outskirts of La Fatarella. There were a handful of Internationals, some Germans and Italians and others who, like me, could not go home, where they would be welcomed by a firing squad.

We were dug in on the outskirts of the village. I fitted in well, as most of the XVth were around my age, plus some older men. One took me under his wing, showed me the ropes. He was quiet, determined. He had no English and I no Catalan, but we were instant buddies, as the American would say, being prepared to die for a righteous cause.

As I recall that final morning it is as clear in my mind as yesterday and I see my every movement, feel every emotion. I walk out of the bunker and look down from the hilltop at the amazing, breath-taking beauty of this land. Despite the horror run amok here I appreciate the sharpness of the air flowing around my face as the sun rises, the birds still coming here to sing to us each morning, the gentle countryside smells that in Glasgow I never knew existed. But 'always' has a different meaning for me, for us, this morning. It will be our last.

With that thought a sob catches me, but I beat it down and smile. I chose this, it was not forced on me. I have become a soldier. I have found family and although I shall never forget my own dear ones, my Helen and my Julie and my brothers, they are lost to me.

We do not know who will live and who will die here today. I know already the enemy is ruthless, uncaring of dignity. They will kill us then march over our bodies and onward. But we shall hold them back for as long as we can.

My friend, my best friend, is humming to himself as he checks his ammunition from his corner of our zig-zag trench. He is grimly determined to fight for the Republic he loves, hates the bastard Franco. I cannot say that, but I have learned the importance of freedom and fairness in my time here. It's a worthy fight and I shall have died for something worthwhile.

We check a glance and smile.

I pull my coat and my tattered scarf around my body. I was hungry earlier, but not now. Not that there was anything to eat. We shared a mug of bad coffee – if that's what it was. It was hot though, whatever it was. The sun is high but the cold is biting.

I feel something under my feet and look down, puzzled. There is nothing there. And again. The earth is buzzing, vibrating just a little, but it tells me … they are coming. We look at each other again and nod. My stomach churns. I bend low and run into the bunker to join the gunners there, looking down the hill towards the ruined farmhouses. I see them. The tanks first, followed by row upon row of men in Fascist uniform, guns ready, marching in step towards us. The first tank fires.

Oh God, I am afraid! I run out of the bunker as the shells shriek overhead, and call down the line 'they are coming'. We take up positions at the designated corners of our trench, guns pointed, grenades ready. From further along the trenches we can hear shouts and screams. Some are running. I will not run.

The shelling quickens, deafening as they fly overhead, landing on the ground above us. Shrieks, as a trench is hit. Then the tanks stop. They cannot reach our positions, it's too steep. The men in uniform begin to run, screaming aloud in a language I cannot understand. We wait. They are close enough for me to see their faces, their hatred. And now I feel excited, ready to fight. My blood is singing. I will kill these bastards if I can. As many as I can. I turn a quick face to my friend who grins back.

I fire, once, twice, three times. I see men fall, clutching at their heads and stomachs. Now I can hardly see for the smoke and chaos.

Their range is getting better. A shell lands behind us, feet away. The noise fills my ears, like screaming. I look around. My comrades are waving and shouting, but I cannot hear for the buzzing in my head. I keep firing until I have run out of ammunition. I get out my knife. Horror! A shell explodes into the bunker. The roof caves in. There were six comrades inside. My friend stands and takes the pin from his grenade and hoists his arm to throw it, but too late.

A moment of distraction: the grenade explodes in his hand, blowing it off. I stare and stare at a hole in his chest, where blood pours. I jump and run to the far end of the trench, and up behind, where the trees used to be. But I didn't know they had moved around our position and are now behind us as well as in front. He runs across the open ground towards me. He grins at me and takes aim. I feel something in my leg. Then he is above me. Another bang and I feel nothing.

I can see now, although I cannot remember opening my eyes. I don't seem to have eyes. I feel such peace. I have no sense of time nor breath. I am somewhere on the ground, or under the ground, I cannot tell. I am as insubstantial as the gentle breeze rippling around me. There are trees above me, the branches swaying, letting shafts of light through in which tiny insects and strange ethereal matter dance together. There are footsteps passing close by. I perceive them. I am curious. A dark-haired woman is walking past me, her hands brushing the tall grass.

She senses me, she stops, frowns, she doesn't understand what she senses. She hurries on.

Then, shouting, blackness, movement, heaviness. I open my eyes. An ancient woman is smiling at me, talking to me but I cannot understand what she is saying. I am alive.

The family hid me and cared for me until I could make a run for the border. Whilst I was in their cellar the Republic collapsed. Hitler had begun his annexation of Europe. I never learned the name of the Catalan family. They would not tell me, so I could never give them up if I was captured, which I was not. My luck held out again. I returned to England, with a new plan.

I have not thought too long or often on it since, but I have never understood what happened on that day, the last day, of the battle of the Ebro, as I lay dying, dead. The strange, unaccountable experience, the pretty dark-haired woman who sensed me there. But, in the end perhaps there are some things it's best not to know.

The End

Thanks and Acknowledgements!

As always, producing a book involves many people without whose help, expert advice and encouragement I would struggle.

My 'first readers', Cheryl, Joy and Rose, as always. Positive criticism, plot holes spotted and excellent suggestions for improvement.

This book has been edited and proof read by Meg Ross, who has done a wonderful job.

Thanks also to Ali Morgan at Alicat Designs for the fabulous cover.

I have used some licence around the pandemic rules as they were in Autumn 2020 but hopefully have retained the substance of what it would have been like to move around during that period of time in both the UK and Spain.

Writing about the Spanish Civil War and the particular effect it had in Catalonia required expert input, and for this I thank Alan Warren of the Porta de la Historia for donating his invaluable knowledge and experience, not only of the history of the war, but of his understanding of the way in which this war affected the people of Spain.

And finally, to Stewart and Alice, my wonderful children, who give me support and inspiration, reassurance and IT support.Both are a constant source of encouragement for my self belief in my writing when I doubt myself, which is often! Couldn't do it without you, kids.

The History of the Front Cover Photograph

The picture of the Spanish Civil War soldier on the front page is from a collection of portraits and action shots taken by one of the official war photographers, Sergeant Harry Randall. Harry was an American from Arizona and was the official photographer of the Abraham Lincoln Brigade of the XV International Brigade of volunteers. The collection is held and curated by the Tamiment Museum in New York, and I am grateful to them for allowing me the use of two photographs from the collection.

When I was searching for a photograph for the front cover of 'The Soldier' I wanted something that would portray more than just war, something that gave a heart and soul to the men and women who travelled to Spain to support the new Republic against the Fascist coup, led by Francisco Franco with the support of the Spanish ruling classes and the Catholic church.

Original black-and-white photograph
from the Harry Randall Collection at
The Tamiment Museum New York (ALBA Photo 11-0944)

The soldier pictured on the cover is Lieutenant William Mitchell Digges, an American from New Orleans, who arrived in Spain in 1937. As soon as I saw this picture, I knew it was the right one: the makeshift uniform, the boots planted firmly in the snow, hands in pockets, the look of determination yet uncertainty. For me, this was the character of so many of the volunteers from around the world. There were believed to be 35,000 at least from over 50 countries, the biggest volunteer army since the Crusades of the Middle Ages. Around 2,000 of them were medics: Doctors, Nurses, Ambulance Drivers.

Digges is an enigmatic character. In truth, very little is known about him. We don't know his age, where he came from or what were his family and background. William Digges's personnel file[1] reported that he was in the US Marine Corps in the 1930's but records under that name have not been found. He was a member of the nascent National Maritime Union (NMU) in 1936. In fact, we aren't even sure if William Mitchell Digges was his real name (it was not unusual for volunteers to use a 'nom de guerre', as many governments, trying to either appease Hitler or keep out of the prospect of another World War that was now on the horizon, did not approve of or permit their citizens to travel to Spain. Most had to go through France and make their way down to the Spanish border). We do know from contemporary accounts that he was a popular man, an able organizer who became an adjutant to the senior commander of the Abraham Lincoln Brigade, Robert Merriman. A colleague described him as '*a sturdy American of medium height with a flat nose and the biceps of a boxer. This American … was always smiling as if he were a candidate for president of the USA.*'

He also seems to have been somewhat carefree and perhaps a little careless, which led to his unfortunate death from an accidentally self-inflicted gunshot wound. He was cleaning weapons with a group of soldiers in a poultry yard near the town of Tàrrega, laughing and joking about the safety of US vs Russian weapons, when his pistol misfired. He died instantly. His funeral took place in Tàrrega in late May 1938, attended by a large crowd of compatriots and International Brigaders. He was buried in an unmarked wall grave in Tàrrega which was lost until the identification of the grave by Jaume Ramon Solé, a Civil War Historian in Catalonia, in 2017. There followed disinterment, the taking of DNA in the hope of finding descendant family members and a ceremony of re-interment, this time with William Digges' name on the wall grave. The Porta de la Historia and the Catalonian historians have made a short film about the war in the area and the death and subsequent discovery of William Digges. It's available on YouTube at:
https://pdlhistoria.wordpress.com/2019/12/04/2179/

The second photograph, which I did not in the end use for the front page is of Walter 'Kid' O'Kane. Walter was a month shy of twenty (born July 28, 1907, in Dixon, Illinois) when he travelled to Spain (where he arrived on June 29, 1937) and did not see his next birthday before he was killed. He was declared MIA (Missing in Action) on April 3, 1938, in Gandesa, Spain, at the end of the period called "The Retreats", along with a group of around 50 other members of the Abraham Lincoln Brigade. Walter's photo I again found very moving, and he inspired the 'face' of the main character in 'The Soldier' – Brodie McAlister.

Work continues in Catalonia to discover information about the victims of the War, and it is possible that, now that the place where this group of US Brigaders was known to have been killed, an excavation can take place. May be Walter's remains will be amongst them. I hope so.

Their memories are not always well recorded. In the UK there are several memorials around the country, and the IBMT (International Brigades Memorial Trust) both keeps a record of the volunteers and organizes events throughout the year with supporters and descendants of the men and women who gave their time and in some cases their lives. In the United States and Canada, the Spanish Civil War is not well known. But there are people there doing excellent work to keep the names of the volunteers in the public eye. I am very grateful to Brian Moyer and Ray Hoff for their help and advice in trying to trace William Digges and Walter O'Kane.

I had little interest in or knowledge of the Spanish Civil War before I began researching for my second book, 'Line of Descent', in the process of which I learned about the missing children of Franco. Since then my interest has deepened. Learning about William Digges and Walter O'Kane has added a dimension of personal interest. Their deep commitment to the cause of the fight against Fascism drove them to travel thousands of miles to fight and die in a foreign country. They did not have to go, but they all felt the need to go.

So, why did these men and women leave their relatively safe lives and travel to Spain? There were a few volunteers whose motives were not ideal, but the vast majority saw the injustice of an uprising against an elected government, the horror of Fascism and the looming prospect of another world war driven and armed by Fascists.

This Spanish war was lost in 1939 and Franco, armed to the teeth by Hitler and Mussolini whilst European nations and others stood by and watched, began a repressive dictatorship that lasted 40 years. Spain then returned to democracy. But the shadow of Fascism has never gone away and is now resurgent again, with tentacles spreading out around the world.

The Spanish philosopher George Santayana is credited with the aphorism, "Those who cannot remember the past are condemned to repeat it." I hope that my small efforts here will help to keep alive memories of events and experiences that should never be repeated.

[1] Russian Social Sciences and Historical Archives (RGASPI), Fond 545, Opis 6, Delo 885, pp. 45-52;

Top and Middle: Walter Elmer 'Kid' O'Kane 1919 – 1938 (ALBA Photo 11-0006 and 11-0934, Tamiment Library/Robert F. Wagner Labor Archives. Elmer Holmes Bobst Library, 70 Washington Square South, New York, NY 10012, New York University Libraries)

Bottom: William Mitchell Digges: 19?? – 1938 (ALBA Photo 11-0944, Tamiment Library/Robert F. Wagner Labor Archives. Elmer Holmes Bobst Library, 70 Washington Square South, New York, NY 10012, New York University Libraries)

Research Sources:

"War is Beautiful" – James Neugass
"The Spanish Civil War "– Giles Tremlett
American Volunteers in the Spanish Civil War – Christopher T. Brooks, ALBA Biographer (unpublished, but these biographies are found on https://alba-valb.org/volunteers/)
"The Spanish Holocaust" – Paul Preston
"Britons in Spain" – William Rust
"The Archaeology of the Spanish Civil War" – Alfredo Gonzalez-Ruibal
"Miners Against Fascism" – Hwyel Evans
"From Abedare to Albacete" – Edwin Greening
"From the Rhondda to the Ebro" – Alun Menai Williams
"Fleeing Franco" – Hwyel Davies
"The Lincoln Brigade" – William Lorenz Katz and Marc Crawford
"Ebre 1938: Imatges D'Un Batalla" – Francesc Xavier Hernandez Cardona & Mar Hernandez Pongiluppi
"For Whom the Bell Tolls" – Ernest Hemingway
"Homage to Catalonia" – George Orwell

Thank you for reading this book!

If you have enjoyed it, please leave feedback on Amazon and/or Goodreads. If there's anything I've missed, or if you have any questions about any feature of it, please leave a message on my website: www.mkjonesauthor.com.

Maze Investigations has its own website: https://mkjonesauthor.com and its own Facebook page. I have an author page on Goodreads, where you will find the occasional blog about my writing.

And if you can't wait, you can catch up with the stories of other cases the Maze Investigations team tackle between the books. These are available when you sign up for my newsletter on the website. You will receive two immediately as a thanks for signing up:

"The Missing Air Raid Warden 1941"

And

"Murder in the Family 1840s"

Following these there will be a new story with each newsletter, in the form of a report by one of the Maze Investigators.

Happy reading!

The Next Book in the Maze Investigations Series

'The Reluctant Chartist'

'On the night of the great Chartist uprising and march to Newport, South Wales, in November 1839, a man with a very different agenda is on the prowl.

He is a thief, who by chance has come across an unusual, potentially priceless item, that could bring him extraordinary wealth. But his plans are scuppered when he is caught up in the march. His subsequent actions will lead to unintended and unexpected consequences, for him and his family.'

Available Now on Amazon

Printed in Great Britain
by Amazon

28247560R00179